Guitar Fac

By

Sasha Marshall

Dedication

For my Grandfather

In loving memory of Malbern

You are the greatest man that ever walked this earth. Your love of music shaped my own. By the age of eleven, music was present in each day of my life. I have always had my own life soundtrack thanks to you. My Christmases are filled with memories of Elvis, and my childhood memories in your shop were sung by every Motown musician ever recorded. Beyond music, your kindness taught me to be kind to others and to give selflessly. Your laughter taught me that life is full of joy. Your love taught me to love with everything I have. Most importantly, your faith and words taught me to chase down every dream I ever had. You saw three of my dreams come true. Here is one more. I love and miss you.

There are character biographies and profiles on the author's website at SashaMarshall.com.

Prologue

When I was four, my love affair with music began. One random day, I wandered into my grandfather's recording studio and watched Uncle Buddy, who is not really my uncle at all, play the guitar for over an hour. I saw him close his eyes and jerk his head from the front to the back, tap his foot, and make the strangest faces. I thought he might be sick and asked my grandfather to take him to a doctor. My grandfather threw his head back and let loose that boisterous laugh he has.

When he composed himself he said, "Baby girl, Uncle Buddy isn't sick. That's just his guitar face."

My grandfather explained to me at four years of age what a guitar face was. I never forgot the words "guitar face" So I observed other musicians to see if they had a guitar face. Each musician I observed had their own guitar face, they were an assortment of dramatic, scary, but most were angelic. I tried for almost a year to mimic some of those faces in a mirror, and I was never able pull off the same effect. I convinced myself that my grandfather would be proud if I could pull off a guitar face too.

By the tender age of five, I deduced my inability to produce a great guitar face was because I did not have a guitar, so I borrowed one of my grandfather's. Standing in the mirror, I realized my guitar face was still scary. Not long after my try at a guitar face with an actual guitar, I realized my guitar face sucked because I could not play the guitar. I decided I must master playing the guitar before my very own amazing guitar face would emerge. I ran to the recording studio to beg my grandfather to teach me how to play the guitar, but I only found my Uncle B.B. there. He isn't really my uncle either. He was sitting on a red leather ottoman playing his guitar and had one of the best guitar faces I had ever seen. I was afraid he would quit playing if he saw me, so I snuck back to the corner of the room and sat in his empty guitar case. I watched him play for what seemed like an eternity. The case smelled like smoke, whiskey, and music. My grandfather's recording studio smelled the same way, and it smelled like home to me. I had a difficult time keeping my lids open, so down in the case and continued to listen.

The next thing I heard was the laughter of men, and when I opened my eyes they all stared back with admiration in their eyes.

"I never seen a child sleep in a guitar case like you do. You been fond of them things since you was old enough to crawl. One day you gonna be too big for it," B.B. said. The men laughed again. I jumped out of his case and walk toward him bound and determined to finish the mission I had set out on hours earlier.

"Uncle B.B., my guitar face don't look good. I have been trying since I was four and can't make it look like yours, or Uncle Buddy's, or my Granddaddy's."

All the men chuckled again, and it made my impatient temper flare. I put my hands on my petite little hips, pressed my lips together, frowned the best frown I could manage, and poked my uncle in the arm.

"It's not funny! I have worked real hard to get a good guitar face but it just don't feel right. I even went and got my Granddaddy's guitar and held it in the mirror, and it still can't do it right! MAKE MY GUITAR FACE LOOK LIKE YOURS!" I stomped my feet for effect, and no matter how good of a job I thought I had done at relaying my anger, they all laughed again.

My uncle picked me up under my arms and placed me in his lap and said, "Baby girl, a guitar face doesn't come from practice or from holding a guitar. It comes from the depths of your heart and soul. You can't decide what your guitar face is gonna look like, the music does. You gotta play that guitar to have a guitar face."

I frowned again, fighting my five-year-old impatience, and took in the men surrounding us in the studio. Their faces were smiling with amusement.

"That's why I came out here. I figured if holding the guitar didn't make my face look right then I need to learn how to play the damn thing, and you were busy playing your own guitar when I got here, and I fell asleep in the case. I need to learn how to play." I could not have been more serious in my lengthy five years on this earth.

My grandfather chimed in, "You better not let your Grandmamma hear you say ugly words. She'll wash your mouth out with soap again."

MY grandfather is never a serious man. I could see him fighting with himself between doing the right thing by scolding me and laughing. A smirk remained on his face.

"I'm sorry Granddaddy, but I'm being serious and everybody is laughing at me. This is important."

My grandfather and B.B. communicated silently with their eyes, and then they simultaneously laughed. I was amusing them!

"I don't know if you is guitar-playing material little girl. Me and your Granddaddy's been playing for a long time, and I ain't never taught nor seen a little girl play the thing."

"So you won't teach me to play because I'm a girl?!!!!! I'm telling my Grandmamma! She says girls can do same things boys can. I do everything better than my brother, and I know I can play the guitar better than all of you! I just need someone with a good guitar face to teach me. So what's it gonna be fellas? Don't be scared of girls or I will tell everyone you are all sissies!" I scrunched my face together and put my hands on my hips to show them I meant business.

With a great deal of effort, the men held back their laughter. "Well, now, little Miss, didn't nobody say nothing about girls can't play guitars. I just says I ain't never seen one. There's a first time for everything. Come on Red; let's go get your Grandbaby a guitar," B.B. said as he put down his guitar, I was ready for my first memorable journey into the musical world.

Chapter 1

"Jesus Christ," he growls in my ear.

He continues to massage my clit and bring me closer to the brink of oblivion. Jesus Christ is about right, I'm about to explode all over his hand. I rake my fingernails into his muscular, tattooed back.

"I can't take this anymore…need inside of you now…going to fuck you like it's my job," he growls again.

Connor Black pulls his fingers out of me and drops his pants down to his ankles. He unrolls the condom onto his shaft and steps back to me. He rains kisses down my jaw line. Connor is the picture perfect bad boy. He is the lead singer in Kellan's Cross, a modern rock band. They sound like a cross between Breaking Benjamin and Five Finger Death Punch if you can imagine such a thing. I'm headlining this tour with my own band, Abandoned Shadow, and I've tried for six months not to fuck Connor. He has relentlessly pursued me, but I have a feeling I'm about to lose the fight. Yup, I'm going to fuck him. It sucks to be the only female on tour with hot male eye candy surrounding you. Talk about a sausage fest! But given the choice, I'd much rather live amongst a sausage fest than struggle through an estrogen nightmare. Bitches be catty.

Connor is now kissing my neck. Should I fuck him? One of three things will happen if I let him shake my wig one good time. Choice one involves him telling everyone he can think of that he shagged me, Henley Hendrix, Queen of rock-and-roll. I know this can be a trophy fuck. Choice two involves him falling in love with me, and it can get ugly. I mean restraining order and publicity battle ugly. Famous people rarely keep their personal matters to themselves. Nope, we crazy, rich assholes are known for using the media to bicker with each other. Think of it as a global Facebook page. I prefer privacy, but letting him stick his dick in me may invite a psycho loon into my life.

Choice three is much more preferable. This preferable choice entails both of us understanding we are two horny, consenting adults who just want to get laid something fierce. Once he gives me an orgasm, and reaches his own climax, we will part ways. If the sex is good I might do it again one day. Other than that, I don't care to see Connor Black again.

Don't get me wrong, Connor is as fine as they come at six feet tall, with dark blonde hair tucked behind his ears, and pretty hazel eyes. The tattoos really do it for me. He has sleeves on both of his arms and a lip ring that is begging for me to nibble on it. Yeah okay, I admit I've thought about it a few times along this six-month tour. I've exhibited willpower and all that motivational shit, but damn a girl has needs. I need to get fucked, like yesterday.

He continues down my shoulder with his kisses and simultaneously pushes my already short dress up to my hips. Okay, so I will probably let him pork me. He rubs the tip of his dick against my lips. Yup, I will ride the baloney pony. He slowly inserts himself in me, and I swear to everything sacred, I almost came. His dick isn't huge. It's average, but thick in girth, and that is on my list of favorite things about a penis. He keeps his thrusts long and slow and kisses me like I'm the only woman in the world. I wish he would hurry though. There's no time for romance shit.

"Open your eyes Henley. I want to watch you come," he whispers.

I wonder how many times he has read Fifty Shades. Dear Connor, men don't really fucking talk like that.

"Let me see you beautiful. I want to feel your soul when you come."

Yup, he is fucking it up for me. I wonder if there's any duct tape in the room. Moaning works for me, and he can still moan through tape. This romantic bullshit is making my vag dry up like the damn Sahara. Okay, desperate times call for desperate measures. I pull him close and press my face to his chest. Now he can't see me and peer into the depths of my soul and all that shit. I grab onto him and rake my nails into his back. He gives a grunt of pleasure and stops spouting all of that 18th century L-O-V-E nonsense. He thrust harder, and I feel it building inside of me. I hear him say something or another, but my impending orgasm has made me partially deaf. I'll pretend he is Bradley Cooper. Nope, not bad boy enough. Shit, I'm in the middle of getting laid, and I can't decide who I want to fuck in my head. Russell Brand? No, too skinny. He looks too much like Jesus for me. George Clooney? No, too refined. Channing Tatum? Nope, he can dance better than me. I might not be able to keep up with him in bed. Orlando Bloom? Nope, not bad enough. David Beckham. Ooohhh daddy yes! He will do it. Victoria will have to forgive me because I'll fantasize about fucking her husband.

And Beckham does the trick. When I imagine his hands running up and down my back and thrusting his pelvis in me, I find the edge again. Tattoos, I need tattoos. I turn my head to the side and watch the tattoos move on Connor's arm and pretend they are Beckham's. Oh yeah, that will do it for a girl. I feel that elusive climax begin building and finally tip over the edge. Digging my fingers into his back, I throw my head back, and close my eyes, screaming out something, but no clue what. Here's to hoping it wasn't David Beckham's name! That would be a rather embarrassing headline. *Rocker Connor Black spills the goods. Henley Hendrix is having an affair with David Beckham and accidentally called out his name during sex.* Welcome to my life kids.

Soon, Connor follows me, and I feel him spasm inside of me. Thank the heavens above we're done. At once he and grabs the condom to dispose of it. A knock at the door startles me, and I race around to make myself presentable. Connor does the same. I open the door moments later when we are both clothed. Neither of us can hide the fresh fucked look, so I don't even try.

Caleb is leaning against the frame of the door. His face is graced with a knowing smile. I wink at him to let him know I need to be saved from myself.

"You ready to head home, Hen?" Caleb asks a little too eagerly.

"Uh, yeah. Let me say goodbye to Connor."

I turn around and Connor has a look of shock etched on his face. Shit, this might not end well. I smile a sexy smile and saunter up to him. I play the only card I have, and it's standing in the frame of the door. I wrap my arms around him for a hug and whisper in his ear.

"Sorry about that. That was amazing! We will meet up soon," I lie.

I kiss his cheek and saunter out of the room. When I pass Caleb, I let the facade drop. Once we are a reasonable distance away he begins his tirade of teases.

"What did you tell this one?" he asks.

"Why do you ask?"

"Because he looks like you shot his dog."

I laugh, "I lied and said it was great sex, and we will get together again soon, and then I apologized for your unexpected arrival."

"Would you like more time with the bloke?" Caleb asks in his best English accent.

"Funny, but hell no. I swear he reads romance novels. I had to pretend he was someone else, so it wasn't a total waste of my time."

"Jesus, that's harsh," Griffin says as he falls into step with us.

Griffin is our bassist, and he enjoys hearing about my sexual endeavors. I don't let it happen often on tour, but when I do, I'm discreet about it. I've been friends with the guys in my band since we were in grade school, but I keep a firm don't kiss and tell policy.

"Who had the honors this time?" Rhys asks.

Rhys is our drummer. Other than being a phenomenal drummer, he is our resident playboy. The girls know it and don't give a shit. They want to be another notch on his bedpost.

"David Beckham," I answer.

"Really? He's married," Caleb says.

"Wasn't a factor. I fucked the recently divorced version of soccer boy," I say.

"I didn't know they are getting a divorce," Griffin says.

"They aren't sweetie, just in my fantasies. It is bad enough I had to pretend to fuck someone else, I can't be a home wrecker too," I say.

"So who wants in on the bet?" Caleb asks as we gather in a dressing room with my brother's band, Broken Access.

"What are we betting?" Kip asks.

Kip is the drummer for my brother's band. He is one of my best friends, but he isn't for the faint of heart. Kip is vulgar and honest. He also has the driest sense of humor on the planet earth.

"We are betting on whether Connor Black will need a restraining order after Henley just ruined him for all other women," Rhys replies.

"You fucked Connor Black?" Jagger growls.

Oh Jagger.

Jagger Carlyle is the finest man gracing this earth. Look, I love my David Beckham's, and all the other pretty men I've met over the years, but none of them have shit on Jagger. I've known this man since the sixth grade and have also been in puppy love with him just as long. At least I understand the difference. He's my brother's best friend and the lead guitarist, songwriter, and backup vocalist in Broken Access. Standing at six foot three, the man is a solid wall of muscle. His body is lean and muscles grace it without being too beefy. He has abs you would want to eat your every meal on. That way you can lick up all your crumbs like a good girl afterwards. Jag's covered in tattoos in all the right places, has crystal blue eyes, and dark brown hair. Jagger's hair is buzzed short, and he is sporting a five o'clock shadow. I've got a thing for five o'clock shadows.

Have you ever seen a man with stubble that makes you want to rub your face against like a dog? This hopefully leads to him rubbing his face against the inside of your thighs, but I digress. Jagger is the man you would want between your thighs, and really any part of him between your thighs is acceptable.

"Can we not talk about my sex life, please?" I beg.

Insert my brother Koi at the back end of this conversation. "What sex life?"

"Dude, she banged Connor Black," Kip says.

Koi looks disturbed. "Dude! She is my sister! I don't want to hear that shit!"

"I do. I want to hear all about it, but every time you would say 'Connor,' insert Kip," Kip says.

"I vomited in my mouth a little. Koi, I'm twenty-two years old. I have sex. I don't make it as obvious as the rest of you," I say.

It is time I change into another outfit and head home. I hate when these guys treat me like I'm void of all things sexual. I'm a twenty-two year old woman with a healthy libido. Jagger mumbles something about killing a motherfucker and stomps out of the room in a temper tantrum. Why do all these men care so much about my vagina? That is a good question. Let me know if you figure out the answer before I do.

Chapter 2

I change out of the little black dress I performed in and then had sex in. We still have fans waiting for a meet and greet. I enjoy meeting my fans in a more intimate setting, but I'm ready to hit the road with Caleb.

All members from both bands are from Macon, Georgia. It's a large city ninety miles south of Atlanta. Macon is so different from Atlanta. Whereas Atlanta is cultured and progressive, Macon is stuck in the 1960's. Apparently conservative Macon withstood the social revolutions of the decade. At some point in history, Macon had more churches per square mile than any other city in the country. This is the same city that claims Little Richard, Otis Redding, and The Allman Brothers Band. I'm sure the latter threw the conservatives off their rockers. Macon claimed the lives of Duane Allman and Berry Oakley, and their final resting places reside in Rose Hill Cemetery on Riverside Drive.

Today, Macon has a mixed vibe. There is a great deal of inner city that come with its own set of problems, but nobody has given up on the city. During the warm months you can hang out with the hippies downtown, catch an outdoor movie, a festival, or a soap box Derby. The most beautiful part of Macon is her musical spirit. We don't forget to embrace our musicians and offer many venues in which you can find them. I've found amazing talent in my city.

I grew up on the outskirts of town, and my grandfather's property has a large stocked pond. Caleb and I want to hit the road as soon as possible so we can fish until the sun rises. Night fishing is one of the best past times.

I finally get to my dressing room, throw on blue jeans, chucks, and a tank so I can set out to find the guys. I locate them in a room designated for the meet and greet. The guys in Broken Access and Abandoned Shadow are already immersed in our fans. I gravitate towards a group of guys who appear to be waiting on me.

I smile for the next hour. Being famous is a delicate balance. I was a guitar prodigy from the time I was twelve, and I live in a male-dominated industry in an almost exclusive male role as lead singer and lead guitarist. This makes men either deathly afraid of me or brave with their tongues.

I spent an hour making light of blatant sexual advances, female fan self-esteem issues, and marriage proposals. I enjoy the fans that tell me how much they relate to my lyrics, but the most amazing part of doing what I do is to have a fan tell me what I wrote saved their life. That makes it worth all the bullshit this job entails.

Once we sign autographs, take pictures with fans, and engage in small talk, we leave. We are surrounded by security as we are walked to the lot behind the venue. Caleb's Porsche is waiting on us. Jagger and Kip are also headed back to Macon, but the rest of the band will party all night in Atlanta.

I give them each a hug, and the guys do the man hug thing. I'm jumping up and down in anticipation of going home. We haven't seen home in six months. Touring is grueling, and not a great deal of downtime. We have a month off and will spend it doing everything we miss, except sleeping. Hell, we can sleep on tour.

Caleb drives through the lot and security opens a gate for him. He cranks the stereo up to drown out the screaming fans on the other side of the gate, and once we escape unscathed the volume dulls. We burst into laughter at the extent fans go to see us for a moment. Caleb finds interstate 75 South and we are Macon bound. My grandfather will wait for us. He loves night fishing too. Caleb is rambling on about two girls who spent their time in the front row flashing him. He grins his best boyish grin. He loves being a musician.

I tease him about me catching the most fish last time we were home. Of course, he says I cheated.

"Oh yeah? Then put your money where your mouth is big boy," I say.

"Name it."

"Hmm, how about you wear a thong bikini for the next six shows? I think hot pink will work."

"I will take that deal. If I catch the most, then you have to wear a thong bikini for the next six shows. Cherry red though," he gambles.

"Fine. But if you get lucky and win, Koi will throttle you," I laugh.

"Then we shouldn't warn him. You just strut your hot little ass on stage and let him brood the entire show. That will be fun to watch from the stage when his ass can't do a damn thing about it for two hours," he roars in laughter.

I notice a slight bump from the rear of the car, so I turn towards Caleb. His smile drops, and his eyes are locked on the rear view mirror. In one second, I see utter horror spread over his face. He reaches for my hand and holds tight.

"Henley!" He screams.

He throws his upper body over mine and pushes me against the seat. I brave a look out the front glass to see what's happening, but the world is turning upside down and then it rights itself for a moment before it turns again. Each time the small car flips on its roof my head hits the top, and the seat belt grabs my torso and digs into my shoulder blade.

Then it all stops. I'm floating. At least it feels like I'm floating. I don't hurt or ache. I float in darkness. Why is it so fucking dark? There are muffled screams. Where am I? Who is screaming? I can't seem to form words or open my eyes. I panic. Am I dead? I can't die yet! I'm twenty-two years old, please don't let me die! Whatever entity or Creator or spirit is out there, please don't let this be it. Shit, you have to at least let me make it to the 27 club.

I hear a cough, and then I realize I felt the cough. That must be me. Then my eyes open. The screams are still muffled, and my vision is blurry. I can't see who is screaming. Where is Caleb? I look to my left and don't see him. My body is hanging upside down, and Caleb is screaming because I'm still trapped. My vision clears up little by little, and then it's as if someone increases the volume. The urgency I hear in the screams is amplified by actual screams.

"Are you awake? Can you hear me? I see someone!"

My voice won't work, but I can see. The seatbelt is holding me in place, so I try to find the release with my left hand but my arm isn't working properly. Placing my feet straight down for leverage and reaching across my body with my right hand, I have to move my body to the left a good bit to reach the release. It doesn't want to let go. Shit. Closing my eyes, I take deep breath. Please let go. I try a few more times before the buckle finally releases. I have to find a way out of this little tin can of a car. Most of my window is smashed and is lying on the ground, completely blocked by concrete.

The driver side window is crushed. How did Caleb get out? I lie down I can get a view of the windshield. Glass presses into my skin, and I let out a whimper. The voices outside become shriller when my voice reaches them, but I can't focus on those people. I have to get out of here. I see an opening big enough for my petite body to fit through, but sharp glass is still jutting from the rubber molding. I kick the glass the best I can and turn my face away to avoid getting glass in my eyes.

I get most of the glass out, but I have to position my body in a painful and unusual position to crawl out. As I place my left arm down for balance, a vicious pain runs from the tip of my fingers to my shoulder blade. I scream in agony.

The people outside are telling me to be still. They promise help is on the way. I don't know these people.

"Caleb!" I scream. "Caleb!"

"Henley!" I hear Jagger. He sounds panicked. "Henley, tell me what hurts."

"Goddamnit Jagger! I can't get out of here! Please help me!" I plead through sobs I'm trying my best to hold back.

"Can you fit through the opening in the front?"

"I already tried. I can't put any weight on my left arm," I say.

"Motherfucker!" Jagger screams.

My heart takes over all other sounds. It flips and flops in my chest, and the feeling is odd. Jagger's voice is tuning out as the thumping takes over my body. Lightheadedness overcomes me, and I realize the blackness is trying to take over again. I need to fight it if I want a chance of surviving. I take a deep breath and shake my head through to consciousness. Jagger's screams slowly grow louder.

"Don't do this baby. Please say something. Henley!" he cries.

"I'm still here."

"Oh, thank God. How are you doing in there?" his voice quivers.

"I need to get free, Jag," I plead.

"I want you to push and then turn yourself into the opening. We found a towel to place over the broken glass. Turn until you can place your right arm out of the opening first, but the front of your body needs to face toward me. Okay?"

"Okay," I agree.

I used my right arm to pull myself up to a squatting position. It takes a minute but I turn myself around in the car. I peer back at the opening, and then I stick my right arm through, where someone grabs my hand.

"Henley, I need to pull you by your arm until I can grab you under your arms. Tell me when to stop. Tell me if I hurt you. You have to push your body with your feet while I pull, okay?"

"Okay."

Jagger grabs my hand and begins to pull me from the car. It doesn't hurt, nor is it pleasant. I push my feet against what was before the passenger seat. My body glides through the small opening. As my back slides over the towel a sharp stab courses through my back. Glass! I let out a yell, and Kip begs him to stop pulling me.

"No keep going. We can't fix it until I'm out of this damn thing," I say.

Jagger grabs me under both my arms and pulls me through the opening. When I see his face, I feel calmer. He sets me down on the ground and assesses me. Kip yells at a group of people about a towel. Jagger looks panicked.

"What's wrong?" I ask.

"Look at me. Keep your eyes on mine and do not move. Please listen, Hen."

He doesn't want me to see my injuries. Kip runs back to us with a towel in hand, and I break eye contact with Jagger. When my eyes find Kip's, I see his fear. He eyes move to my left side, and my gaze follows his. Jagger grabs my chin before I can see the reason behind his panic.

"Keep your eyes on me, Hen. Your arm is broken. You shouldn't see it. There is a lot of blood, but we're going to fix it. Kip will wrap the towel around your arm and then tape it. It might hurt but he has to stop the bleeding and keep anything else from getting in it. Hold on, and you scream and swear if you need to, just please don't move your arm." Jagger turns to Kip. "Wrap it as tight as you can, man."

"I can't do this," Kip declares. It must be bad.

"You'll have to wrap it, man," Jagger pleads.

"No. I'll hold her. I can't hurt her," Kip replies.

My eyes stay on Jagger, afraid to see the damage to my arm. He walks to my left, and Kip stands in front of me. He pulls me to his chest. Jagger picks my arm up by my hand and an excruciating pain screams through every cell in my body. I quell my scream into a whimper, but when the towel tightens around my arm, the pain becomes unbearable. As Jagger places the last of the tape around my arm, a young guy around twenty-five approaches to my left and he looks glum.

"They found him. He was thrown across the interstate," he says.

I follow his eyes across the interstate to where I know Caleb lies. Without thinking about it, my legs take over, and I sprint across the lanes as quickly as my body can move. I push through the people hovered around Caleb and start my prayers. Please let him be okay. He has to be okay. I find Caleb lying on grass, his eyes closed. I fall to my knees and place my ear on his chest. There aren't any breath sounds. I can't hear his heartbeat. Okay. It's okay. I took CPR in high school. Remember Henley. It's.... um... it's… thirty compressions, two breaths, and repeat until help arrives.

I tilt his head back and open his mouth to clear his airway. I count thirty compressions, and my arm screams with every single push. I lean down and give Caleb two breaths and then begin my compressions again. *Come on Caleb, open your eyes.* I continue ten sets of compressions and breaths when I see Kip lower himself to the ground beside me. When I catch his movement out of my peripheral vision, I turn and nod. I need to concentrate on the count, so I turn back to Caleb and count. Jagger lowers himself to his knees on the other side of Caleb. I don't take my eyes off Caleb though.

Please Caleb. Please breathe for me. I need you to open your eyes. I don't know how much longer I can do this with my arm. Please be okay. I can't do this. I can't lose you. Where is the fucking ambulance? It should be here by now. I just need to continue CPR until they get here. They will take him to the hospital and fix him. God, they have to fix him. He will be fine. When he gets out of the hospital we will fish every day for a damn month. Come on Caleb! Fight for me, please! Fight for your parents, our fans, our friends! I can't fight by myself.

Movement catches my attention out of my peripheral vision again. A man with salt and pepper hair lowers himself in front of Caleb's head. He gives me a sad little smile. He has on a uniform, but I can't keep count of compressions and figure out who in the hell he is. Shouldn't he be jumping in now?

"Kip, can you please count the compressions?" I ask.

Kip counts. I keep pushing on Caleb's chest and giving two breaths at a time. I can finally give the man beside me a little of my attention. He is just sitting, watching me intently. The patch on the side of his uniform shirt says "EMT," he should help Caleb.

"Why aren't you helping him?" I snarl.

"What's your name?" He asks.

"Henley," I hiss.

"Henley, my name is Manuel. I've been an EMT for twenty years. I will take over compressions when you decide. Once I begin CPR, I cannot stop until he reaches the hospital, and a doctor determines whether the lifesaving measures have any chance of working. I will take over compressions if, and when you tell me to," Manuel says.

"Why wouldn't you?" I ask.

"Henley, you are in shock. You appear injured, and your adrenaline is pumping from the trauma of the accident, so I need to ask you a question. Have you looked at Caleb, darling?"

"YES! I'm looking at him now!" I scream.

"Henley, focus on his head and neck," he says.

I can't bring myself to look at Caleb. I'm not sure I want to see more than I've already seen. I continue my compressions and breaths. No one makes any attempt to speak any further. I realize at this point that emergency lights are flashing everywhere, and traffic is backed up on both sides. The scene around me comes alive as though it were all paused for a moment. Bystanders are watching and whispering, and emergency workers are surrounding me. I listen to Kip count the compressions while I glace around, and take in firefighters, paramedics, and police officers standing around the scene. They are just standing around watching me save Caleb's life. I realize by the expressions on their faces, they know who I am. They know who he is. I get sad, sympathetic faces from each of the men standing behind me. I have no idea how I didn't hear the damn sirens.

I stop compressions long enough to give two more breaths, and as I rise up to start compressions again, I see Jagger's face. Tears are falling down his face, and he seems so helpless. I can't see him like this, so I glance over to Kip who is still counting. His face is stained with tears as well. No, I won't give up on Caleb. I wish I was more religious, and then maybe this wouldn't be happening. I'd have a firm idea of what I believe in, and I would know who in the hell is in charge, so I could take my requests… no orders… directly to him or her. *Save my best friend.*

I peer over at Manuel, and his eyes are glistening with tears. They haven't fallen over just yet, but the emotion is clearly there. When I see his tears, I know. I have to look at him. I complete several more sets of compressions and breaths until I find my courage. When I finally take in the man who has been my best friend, my partner-in-crime since the 1st grade, I can't believe what I see. The right side of his head and face are sunken inward. His neck is severely cut. I can see things I shouldn't be able to see. Those things mean the person is dead, right? I don't understand. Caleb was wearing his seatbelt. How was he thrown so far? Why isn't he in the car? Why did it take so damn long for someone to find him? Why did it take so fucking long for the paramedics to get here?

Why won't Manuel help him? I look back at Manuel's face when I come back up from giving Caleb breaths. His tears have finally fallen over his lids. He knew as soon as he saw my best friend he was dead, and he could not be saved. I can't bring him back. His injuries are too extensive. As reality dawns on me, the tears form and spill in steady streams down my cheeks. He is gone, but I keep pushing and Kip keeps counting. Everyone around us quietly waits. I don't know what they are waiting to happen.

"So, how do I do this? Do I just stop?" I ask.

Manuel's lips press together. "When you are ready, you stop."

"When I'm ready?" I ask unsure of what he means.

Manuel slowly nods his head. "Yes. When you are ready to let him go, you stop CPR."

"But you said you would take over if I ask you to," I plead. It is my last-ditch effort to save him.

"And I will keep my promise. You say the word, and I will take over," Manuel says.

"Okay." But I didn't move or stop CPR.

My eyes found Jagger's beautiful crystal blues. His eyes are puffy and red from crying, but they seem more brilliant through his tears. The things one notices in times like these are almost absurd. Jagger focuses on me with agony in his eyes. When my eyes fall on Kip, he is doing the same. Kip is still counting compressions. Jagger places his hands on top of mine as I continue another twenty sets of compression and breaths. I dip down to give Caleb another two breaths, but when my lips touch his, his skin is cool. It is this moment, right now, I realize he is dead. He cannot be saved, by me or anyone else.

When my hands stop pushing on Caleb's chest, Jagger's holds both of my small hands in his. When I find his beautiful face, I see what sorrow, pain, heartbreak, and anguish look like. Jagger looks like I feel. Heartache sets in, and it feels as though a ton of bricks are now sitting on my chest. The tears spill down my face, and Jagger frees a hand to wipe them away.

"Oh baby, I'm so sorry. I'm just so sorry," he says.

His words carve into my heart like a dagger, and whatever gate was holding my sanity firmly in place has slipped. The hysteria slowly sets in on me. I lay my face down on Caleb's chest, hug him, and sob.

"No! Caleb, no! Please don't leave me! I can't do this! Please!"

Caleb doesn't hear my cries though, and he won't come back. So, I try to pick up his head, but my left arm is hindering. Jagger and Manuel help me pull his body to mine, and I hold him. I hold him and I sob. My best friend is dead.

"Please don't leave me. I don't understand why this happened. I don't understand. I don't want this. This isn't okay. Please Caleb, come back. Don't leave me. Why? Why did you leave? Why did you leave *me*?"

I rock him back and forth as I sob and softly speak to my best friend who can neither hear me nor respond. He never will again. I'm not sure how I'm supposed to live without him. Why didn't I die instead?

Since my pleas to Caleb went unheard, I try Jagger. I find his crystal blue eyes, and beg, "Jagger, please make him come back. He will listen to you. Please bring him back to me."

Jagger tenderly touches his hand to my cheek, and sighs. "I'm so sorry Henley. I'm just so sorry." He chokes on his sympathy.

I don't know how long I stay wrapped up in Caleb, but Manuel keeps telling me to take my time, so I do. I can't bear to say goodbye. I can't figure out how. What words can express the way I feel right now? None of them do the reality of this moment any fucking justice. Kip breaks my trance.

"Henley, the emergency workers have been holding the bystanders back, but people are taking pictures and filming this. We need to let them take Caleb baby," he worries.

I lay Caleb's upper body down with help from Jagger and Manuel. I touch his face, not wanting to forget what he looks like. I kiss his cheek and tell him how much I love him. I tell him how much I will miss him and that he is the best friend I could've ever asked for. I thank him for everything he did for me in this life, and I stand up, and turn away from Caleb and begin walking towards a nearby ambulance. The world spins beneath my feet, and I reach out to steady myself against someone.

"Henley?" Jagger panics.

I avert my gaze in his direction, but I can't see his face. It's blurry, and the world spins faster and faster. My heart beats loudly in my ears, and then blackness sweeps in on me.

Chapter 3

King, 23 Dead; Hendrix, Critical Condition

E! News

It is with much regret we report today on E! News that Caleb King of Abandoned Shadow has been killed in a car accident. It is also reported that Abandoned Shadow's lead singer and guitar prodigy, Henley Hendrix, was a passenger in his car at the time of the accident and is in critical condition at a local Atlanta hospital. Sources close to the band members cite the two left together after an Atlanta concert early this morning. The two were struck on Interstate 75, where King was thrown from his car. He was pronounced at the scene. We will bring you more details as they surface.

Videos of King and Hendrix Crash Surface

Atlanta Alive News

Videos of the car crash that claimed Caleb King's life early this morning are now surfacing on the Internet. The videos are graphic. Caleb King, 23, was killed early this morning in the crash when he was thrown from his Porsche across the interstate. Neither camp from Abandoned Shadow or Broken Access has released a statement on the death, or the condition of Henley Hendrix who is rumored to have sustained serious injuries in the accident. More news to come about Georgia's rockers soon, on Atlanta Alive News.

Caleb King killed by drunk driver

August Reaves

New York Times

Early this morning, rockers Henley Hendrix and Caleb King were struck by what authorities are saying was a drunk driver. The two were struck in King's Porsche, and the car subsequently flipped fifteen times down Interstate 75 in Atlanta, Georgia. The two played Phillip's Arena last night and left together reportedly bound for their hometown of Macon, Georgia. Hendrix is reported to have required help to escape the vehicle, but King was thrown from the car. Bystanders state King's body was thrown from southbound traffic to the northbound side. King, 23, was pronounced dead at the scene, and Hendrix is receiving medical attention at Grady Hospital. It is unclear what injuries Hendrix has sustained, but she is listed in critical condition. Videos of the fatal crash have surfaced on the Internet from bystanders. It is unclear what the videos contain. In my opinion, it is distasteful to post such a tragic event on the Internet. Something so tragic is a private moment. While reporters around the country will write articles and record news segments on the contents of the videos, I remain steadfast in my disapproval.

Carlyle and Paxton Help Hendrix Escape Car
TMZ

As videos of the crash that claimed Caleb King's life went viral this morning, one thing became clear. When traffic came to a standstill stop in Atlanta in both directions for two hours because of the accident, bystanders made use of their time by filming the events that ensued after the crash. In this segment, Jagger Carlyle and Kip Paxton are helping Henley Hendrix escape the vehicle that flipped fifteen times down the interstate. The vehicle is almost unidentifiable, but the individual captured the entire rescue on video. Audio is not the greatest, but subtitles have been added for what can be understood. The video ends as Carlyle pulls her out of the car.

Hendrix's Arm is Broken, and She Loses Consciousness.
E! News

The Hendrix and King camps have remained silent all day. As videos continue to surface of the crash and events surrounding the crash, everyone linked to the bands have remained eerily quiet. The latest video to go viral shows Henley Hendrix, 22, escaping the Porsche Caleb King was thrown from in the collision. Once Jagger Carlyle and Kip Paxton, of Broken Access, help her escape, this video's author captures Hendrix with a bone protruding from her arm. The video also catches Paxton embracing Henley while Carlyle wraps the wound with fabric. It is still unclear what injuries Hendrix has sustained, but Grady Hospital has not changed her status from critical as of late. Another video posted online an hour ago, shows Hendrix covered in blood and collapsing. Jagger Carlyle scoops her up and rushes her to a nearby ambulance. While Carlyle and Paxton were not passengers in King's car, the two were also Macon bound after their Atlanta show last night. It is unclear how close the two were to Hendrix and King's car when the accident occurred. They did not appear to be injured in any of the videos.

This just in.... publicist and long term friend of both bands, Samantha Davenport, will issue a live statement tomorrow morning in front of Grady Hospital. We look forward to receiving news of Hendrix's health. Don't forget to watch for the statement tomorrow morning on E! News.

Caleb King, drunk! Scheduled to Enter Rehab Day of Death!
The Sun

An inside source states Caleb King, 23, was drunk when he crashed his Porsche with Henley Hendrix in it. Apparently, King has long fought with his addiction to alcohol and is rumored to have caused problems with his band, Abandoned Shadow, as a result. Three days ago, King was given an ultimatum from his band mates. He was either to seek treatment for alcoholism, or leave the band. King was scheduled to enter rehab the same day he crashed his car, and his alcoholism could have led to the death of Hendrix besides his own. She remains listed in critical condition at Atlanta's Grady Hospital.

Hendrix tells King Goodbye on Video! Holy Shit!
CelebStalker Blog

The videos that keep surfacing all day are crazy! I've seen every single one of them and keep waiting for more to post. So far I've seen a drunk driver swerve and hit Caleb King's Porsche. There is also a video that shows King's body literally fucking flying over the interstate. It looks like something out of Jackass! The car flips, count with me on this video, one, two, three, four, five, six, seven, eight, nine, ten, eleven, twelve, thirteen, fourteen, fifteen times! I can't believe she is still alive! Jagger Carlyle and Kip Paxton are caught on video helping Henley Hendrix escape, and when she does her fucking bone is sticking out of her arm! WTF? My favorite video is the one of the Guitar Goddess herself, leaping across the barrier between the two directions of traffic and bounding to her best friend. Watch this shit in slow motion. I bet we can add a badass song for effect to this one. That will come later though. Now the newest shit is of Hendrix holding King's dead body crying, and all I love you and shit. At what point did this crazy chick not go, oh a dead body? Gross! You can hear and see snippets of the drama unfold because the emergency workers crowd around here. Cock blockers! Anyhow, is this bitch crazy or what? Leave your comments.

Statement from Samantha Davenport
(The morning after the collision)

Thank you all for coming today. I will read directly from my statement.

Yesterday morning at 2:35 am Eastern Time, Caleb King and Henley Hendrix were struck by a drunk driver on Interstate 75 Southbound in Atlanta, Georgia. The two were leaving a concert they performed at Phillip's Arena. Caleb King was thrown from his car after the collision causing the vehicle to flip many times. Authorities state Caleb was wearing his seatbelt, but due to the momentum of the car while flipping, the seatbelt broke against his weight, and he was ejected from the vehicle. Henley was able to exit the vehicle with the help of Jagger and Kip. Neither Jagger nor Kip were involved in the accident or injured in any way. The two left the venue shortly after Caleb and Henley did and were mere seconds behind the collision. Henley attempted to revive Caleb for close to an hour after she emerged from the vehicle. Caleb was killed instantly from the trauma of being ejected. His preliminary toxicology reports state he had no alcohol or drugs present in his system. He did not have a problem with alcoholism, nor was he given an ultimatum to enter rehab. Caleb rarely drank, and the rumors that say otherwise are malicious and untrue. Henley's toxicology report had the same results; she had no alcohol or drugs in her system. Henley has sustained a broken arm that required surgery to fix. She suffered internal hemorrhaging from the impact of the collision, and she is in a coma due to a hematoma on her brain. The next several days are critical for her as she fights for her life.

Christopher Johnson, 28, of Raleigh, North Carolina was arrested yesterday morning on suspicion of drunk driving. He registered a blood alcohol content of .30 on a Breathalyzer test after the collision, and is charged by the Atlanta City Police with driving under the influence, driving on a suspended license, and first degree homicide by vehicle. Johnson is scheduled to be arraigned tomorrow morning, and a bail hearing will be set.

The band members, family, and friends of Caleb and Henley would like to thank you all for your support, sympathy, prayers and well wishes during this dark time. It is requested that all videos of the collision and events surrounding it be pulled from the Internet out of respect for Caleb, Henley, and their families. The family would like to thank the paramedics on scene, Atlanta Police Department, and Atlanta Fire Department for shielding prying eyes from seeing the most private and heartbreaking of moments when Henley said goodbye to her best friend. No individual was given permission to record either of them, and legal action will follow if videos are not removed within twenty-four hours.

Funeral arrangements for Caleb have not been made. The parents of Caleb would like to thank everyone for their deepest sympathies. They have postponed arrangements pending Henley's recovery. An announcement will be made at a later date. Thank you all for coming and please continue to pray for the families of Caleb and Henley.

Hendrix Awake After Fourteen Days

Atlanta Journal Constitution

Henley Hendrix's publicist has issued a statement notifying the public of Hendrix waking up from a comatose state. She remained in a coma for fourteen days after a vehicle collision that claimed the life of longtime friend and band mate, Caleb King. An earlier statement by the publicist stated Hendrix suffered from a broken arm and internal hemorrhaging. Funeral arrangements are still postponed for Caleb King. Fans have poured out in masses to show respect to Hendrix and King at the site of the accident and at Grady Hospital.

Hendrix rose to fame as a guitar prodigy at the tender age of twelve. Her legendary grandfather, Red Newman, taught her to play the guitar, and she was first noticed on stage with close family friend Buddy Guy. Guy has always joked that she played him right off the stage. King, also rose to fame as a guitar prodigy at the age of fifteen, and the two childhood friends formed the band Abandoned Shadow. The two recorded their first album with band mates Griffin Hughes and Rhys Ryan and were touring by the age of sixteen. Their following grew quickly, and they remain one of the top grossing rock acts in history. Her brother, Koi Hendrix and his band Broken Access, rank right behind Abandoned Shadow. All members from both bands have roots in Macon, Georgia. It is reported King will be buried in his hometown.

Hendrix Hysterical after Miscarriage

The Sun

Sources close to the Guitar Goddess report Henley Hendrix is devastated after losing her unborn child while she was comatose. The sources disclosed Hendrix was around three months pregnant with Caleb King's child. There is a clear link to our earlier reports that King was being forced into rehab, and his expecting a child is a prime motivator for the intervention and ultimatum given to him. Funeral details have not been reported for King.

Statement issued by Jagger Carlyle

It is common knowledge that members of Abandoned Shadow and Broken Access have all been linked since childhood, so it is with a heavy heart that I thank our family, friends, and fans for the outpouring of love and support in the three weeks we have endured the loss of Caleb and the near loss of Henley. I felt it necessary to clear up rumors about the tragic accident and later injuries that claimed Caleb's life and nearly claimed Henley's.

Henley is not pregnant, nor has she ever been pregnant. She and Caleb have always been friends and have never been romantically involved. I find it abhorrent that media outlets find it necessary to report false information in an attempt to further financial gain. This is a time of grieving for our friends, families, and fans, and we ask our privacy be respected so we may have time to remember, mourn, and heal. Funeral arrangements have not yet been scheduled because of Henley's injuries. She and Caleb have been friends since the first grade, and Caleb's parents would like her to be able to attend.

I would like to take a moment to ask the world to consider other options when intoxicated. Drunk driving claims innocent lives and is a senseless act. Caleb touched so many people around the world in his short twenty-three years, and his life was cut ridiculously short because someone made a selfish decision. Please call someone for a ride, walk, or call a cab if you are intoxicated. I urge you to think of the possible consequences your actions can have on others. If you are prone to drink and drive, surrender your keys before you drink.

I appreciate all the support during this difficult time. Our parents have held us together, and our friends have been our rock. Henley is awake and doing as well as can be expected. She is healing well physically, but is still coming to grips with an immense loss. Thank you to all of our fans who have poured out their hearts on social media for us. Your words do not go unnoticed. Please continue all positive thoughts and prayers as we endure the days, weeks, and months to come.

Chapter 4

Four Years Later

"Henley! Look this way."

"Who are you wearing?"

"Your dress is gorgeous."

The lights flash all around me as I walk into the awards show. I was taught a long time ago to look straight ahead. You can't see a damn thing when the masses of photographers aim their incessant flash at you. So you just smile and look ahead. When you join the league of the rich and famous, your life belongs to the world. You are superhuman, and all around eyes lurk in the shadows watching and waiting for you to fall gracelessly from the top. It reminds them of their own humanity, their own impermanence.

The red carpet always turns into the lights on the dash. Caleb is laughing about the gig we just left. A girl in the front row flashed him all night, and he loves being rich and famous. We cruise down Interstate 75 South heading for Macon, home. The bump startles me. Caleb's smile leaves his face, and he peers in the rear view mirror. I see horror take over his beautiful face. The world is upside down, and I'm trapped. I can't breathe. Where is Caleb? I have to get out of here, but the seat belt is stuck. Something is oozing down my face, and it stings my eyes. I begin to pour sweat as I work to free myself. What is wrong with this damn seat belt? I grow frantic, and I want to scream, but I cannot seem to push it from my belly. Then I see him. Caleb! I finally scream for him. I finally free myself and kick my way out of the car. There are people everywhere, and they are in my face. Get out of my way! I finally get to the other side of the car, but Caleb isn't there anymore. Where is he? I scream for him. I beg him to tell me where he is.

I launch myself into a sitting position on the bed, covered in a sweat, attempting to catch my breath. It's always the same dream. He's always gone at the end, and I can never find him. I sit on the edge of the bed and take a drink of water from the table beside where I lie. My cell starts ringing.

"Yeah?"

"Hey, gorgeous!" Jagger says.

"Hey, you," I croak out.

"You okay?"

"Yeah. Bad dream."

"You want me to come down?" He asks, and it sends all kinds of naughty thoughts through my head. Yes, I want you to go down.

"Nah. I'm good. I will see you tonight."

"Good. I'm calling to make sure I'm still going to see your gorgeous face tonight," He says with that raspy voice that pours sex. I can always sit on your gorgeous face, I think.

"I wouldn't miss it." Sitting on his face, or seeing his face.

***

The last four years of my life are scarred by the tragedy that took my best friend. I left music. I was rock-n-roll's favorite child, and I left it all behind because I refused to fall apart in front of the entire world. It isn't any of their fucking business. They don't know him, and they didn't lose him. I also can't muster the courage to play music again without him. It took me a year to decide suicide isn't an option because I'm too much of a coward to go through with it. It took me another year to find something to scratch my itch. My itch is needing to find something to do every day that doesn't require me to be the guitar prodigy anymore. I went through every hobby known to man. I couldn't find fulfillment no matter what I tried.

My dad suggested I pick my camera up and find something to do with it. I photographed my entire life before Caleb died. I managed to maintain control of most of the photographs that were released of our band and even our private lives. I love photography as much as I loved music. It is a big deal to maintain control of our pictures, and it further showed the deep artistic qualities of our band. When I finally picked my camera back up, I went backpacking through Europe for six months. I saw everything I ever wanted to see from the Irish Countryside, medieval castles, Rome, and I even ran with the bulls in Spain. I slowly began to feel alive again, but the numb isn't completely gone.

My travels taught me how to embrace how others live. When I was in Italy, I learned to let go of the American picture of beautiful. Italians eat and drink with indulgence. They enjoy every bit of food and drink that touches their taste buds. I didn't really learn to enjoy food until my time in Italy. The French taught me that it is acceptable to have a filthy mouth. I appreciate their country for that. This beautiful country can teach anyone how to live passionately. If you leave with nothing else, you will use filthy words passionately, and you will do so in style. You won't ever catch the French slumming it. The British taught me to embrace my sarcasm. They aren't easily offended, and after living most of my life in the Deep South, it was refreshing. They also expand your vocabulary; simple requests become a fucking poem by the end. The Irish taught me to love whiskey, and that every occasion is worth drinking for. I also learned if you can't beat them, fuck it; beat the shit out of them… most likely you will be friends tomorrow. The Germans taught me to be proud of my own country. Germany is a country full of people with feelings of nationalism. They also know how to drink like sailors, and they do it with such fervor. The ideals of socially acceptable alcohol use in the States fall to the wayside in Germany. Live and let live.

While I was in Germany in my sixth month of travel, I was approached by a Buddhist Monk. Jagaro approached me at a coffee shop as I was considering going back to Georgia.

"Life is full of suffering," he said with an Asian accent.

He then motioned for the chair on the other side of my table. I nodded to let him know he could sit. *Life is full of suffering.* Why yes it is my new, enlightened friend. I didn't need a monk to tell me; I live it every day.

"The death of a loved one, reminds of us of our own impermanence. It is alright to be sad about your friend, but he will not find peace until you do," I stared at this man as my mouth dropped to the floor. If he had been anyone else, I may have decked him and been thrown out of the country, but somehow I knew he meant well. He was concerned for me, a perfect stranger.

"Caleb is not at peace?" I asked.

"He is not suffering, but his soul will not find total peace until you do," he replied.

I pondered that for a beat. "I don't know how. It hurts so much."

"Tell me, what did you leave behind? I see you live a different life now," he asked.

I smiled a nervous smile. "I don't really live at all anymore."

It was the first time I realized this for myself. What was I doing with my life? Caleb would be so pissed at my choices.

He stood and offered his hand. Now I was raised with the same rules as you were, don't talk to strangers, don't take candy from strangers, and don't take drinks from strangers. But I gave him my hand anyways, and I followed him back to the Muttodaya Forest Monastery. There, I lived for three months adapting to the Buddhist lifestyle. I worked, I meditated, I studied, and I worked some more. Anyone who has ever thought **that being a monk wa**s easy work has no clue what the calling is about. At the end of month three, I felt more peaceful and calm. I smiled and laughed, and I felt like I really understood why Caleb had to go. I approached Jagaro and told him I would be departing back to the States the next week. He hugged me and we smiled at each other, a knowing smile full of genuine love.

"You have found so much peace. Continue your studies and meditation, and as life throws you more suffering, you will be strong. You are strong Chiko." This is what Jagaro calls me.

"Why Chiko?" I asked for the first time in three months.

"It means small tiger. Some believe a tiger represents strength. Some also believe this animal represents changing one's anger into wisdom and insight. This is you Chiko."

He smiled at me again with love. He is very observant. I slowly but surely found a way to transform my anger at Caleb's death to an understanding I never thought I would find.

My departure from the monastery was a tearful one. I said my goodbyes to each of the monks. They all gave me a gift. I had prayer flags, malas, and amulets for protection and happiness. It is Buddhist custom to give a donation when you are given a gift, so I handed Jagaro a three million dollar check. Three million dollars is not nearly enough for what he helped me find… peace. I spent most of my teenage years and adult life as a rock star, so three million wasn't going to set me back.

I returned to the states having done the *Eat, Pray, Love* thing, and spent some time with family and friends in Georgia. I was only home three weeks when my itch needed to be scratched again. I decided to travel to Africa to volunteer helping out a local village. I helped build a school, a clinic, and helped teach the children. I educated the villagers on HIV and AIDS and how to prevent the virus from spreading. I used my contacts back in the States to provide condoms, and medications to manage those who already have the virus. I remained in South Africa for almost a year before I returned home. I stayed in contact with my friends, but especially my brother Koi and Kip.

Koi has his own majorly successful rock-n-roll story. Our grandfather is Red Newman. He is a fucking legend. We were given instruments when we were toddlers. Our grandfather wrote some of the most notorious songs in music dating back to the 50's. He was a highly respected musician, songwriter, and eventually a producer. Koi is 18 months older than me and is the front man for Broken Access. He plays rhythm guitar and writes half the songs for the band.

Jagger is the epitome of a rock star. Every man wants to be him, and every woman wants to fuck him. He can't be tamed. He is known for his love of women, lots of women. Google his name. Did you do it yet? You won't see him in a picture with the same woman more than once. He loves to party hard and has been thrown out of his fair share of hotels for being loud and destructive. He is covered in tattoos and is a guitar god. There isn't one ingredient in the bad boy recipe that Jagger isn't made of, and last year he showed off most of those ingredients in his cover of People's *Sexiest Man Alive* cover issue. Jesus, those hipbones. It should be a crime to be that damn fine. Those hipbones, abs, and tattoos did things to me all the way on another continent. He is six foot three, tan, lean, with tattoos in all the right places, and crystal blues eyes that sparkle. He has a panty-dropping smile. I mean it. If you were at a party standing in the corner talking to a friend and minding your own damn business; you could make eye contact with him and as soon as he smiles… BOOM! You're standing in a room full of people with your drawers around your feet.

When my girly bits started to come alive in eighth grade, Jagger was the boy who starred in my fantasies most nights. I only deviated to Johnny Depp or Jared Leto when I saw Jagger with another girl. I suppose it was my way of punishing him in my teenage mind and heart even if he didn't know it. Jagger never saw me the way I saw him, but there is always a place in your heart reserved for your first crush.

Jagger happened upon the scene of the accident that claimed Caleb's life. He left the venue our bands played shortly after we did, and when he hit traffic he began calling our phones. Apparently, when neither Caleb nor I answered our phones, his intuition told him to park his car on the shoulder, and he ran until he found the accident. I have no idea what Jagger thought or what he went through that night, I only know I couldn't have made it without him. That night forever solidified our friendship.

***

Broken Access is playing Verizon Wireless Amphitheater in North Atlanta tonight, and I promised Koi I would photograph the show. I might as well get my ass in gear. I have a two-hour drive to Koi's hotel. I'm wearing a dress that could probably be longer, but I'm 26, and I have a nice body. This shit won't last forever, so I might as well flaunt it while I can. I'm also sporting my knee high black leather boots with a four-inch heel.

I make the drive to Atlanta from Macon, turning my iPod all the way up and rock out to Sevendust, Chevelle, and Jimi Hendrix. I finally arrive at his hotel, but not before he and his band mates send heaps of texts requesting my ETA. I meet Koi in his room and throw my arms around my brother. Women love him. He has darker features than I do. His dirty blonde hair and chiseled jaw encase his dimples and dark blue eyes.

"Jagger says you had a bad dream," Koi says.

"He has a big fucking mouth."

"You okay?" He frowns.

"Yeah. I don't have them as much as I used to. Everything is fine," I lie.

There is a loud knock on his suite door suddenly. Koi opens the door, and Jagger bursts through all smiles.

"Henley!" He rushes to me and lifts me off the ground. He hugs me tight and doesn't let go for a beat. God I love the smell of him. He smells the same as he always has since we were teenagers. A touch of patchouli, a hint of cigarettes, a dab of leather, and spicy like saffron…. yes that describes Jagger.

"Stop mauling my sister," Koi says.

"Your sister is hot. I can't help myself. She is all powerful and classy and it just makes me all touchy-feely."

He winks at me. He loves taking jabs at my brother. I guess they are really more like brothers than friends since they have been friends for fifteen years.

I look at two of my favorite men in the world and give them the biggest smile I can muster. I really miss these guys, and my eyes get all fucking misty. Damn allergies. I avert my eyes down at my shoes to hide my emotion. Jagger lifts my chin to force eye contact. He never misses a damn thing.

"What's wrong gorgeous?"

I smile again. "I just realized how much I miss you two. It has been a long time since we've hung out. It feels like old times, well sort of." Sort of, without Caleb.

Jag really is gorgeous. His crystal blue eyes shine back at me.

"I'm only ever a phone call away, Hen." He strokes his thumb up my cheek. How does he do that to me? I think I need to change my panties.

He keeps rubbing his thumb down my jaw line, and oh dear Lord Jesus, Buddha, and Allah, I think my vagina is on fire. I quickly assess how I can get my brother out of the room, disrobe Jag, have amazingly hot and dirty sex, and then get myself in order so my brother never knows. I muster the best smile I can and hope Jag and my brother can't read my thoughts. He probably shouldn't touch me again. It is highly likely that I will start humping him like a damn dog. Down girl.

Koi interrupts my reverie with tirades about the girl he recently split from. We start discussing issues with his current flame. He just broke up with a makeup artist, Reagan, who is the spawn of Satan. Seriously, the bitch is certifiably psychotic. He speaks to Jagger in an attempt to finish telling a story, but Jagger doesn't respond. Koi launches a pillow from the nearby couch at his best friend, and Jag finally seems to snap out of it.

"Sorry…shit... what?" Jag asks irritated.

"Dude! You are so checking out my sister's ass," Koi is disgusted.

"No. I'm checking out your sister's ass, legs, feet, back, shoulders, hair, and all the places I can only imagine in between," he retorts.

Oh daddy.

Koi's jaw tenses, and I can see his aggravation.

"I'm going to find the rest of the guys. I will call when it is time to load up on the bus and head over to the venue. Try not to rape my sister while I'm gone." he smirks.

I look back to Jagger, and he is staring again. "I'm going to have to kill any motherfucker who looks at you tonight. Maybe we should cover your shoulder up. Jesus! While I'm redressing you, we should just buy you a jibab and hijab. We can even buy you the Moroccan version so it has all that pretty stuff on it." He looks serious.

"Jag, I'm going downstairs for a smoke. If I see you with a jibab or a hijab, I'm going to put my cigarette out in your eye." I give him my serious face, hands on hip and the whole shebang.

Jagger takes a few steps towards me with his long legs and pulls me into a tight hug. He holds me for a long time and strokes my hair with his free hand. Just as I think I'm about to spontaneously combust from the sexual frustration coursing through my body, he draws back and places the sweetest kiss on my forehead. Like I said, he sees me in a platonic way, while I see him in a very naked way. Yup, right between my legs. Hell, I couldn't care less what part of him is between my legs, as long as he is there. He offers me his arm with a smile, and I take it.

He shakes his head and mumbles, "I'm going to jail tonight."

We wait for the elevator and then enter the car when it arrives. Jag leans into the back corner of the car and when I look up, he has an intense look on his face. He holds my gaze. I would normally break the ice by saying something witty, but I can't seem to muster up the words. His crystal blue eyes are making my vagina pull out her Sunday church fan to fan the flames. If he continues looking at me so intensely, I'm going to *rape* him. The scene plays out in my head…. Mmm. Before I know it, Jag crosses the car and puts his hands on either side of my head, and he leans down into my personal space. I mean up close and in my face. I really love the way he smells. Have I mentioned that before now? If not, I should have. He smells like sex on a stick. Speaking of sticks…. I wonder how big his is. I do a mental headshake, focus grasshopper.

I look down at his chest because his proximity is making me all light-headed. Am I in high school again? He lifts my chin again, and I look into those crystal blues. I really can get lost in them.

"I'm so glad to see you. I don't mean your presence, I mean the Henley who threatens violence, like putting a cigarette out in my eye. You are so fucking gorgeous." He leans down to my neck and sniffs.

"You even smell amazing. I love the scent." Goosebumps spread down my arms.

Oh, daddy I have a scent for you. If I speak now, I will stutter like a damn fool, though. He leans back up and makes eye contact. He is really close to my face. He looks at my lips and back to my eyes. Oh, in the name of everything holy, please jack me against this wall and have your way with me. Is he going to kiss me?

The elevator car pings, and it stops on the tenth floor. He pulls away slightly and then tucks into the corner behind me as the elevator quickly fills with roadies. They instantly notice me, and I'm enclosed into hugs and greeted with endless smiles. The elevator quickly makes its way down to the lobby, and I follow the masses of men out to the smoking section, all the while wondering what just fucking happened in that elevator. I should have worn extra thick panties tonight, to soak up all the hot mess Jagger causes between my legs.

Once I enter the smoking section, I light up a menthol and enjoy the first drag. Camden and Kip emerge around the corner of the smoking section with Koi, and their faces light up when they lay eyes on me. Camden is the bass player, and Kip is the drummer in Broken Access. Camden is more on the quiet side, and Kip is a fucking riot. Camden pushes Kip back as though they are still kids and gets a head start on me. He picks me up, swings me around, and hugs me tightly. Kip yanks me from Camden's embrace and throws my petite body over his shoulder.

He walks away from the guys with me yelling. "I'm wearing a fucking dress you ass hat!"

"Bring her back Kip!" Camden growls in mock irritation.

"Go get your own!" Kip yells back.

"There isn't another one asshole!" Camden replies while I'm being manhandled by Kip. He finally sets me down when we turn another corner, and I quickly pull my short dress down. He steps back, looks me over, and smiles.

"Looking good girl. Miss you so much," He says, and then he embraces me in another hug. In this moment, I feel a major rush of guilt for barely being around for the past four years.

Camden rounds the corner with Koi and Jag and immediately picks up where he left off. He wraps me in a big bear hug and sets me back down and smiles at me. Cam quickly kisses me on my cheek.

"You are the most beautiful woman I have ever seen. Why just the other day, I was telling your loving brother how your poster from the Rolling Stone cover in 2005 is my favorite jerk off material for like ever."

I feign a gag, and the guys laugh.

"Yeah your brother was none too happy about that revelation. Jag was about to pummel me, and Kip tried to one up me by…."

"Shut up fuck face," Kip warns.

"What you don't want my baby sister to know you jacked off to her 2006 Maxim Magazine photographs?" Koi laughs.

Kip is immediately face to face with me, lifts my chin to meet his eyes, and I knew by the mischievous grin on his face he is up to no good.

"Don't let your brother fill your pretty little head with all this nonsense. I worship you as the goddess you are. It isn't my fault you graced that cover in lacy boy shorts and a mesh shirt that left everything to my imagination. I'm a man and let me tell you… I imagined it all! I'm a visual creature, and ma'am you were very visual to me in the 2006 Maxim article. I really enjoyed the article as well. Although, I did have to memorize the article because the pages began to stick together."

"Jesus, Kip. I just threw up in mouth a little," I shot back.

"You hurt my heart lady. You hurt my heart. I stand here and bare my soul and you rip it from my body. I really did memorize your amazing intellectual article," he chuckles.

"Oh dear sir, I do apologize for my lack of couth. Please do tell me, what is your favorite part of the article?" I ask.

His face drops into a frown, and he considers for a beat. The lively banter is gone. The tension coming off him now encases me. "When the interviewer asks you how you feel about being called *The Guitar Goddess* all these years, you say, 'It really is an amazing gift my fans gave me. It let me know they enjoy my lyrics, music, and our band. I have been a musician for as long as I can remember, and I can't imagine doing anything else. That being said, I think people often forget, even the people who know me best, that I'm human. I hurt, I bleed, I cry, and I feel just like everyone else.' I love that you showed the world you are human, no matter how they try to immortalize you Hen."

"Well thank you love. I'm just a girl ya know?" I thank him lightheartedly to avoid the serious turn of direction.

"If you are done trying to get into her panties, maybe we can all head to the venue," Jagger says to Kip.

"Carlyle, don't get jealous. Henley has always been in love with me. Tell Jag, Henley," Kip teases with a straight face.

Before I can retort, Koi jumps into the conversation. "Jesus Christ. She is my sister for fuck's sake. Do any of you ever take that into account when you talk about her like she is a piece of meat?"

"No!" His three band mates say in unison.

Chapter 5

The bus ride to the venue takes close to an hour with Atlanta traffic. Broken Access is headlining the entire tour, so they won't go on stage until ten. When I toured, I always enjoyed arriving early enough to catch some of the other bands. It also gave me a chance to photograph them on stage. Koi and the guys make a habit of arriving early too. The guys are each doing their own thing on the bus. Cam and Jag are playing the Xbox. Koi is talking to his publicist on the phone, and Kip is watching Dexter. I watch TV with Kip.

When the bus finally parks at the venue, the road manager Randy comes on board.

"Listen guys, there is a crowd near the entrance. We are waiting on more security staff to help walk us there. Get your pens out and get ready to sign." He lowers his eyes to me, and smiles. "Good to have you back, Henley. You have no idea how much we miss you."

I smile back fighting those pesky damn tears in my eyes.

Jag pulls his shirt off and I think my jaw hit the floor. You have to see Jagger in the flesh to fully appreciate all this man encompasses. I thought he was gorgeous as a teenage boy, but the man he has become has surpassed all that I could have hoped for. I think I might be drooling. Close your mouth Henley. He is looking through a small closet and each time he moves a hanger on the rack, his muscles move, and just DAMN. Jag isn't a meathead. He is just lean and in great shape, amazing shape really. Oh my, look at those washboard abs. I can lick all sorts of things off those: whip cream, every flavor of syrup, ice cream, cream cheese, icing… focus grasshopper. His dark brown hair is buzzed, and he has an olive skin complexion that will make any woman sick. You should see that skin when it is all tan during the summer, yummy. He towers over my five feet four inches at six foot three. He has strong arms that make you wonder just how capable of a man he must be. His arms are covered in beautiful tattoos, and that muscular back would make the gods weep.

I quickly take a peek to make sure no one saw me ogling Jag. Good, they are all busy. I better not chance it again. I hear Jag's steps coming towards me, and I keep my head down pretending I wasn't just looking in his direction.

"Stand up woman," he orders with a smirk on his face.

Hell, he can order me to do lots of things: bend, up, down, on me, under me, open, lick…. I digress. I do as I'm told, and he pulls a familiar looking messenger cap from behind his back.

"You left this on the tour bus. It's from the last tour we did together four years ago. I figured you might need it when you came back out with us again."

He puts it over my head and fixes my long blonde hair hanging from under it. His hands brush my face when he does so, and I swear to you I almost cream in my panties.

"When?" I ask.

He pursues his lips in sympathy. "Yes. When. I knew it would take you some time to feel comfortable touring again. I never knew how long, but I knew you couldn't stay away from music for the rest of your life. Regardless of how much you have put between yourself and the industry, our fans were your fans first. We don't ever forget that. They still love and want you. They will recognize you in a heartbeat. Your face has been in the media since you were twelve years old. You are America's guitar prodigy, rock-n-roll royalty. Just because you want to stop being *The Guitar Goddess,* doesn't mean they will let you. When you are the President of the United States, you are always the President of the United States," he chuckles. "We are going to have to flank you on all sides so no one catches sight of you. Unless, you want them to?"

"No. I'm not ready for that Jag," I know my eyes plead with him.

His eyes soften. "It's okay not to be ready. You being on this bus, at this show… that's big. It can't be easy to walk away from the only thing you have ever known. It can't be easy trying to figure out who you are as a person and a musician without him."

"If you are done whispering sweet nothings to my sister, we can go inside now. Security is waiting outside the door," Koi laughs.

"I'm discussing her being noticed," Jagger says with a little gruffness to his voice.

I guess my brother hadn't thought of that. Hell neither had I, but Jagger seems upset with Koi for it.

"She needs to be heavily surrounded by security going in. We can see about ourselves. We need to sign autographs anyway," Jagger says.

"Most certainly not. You guys are not going out there unprotected. I, of all people, know how crazy fans can get. We need to figure something else out," I demand.

All eyes are on me, and Randy is back on the bus. "Shit," he says. "Henley, forgive me. I hadn't thought about this being a problem. I will figure something out."

"No. You are my sister; I should've been more proactive and thoughtful. Shit." Koi runs his hands through his hair obviously frustrated. "Everybody sit still for a minute." Koi exits the bus. Luckily, our bus is parked between two others, so no one who shouldn't have access to this area will see him.

Thirty minutes pass before Koi boards the bus again. I'm left to my own negative thoughts about being noticed. I wonder why I didn't worry about this before now. Perhaps, I was too consumed with all things Jagger to think about anything else. My brain synapses do not fire properly when he is around.

What if someone asks me to sing or play? Until six months ago, I hadn't picked up a guitar in years. I have been focusing solely on healing. I feel panic begin to creep up, so I start a little chant Jagaro taught me in Germany and focus on my breathing to stay calm.

"I got it worked out," Koi happily announces. "Come on guys. Let's do it to it."

Jagger motions for me to step in front of him. I exit the bus and follow behind the band as they walk towards the back of the bus. I am not prepared for what is waiting for me. Every band and staff member on tour is standing there, waiting. Waiting for me. If you have never been on tour or seen the inner workings of a tour, the amount of people musicians rely on to make this happen each night is enormous. We depend on a lot of people. They make it possible for musicians to walk out on stage every night and sing and play their hearts out. I look behind me to see Jag smiling. He is smiling at the hundred or so men standing in front of me. I turn back towards the men, and see they have their hands on their hearts, for me. The notion was started when I was fifteen; my Grandfather was photographed with his hand over his heart while I played a forty-minute guitar duet with Buddy Guy on stage in Chicago. The notion stuck, and it is how people began to show respect for me. What stands in front of me now is overwhelming respect. I focus on my breathing again, and I simply nod my head at the crowd and offer a smile. To show respect back, I place my hand over my heart and mouth a "thank you."

"We are putting you in the middle of that very huge crowd. You won't be noticed. The musicians in the group will cover the inner part closest to you so they can avoid heat from the fans. The staff will cover all the musicians. This will give us all coverage," Koi says.

I will never know how he did this in thirty minutes. We spend a minute or so getting into some semblance of a circular crowd and then follow Randy to the building. Someone grabs my hand after we walk a few feet. I look up to see Jagger smiling sweetly at me. He focuses on moving forward and getting me inside the venue. He has his serious face back on moments later. He rubs the pad of his thumb on the inside of my hand. He is nervous about me being seen. Jag has always been sweet to me, but this is a new level of sweet. I like it!

We make it to the venue without much fuss. Jag keeps my hand in his. The guys still flank my sides as we are ushered into their dressing room. Once inside, I feel relief. Jag still holds my hand, and Kip looks between us with the oddest look upon his face.

"Henley, if you want a real man to hold your hand, all you have to do is ask." He crosses over to us and takes my other hand pulling me away from Jag. I burst out laughing.

"Now boys, let's play nice with each other. I love you all."

"Yeah, but you love me just a teeny-tiny bit more, right?" Kip asks with two fingers in front of my face.

"Dude, are you showing her the size of your dick right now? You are supposed to surprise women with that kinda shit or you will never get laid," Cam says.

"It's the motion in the ocean fucker," Kip fires back feigning hurt. "Isn't that right girl?" He elbows me as a prompt.

"Um… Kip, you see…. That isn't always true. Sometimes you have to possess a big enough boat to even make waves before the motion even becomes relevant." I pat him on the cheek and he puts on his best, shocked face. "I'm sorry to be the bearer of bad news sweetie," I chuckle.

"See she called me sweetie. I'm sweet. At least I have that going for me, right?" He looks down to me with big puppy dog eyes.

"Yes, you most definitely have that going for you," I say with another pat.

"Stop trying to get in my sister's panties. Fuck, SHE IS MY SISTER!" Koi yells.

"Dude every man who has ever walked planet earth wants to get in your sister's panties. Hell I would prefer if she just wouldn't wear any, easier access and all," Jagger says with a shit-eating grin on his face.

I think I'm blushing.

Thankfully my parents enter the room and take all attention off of me. My mom and dad are carrying a suitcase. They hug each of the band members and a few roadies who are in and out of the room.

My dad pulls me into a hug and whispers in my ear. "I'm so proud of you Henley. You will find your happiness back on the road with your camera in hand. Maybe you will even find your way back to music."

On the road? What the hell? I pull back from my dad's hug a bit and look him in the face.

"Dad, what are you talking about?" I must've said it harsher and louder than I meant to, because Kip, Cam, Mom, Jag, and Koi attempt to exit the room in that order.

"Get your conniving asses back in here."

They all stop, turn, and look at me. Oh someone is about to get the ass kicking of the century. So this is what a set up looks like. I look around at the faces to see who the guilty culprit is. Their faces tell me they have all played a part in this scheme. Jag has the guiltiest face of all though. Hmm.

"Everybody out except Koi and Jag," I order.

My dad kisses my cheek and pats Koi and Jag on the shoulders. He knows the tongue-lashing they are about to get is going to be unpleasant. Once everybody exits, I find the table that holds alcohol in the corner of the room. I down a beer in a few seconds. That should take the edge off.

"What in the hell do you two think you are doing?" I spit at them. It looks as though they are both hoping the other would speak first. Pussies.

"No, Henley. This is between you and me. I did this," Jagger says.

Koi takes that as his cue, so he promptly exits the room.

"Jag, what the fuck? You can't bully me into going on tour with you. I have a life. I have appointments all over the country to photograph clients. I can't just stop everything because you tell my mom to pack a bag. What are you thinking?"

Jagger doesn't answer me. He stares at me, and he seems to be carefully choosing his words. He takes a few steps towards me, and stops. He doesn't speak immediately, but instead lets out a big sigh.

"My dad has his hopes up that this will lead to some miraculous return of me to this scene. Why would you do that to me? Do you have it out for me?"

Jagger frowns and gives me his puppy dog eyes. Shit. When he gives me those eyes, what in the hell am I supposed to do? Kiss him? Perhaps. No, no, that is the worst idea ever. Focus. He tenderly touches my face again. You see this recurring theme too, right? Or, am I just imagining all these intimate touches? I really need to get laid.

"I miss you Henley. I just… shit I don't know what I was thinking. I just know we all need you. I have seen you more in the last year than I have in a long time, but it still isn't like the old days. We grew up together, and I saw you almost daily from the sixth grade forward. I guess I feel like I lost you too when we lost Caleb, and I selfishly tried to force you back into my life the way I want you in it. I'm sorry. Forgive me?"

"Fine. But next time, how about asking what I want? Let me know what plans you have for my life, yeah?"

"So does this mean you are going on tour with us?" He asks hopefully.

"Jesus. Yeah, I will go for a bit. I miss you guys too. I really do,"

"My reasons may not be good enough for what I did, but they are all I have. I should be sorry that I went behind your back to get you on tour with us, but I'm not because it worked. I get to spend every day with the girl I grew up with. The girl I had my very first crush on."

"Crush?" Yes, that is the only part of the conversation I can focus on at this very moment.

"Really, Henley? You didn't know?" He asks in genuine shock.

"No. How was I supposed to know? You never gave me the slightest hint. You never told me."

"Jesus. I was scared to death to be around you. Your life in middle school was already bright lights and guitars. Your family is well known in our parts, and when I was in the same class as you in middle school, I think my dad was actually jealous. You intimidated the shit out of me. I was a teenage boy who got wood if the wind blew the right way. If you walked into a room, I had to sit down and hide it. When I met your brother and started the band in the ninth grade, I was hoping I would get close enough to you. By the middle of tenth grade you were home schooled and recording your own album. You were so out of my league it isn't even funny," he says with a chuckle.

I say the only thing I can think of to break the ice and hide my own embarrassment. "So which is your favorite magazine cover?" I give him my best sexy grin ever.

He throws his head back and laughs a big boisterous laugh, but sets his crystal blue eyes back on me, and they are serious and heated. "Spin Magazine, August 2009. The only thing covering the bits every man alive wants to see is a 1964 Gibson. You had a cigarette hanging in one hand, and a sleeve of tattoos on your arm. Your right leg is bent, and your foot is in front of the guitar holding it in place, while your left leg is laid out for inviting eyes to only imagine the unknown. But my pages aren't sticky. I bought five copies so I always have at least one memorabilia edition."

It is my turn to burst out laughing. That is actually one of my favorite shoots ever. I felt like the sexiest woman alive. I feel giddy now. I'm his first crush too. I need to devise a clever way to let him know.

"And now I have my own cover for eye candy, Mr. Sexiest Man Alive," I tease.

"And none of it changes a damn thing."

"What do you mean?" I ask.

Before he can answer, a roadie enters the room and requests his presence in another part of the venue.

Chapter 6

I walk down the back halls of the venue to the backstage area. This walk is always my favorite. You walk towards your screaming fans. You walk towards doing the one thing that matters most in life, playing music. I follow behind everyone else. The guys are at the front of the crowd. All of our parents are here following behind their sons, and then the roadies, technicians, and other staff follow suit. I follow behind the group with camera in hand. I hear someone walking behind me and turn to look as I feel a presence getting closer. I'm pulled into a side room, and once inside I realize Jagger's hands were on me. Yeah, I said it, that fine ass man's hands were on me. When he opens the door, several members of Resin are sitting around a table. I hate that I missed their show. I really love their music. Shaun isn't hard on the eyes either.

They look a bit stunned to see us. "Can I have the room for one minute guys? Sorry to bust in here like this. I didn't realize anyone else was in here."

The guys are instantly accommodating, and as they exit, Shaun turns to me. "You are the most amazing guitarist I have ever had the pleasure of seeing live. I know death, and I know loss, so I hope you find your way back. We miss you." And with a smile he is gone. Swoon!

I don't have time to get emotional because Jagger gently grabs the sides of my face again. I really like this touchy-feely stuff. He shows me my "All Access" pass with the name, "Jagger's 1st Crush" typed across it. I burst out laughing as he places the lanyard over my head.

"I guess you can't very well put Henley Hendrix on it. Thank you Jagger." I lean up and kiss him on the cheek. He stills, so I stand on my tippy toes and hug him tightly. "Now go rock their faces off."

He smiles and we walk to the side of the stage with him carrying my camera case, and my arm through his.

I forgot how much I enjoy the first moments of live rock-n-roll. The moment when all the lights go down and you hear the first guitar riffs through the speakers. The riffs sound more powerful, harsher, and more real than the recorded music. When the lights come on, you see the love each musician has for their own music. They create this. It is theirs, and this is the moment to own it. I wait for the first song before I go to the press pit. I want to enjoy watching them play for the first time in four years.

I wind my way down to the gate between backstage and the audience. The security guard lets me through, and points me to the press pit. There are eight others in the pit. I have never fought for space with them since I usually wait until they are gone to start snapping shots. Industry standard for concert photography gives the photographers only the first three songs to photograph with absolutely no flash. I didn't realize how cramped it would be. I might as well get used to it. I push through the men and start shooting the guys rocking their faces off. They are playing one of their earlier hits and my brother is singing lead. I love this song. I photograph each one of them in their element. When Koi and Jagger back off the mikes and start playing close to one another, I capture every second of it. Through my lens I can tell they are laughing at one another. They are enjoying every second of this. As Koi steps back up to the mike, Jag joins Cam on bass, and I capture their serious guitar faces. Then I focus on Kip at the drums. His shirt is already off and sweat is starting to show up. That's how I like my drummers… shirtless and sweaty. But don't we all?

The second song winds down, and the photographer beside me yells. "Hey, are you Henley Hendrix?"

Shit. I shake my head and pull my hat down a bit more. I will wait on the side of the stage while they finish up photographing their last song. I begin to make my way across the length of the stage to the back stage door when someone from the crowd grabs my shirt. They must've heard him. The photographers are all in my face by this point clicking away. I'm trying to cover my face and protect my camera at the same time. Hands continue to grab me from the front of the crowd. I'm stuck between the metal divider that keeps the crowd back and eight grown men, double my petite size. When the dim lights brighten on stage, I'm really in trouble.

"Get the fuck off of her!" I hear.

A sweaty man picks me up. I hear Koi screaming at the photographers behind me. I'm quickly carried to the end of the stage, and through the door. The area between the end of the walkway from the side of the stage and the door at the bottom is dark, but I know who manhandles me. I could bottle up that smell and sell it for hundreds of dollars.

I'm sat on a crate. "Jesus Christ! Are you okay Hen? Are you hurt?"

I feel Jag's hands on my face, and I instantly know he is shaking. From fear or anger, I don't know. He can't see me in the dark. He can't see my fear. I shouldn't have gone out there with those other photographers. I knew better.

"I'm fine Jag. Thanks for getting me out of there," I muster.

All of a sudden the door opens, and from a brief sliver of light, I see Koi, Cam, Kip, Randy, and several roadies walking back stage. They look as pissed as Jag sounds. I don't get to look at Jag before the door closes. Koi grabs my hand and ushers me to the side of the stage. He sits me on a speaker box, and flashlights shine in my face and all over my body. The lights are blinding, so I squint my eyes. I notice the crowd getting restless.

"I'm okay, guys. Thank you for saving my ass, but you need to get back on stage." I shoo them away.

Jag is the last to leave. His eyes bore a hole through me. He still looks pissed. Jag doesn't lose his temper often, but when he does he has a hard time reigning it back in. The lights come back on, and Koi is breathing into the mike. He looks over at Jag, and Jag nods. I feel my mom and dad each throw an arm around me. I smile to let them know I'm unharmed.

"Sorry about that folks. Some of you may know my little sister, Henley Hendrix," Koi says to the audience.

The crowd goes wild. I hear my name. It has been so long since I have heard those sounds. It is still as exhilarating as it always is.

"Tonight she is watching us play for the first time in four years. It's a really big deal when the guitar goddess shows up to watch you play whether she is your sister or not, or whether she grew up with you or not. As many of you know, Henley is also a really gifted photographer, and we asked her to take pictures of us tonight, but some asshole photographers in the pit trapped her and took her photograph instead. A few of you in the crowd pulled on her clothing and further trapped her in the pit. As much as I love my fans, it is not okay to harm my sister. The people responsible for harming her have been escorted from the premises. There are some of you out there who tried to help her and succeeded in pulling people off of her. I just wanted to say thank you. I know she appreciates it too. How about we get back to playing some music for you amazing people tonight?"

The crowd roars and my heart swells. I'm stuck on two sentences he said. *It's a really big deal when the guitar goddess shows up to watch you play whether she is your sister or not, or whether she grew up with you or not.* These men mean the world to me, and I haven't shown them that in a really long time. I need to make up for it, and I will start by touring with them.

Broken access plays two more songs, and then Koi makes a quick appearance in front of us.

"I don't want to take a chance with you going down there again tonight, okay? They know you are here," Koi says.

"That's fine, I can get some shots at the next stop," I say with a smile.

"You are going on tour?" He all but shrieks.

"Appears so."

"Fucking A! This is going to be so fucking awesome Hen. Jesus, I love you." Koi is overcome with excitement and he picks me up and swings me around like a child. He sets me back to rights, and kisses my forehead. I have the greatest brother in the world.

"Shit. I gotta go play." He turns on his heel and rushes back to the stage.

The rest of the show is absolutely amazing. I'm happy I came to see them play tonight. Little by little I feel my walls coming down. I feel more alive tonight than I have in four years. I forgot how much I love life. I love the good, the bad, and the ugly. It feels good to be alive.

After the show, the guys make their way to the complimentary room where the food is held. All bands and anyone with an all access pass are allowed here. The food is catered, and the room is usually stocked to the gills with alcohol. I'm famished, so I stand in line with my parents and load up on grub. I fill my plate with fruit, veggies, and steak skewers. I grab a bottle of water and sit at a table with my parents and Kip's parents. We eat, talk, and laugh. The guys grab beer, and leave quickly to sign autographs. I help the moms make plates for the guys since they usually opt to eat on the tour bus. I grab as much beer as I can and help the moms move it all to the bus. My mom and dad sit with me on the bus for a while since the boys aren't back. I'm really close to my parents, and Koi is too. My mom grew up in rock-n-roll, so our lifestyle isn't exactly crazy in her eyes. Dad joined the family when they were both young, only twenty. He was a session guitarist at his young age and my grandfather really respected his ability. He was hired on and my parents fell in love shortly after. They are still deeply in love with each other. I hope one day I can find that kind of love.

"How many other photo shoots do you have booked?" Dad asks.

"I don't really have much I can't reschedule. I plan on shooting some friend's headshots for a modeling agency, but I can hook them up with another photographer. I think I really want to just try to enjoy being on tour again. I don't want to travel back and forth any more than I have to."

"That sounds great baby. Red was excited about you touring. He also asked that I tell you to call him if any of these boys get out of line. He will personally kick their asses," my mom says.

"The man is seventy, and I don't doubt he could hand these boys their asses," I say.

Mom and Dad decide to head home before the boys get back. We hug and I wish them a safe trip. Since my own car accident, I have become fully aware of how much can happen in a small time frame, much less in a two hour drive back to Macon. I must have fallen asleep before the guys got back. I hear them loudly climb on the bus, so I sit up and rub the sleep out of my eyes.

"Sorry we woke you kid," Koi says, and they all quiet down.

"Don't be on your best behavior on my account," I smile. "I figure it has been way too long and the least I can do is stay up all night and play cards and get drunk with you rejects."

"Cards?" Kip asks hopefully.

At one time, we all yell "Bullshit!"

Cam hands me a beer, and we start the night off with a shot of whiskey.

"Since it is your first night back with us, the honor of the first toast goes to you Hen," Cam says.

I raise my glass and say the first words that come to mind. "To peace, love, and rock-n-roll." We all clink glasses and throw them back.

We play Bullshit for hours, and it comes down to me against Jag. Koi and Cam retreat to bed as soon as they are out. Kip falls asleep on the couch not long after.

Jag kicks his foot. "Take your ass to bed before I have to hear about how you have a crick in your neck tomorrow."

Kip stands, stretches, and fires back. "Yeah, I got a crick for you asshole. You know it is only fair for me to take some of your cards, otherwise you can't truly bullshit each other." He snatches Jag's hand from him and takes some cards after careful consideration. "May I see your cards lovely lady?" I hand over my cards.

"You just snatched mine. You didn't ask nicely." Jag says.

"Well you don't have a nice rack like Hen does, now do you?" Kip says with a grin.

"Valid point." Jag agrees.

"I heard that! Go to bed before I beat your skinny ass!" Koi yells from his bunk.

Kip retreats to the bathroom and then to his bunk.

"Two 2's," I say as I lay my cards face down on the discard pile. Jag looks me over for a beat.

"Hmm," he says. Shit, I'm drunk. I know my poker face isn't at its best. "Bullshit." He says. Fuck, I'm lying. I laugh and pick up the entire discard deck.

"Asshole," I murmur.

"Hey don't get all mad because you have a tell," he replies to my insult.

"I don't have a tell," I say. "And if I do, it's because I'm drunk," I add.

"You do have a tell. Not many people see it. It is more pronounced when you are drunk, but it is still there even when you are stone-cold sober sweetheart."

"Sweetheart?" I lift my eyebrow at him. Shit, am I flirting with Jagger Carlyle?

"You don't like when I call you sweetheart?" He asks with mischief in his voice.

"No, I'm not a sweetheart kinda girl," I reply.

"So what kinda girl are you?" he asks.

"Well you seem to have your own ideas after the Spin cover. Why don't you tell me?" I flirt.

Something changes in his eyes. If I had not been looking directly at him, I would've missed it. He doesn't say a word. He looks instead down at his cards. Do they hold the answers?

"Jag?"

"You don't want to know what I think, Henley. Can we just leave it at that? Shit, I really am tired. Care if we finish this game tomorrow?" He asks. He refuses to make eye contact with me.

"Sure." I muster through hurt feelings. I don't know why they are hurt, but they are.

I make my way to the bunks and quickly realize I don't know which one is mine. Jag comes up behind me. "Yours is on the bottom like you like it. I remember that you like to hear the bus," he says.

I can't look him in the face, so I just whisper a thank you, and climb in my bunk. I won't forget my place again. I won't forget that this attraction is one-way. I can't believe I let myself think all of Jagger's touches could mean something more than the friendship we share. He looks at me like a sister. I shoved my wounded pride down and found sleep.

Chapter 7

I hear my name. Ouch my head hurts. Damn you Crown Royal.

"Henley!!!!" Kip sings from his bunk above.

"Kip," I groan.

"Good. You are awake," he says.

"I am now. Thanks for the wakeup call," I shoot back.

"Not a problem. I bet you are thinking… 'Then what the hell is the problem, Kip?' Well, I will tell you. I woke up to the most magnificent morning wood. I turn to look at the top of my bunk where your magazine pictures are so ceremoniously placed, and I think about rubbing one out, but then I think to myself. 'Kip why would you do that when the real thing is right under you?' Good thinking, right? So, I was wondering if you could somehow reenact one of these sexy poses, you little vixen. Then can I come on your leg? I mean I would ask for intercourse, but with your brother on the bus I think it is just plain out disrespectful. We can get to that later tonight you little sex kitten."

"Do you ever shut the fuck up?" Koi asks from his bunk. Cam and Jag are laughing from their own bunks.

"You know what Koi? I'm telling your mom. Henley and I are having a very serious conversation. We are having a moment and you just interrupted us. Didn't your mom ever tell you not to interrupt adults when they are talking?" Kip replies.

"Yeah I would like to have my mom and dad present when you repeat the conversation you forced Henley into." Koi laughs. I can just imagine the looks on my parent's face, right before my dad decks him.

"Koi, I'm of the belief that your parents would understand our conversation. They would love to have me as their son-in-law. I'm lying here, pouring out my heart and soul to Henley. I'm showing her mad love and romance and all that shit, and you just rained on our parade. You should really get laid so you aren't so angry about our love." The sad thing is Kip probably says all of this with a straight face.

"I swear to God, if you marry that ass hat, Henley, I will disown you," Koi says.

I open the curtain to my bunk so my voice can carry a little better. "Kip, I really appreciate your romantic notions. Really, I do. I'm just not ready for a committed relationship. It's not you, it's me. Maybe one day, when I really am ready to give you everything you deserve, we can try a relationship. Can we still be friends?" I ask.

The guys all burst out into a fit of laughter. Kip is silent until they are finished. "So what you are saying is we can have raw sex, porn star style until you are ready to give me your heart too?"

I hear and see Koi's feet hit the floor from above Jag's bunk. I see him reach through what has to be Kip's bunk above mine, and Kip begins yelling. "Stop it you heartless pig. Henley will be mad if you hurt my nipples. She likes to suck them. Tell him Henley!" Then I hear Kip really let out a yelp, and I know Koi has given him the titty twister of a lifetime.

I push out of the bunk to make a trip to the bathroom. When I exit the guys are all seated in the common area in the front of the bus. Kip is still rubbing his nipple. He smirks and winks when he sees me.

"Darling, I really think you should talk to Koi about us. He needs to find peace with our relationship. He really hurt my feelings when he assaulted my nipple. I would like an apology," Kip says.

I ignore his sarcasm and turn to the cupboards. I need coffee and Advil. "You have to be fucking kidding me." I murmur when my search turns up empty. I lean my head down to the counter with my head in my hands.

"See Koi, you hurt her feelings too. You should apologize," Kip says.

I stand up straight, turn to Kip and give him my serious face. "Kip darling, I love you. I adore you, even, but I need you to shut up until I can get coffee and Advil." The guys crack up. "How is it that you four have managed to live on this godforsaken bus without coffee and Advil?!!"

"Why does the bus have to be god forsaken, pumpkin?" Kip asks.

I point my fingers at him. "Shut your hole now. I mean it Kip. If you think what Koi did is hurtful, I will do the same to your dick if you say ONE. MORE. WORD." He pretends to zip his lips and throw the key away. Then he winks at me. I can deal with winks.

I look at Koi. "Help?"

He looks through the cupboards and finally finds a bottle of Advil I hadn't had the patience to find. He pulls out his phone and speaks into it. "We need the Escalade. Henley needs coffee and food before she kills Kip. Or before I kill Kip. Then we need a grocery store." He hangs up and smoothes my hair down.

I throw my arms around him and whisper. "My hero."

They all chuckle, and I jerk my head out of my hug to give Kip the evil eye. He immediately stops laughing and begins to look around whistling a silent little whistle instead.

I jump in and out of the shower quickly so the guys can also have a turn. I take over the back room of the bus. Some bands use it as a master bedroom. This bus has another common room with sofas and every electronic known to man. I use a mirror in the small closet of the room to do my hair and makeup. Once I dry my hair, a knock came at the door.

"I'm dressed." I announce.

Jag enters with a pack of my cigarettes and a soda.

"It's not coffee or food, but I figure it might help," he smiles.

I haven't forgotten about last night, but I need to put it past me. I grab the smokes and soda, utter a thanks, and take a swig. This is definitely better than the dry mouth I've been sporting all morning. I light a cigarette and inhale deeply. I close my eyes and enjoy that first drag and then exhale slowly. When I open my eyes, Jag's are on me. He looks bothered. I ignore it and start working on my makeup.

"What the fuck Hen?" His question has my head spinning around to him. He touches my jaw line. "Did this happened last night?" I take a closer look in the mirror. A bruise is beginning to appear on my jaw line. It must've happened last night, and I say as much to him. He looks pissed, and mumbles something about a motherfucker and exits the room in a fit. Men are so dramatic sometimes.

When I emerge from the back, the guys are itching to go. We quickly exit the bus, and then I remember we are in Jacksonville. The Florida sun and heat are brutal. I turn to the guys to ask for two minutes to change. I quickly grab my sunglasses, and change out of my jeans into a short denim skirt, and a pastel green tube top. I throw my aviators on and meet the band, which are loaded up and ready to go. Randy sits in the front passenger seat while their head security guy John drives. I sit on the second row seat between Jag and Koi. Another Escalade will follow behind us for further security.

We find an IHOP close by, where I drink a pot of coffee and devour pancakes and bacon. Next we find the closest grocery store, and I stock up on food and other necessities. Whatever I want, I buy two of since the guys will eat most of it. I buy things to make sandwiches and dinner. I also buy an ass load of coffee, sugar, and breakfast food. Once we finish shopping, we find our way back to the tour bus where we unpack groceries. Since the bus is parked in the lot of the hotel the band is staying in, we grab our things and head to our rooms. I decide to take the extra room Koi has in his suite instead of getting my own room. Randy who normally bunks with him, stays in Jag's suite. I immediately find the bed and take a nap. Hangovers get worse each year I get older.

I wake up and immediately notice it is dark outside so I reach for my phone. It is 8:00. Shit! I slept the day away. I find a note taped to the lamp.

We are headed to the beach for a bit. Didn't want to wake you. Hope you enjoy your rest. Call me if you need anything. See you this evening for dinner. Love you, Koi.

It sucks I missed out on the beach, but I wouldn't have had much fun in the sun being hung over. I'm glad the guys got some downtime though. Touring can be rough.

I shower again and redo my hair and makeup for dinner. I throw on a black halter top dress, and some silver wedges. I put a few pieces of jewelry on to complete my look. I decide at the last minute to put my hair up since it is so humid outside. I twist the tops into two sections and then the back into another. I really love the whole 30's look in my hair. I suppose I will sit on the balcony, smoke a cigarette, and read a book while I wait on the guys to return. As I take the first drag off my cigarette, the front door opens to our suite.

Kip is already calling for me. "Henley, darling. Honey I'm home."

I can't help smiling, because Kip is pure entertainment. I stand inside the balcony doorway and give a little whistle so they know my location. When I spot what Kip holds in his hand, I zero in on the Starbucks cup like a tomcat would a pussy in heat. Kip notices immediately.

"Oh pumpkin, I brought you a skinny cinnamon dolce latte. Come give daddy a kiss," Kip teases.

"A kiss?" I ask. I immediately know we are going to war over that precious cup in his hand.

"Well if you aren't willing to give me a kiss, what are you willing to give for my sincere hospitality and thoughtfulness?" He asks wiggling his eyebrows.

I think about it for a beat. I have to speak in Kip language here. "Well, *muffin*, since my heart is so unavailable to you, due to my still sowing my wild oats and all, why don't I be your wingman tonight? You know I can bring in hot ass."

Kip thinks about it for a minute, and even rubs his chin to feign his deep thought. "Define hot."

"Well, since I know you so well, as I should the love of my life, hot to you my stud muffin, would be leggy, fake breasts, nice ass, skinny waist, and blonde," I say with a coy smile on my face.

"Blonde would feel too much like cheating on you now that everyone knows about our relationship. I should really stick with brunettes so I don't hurt your feelings," he says.

"Deal, now give me the fucking coffee before it gets cold," I order, and he complies.

The men are famished so we find a local steakhouse for dinner. Jagger and I sit in the third row seat of the Escalade, and he throws his arm over the back of the seat. Ten minutes into our trip, he rubs light circles on the top of my shoulder. I pretend not to notice since this will only end badly for me. The more I pretend not to notice, the more the lower bits of me sit up and take notice. I'm so glad I don't have a penis, otherwise, I would be sporting a hard on the size of Europe. Conversation around us flows freely, but I abstain from involvement because words may not be coherently strung together.

I lean forward and make up something to say to Koi who is sitting directly in front of me, so Jag's happy little thumb will quit rubbing circles of fire in my shoulder. It works, but when I lean back because the conversation comes to a natural end between my brother and I, Jag places his hand at the crook of my neck. Shit. Not the neck, anywhere but my neck.

"You're all tight and bound up," Jagger whispers incredibly close to my ear.

Oh you have no idea, Skippy. "It must be the whiskey from last night," I say without making eye contact.

"Relax Hen," he whispers.

Yeah right. You relax while I stroke your dick. Let's see how that works out for you, hoss.

At dinner, he plants his ass in a seat right beside me. Oh sex gods, you are fucking with me. Ha! I shake my finger at them in my head. After we order drinks and food, he leans back in his chair and that damn naughty little thumb of his starts up again. I look around the table to see if anyone notices the up and down motion he has begun making in the middle of my back. I'm almost positive beads of sweat are forming on my forehead. My breathing is labored, and I'm fanning myself, but no one notices. I lightly touch my forehead and the sweat is not there. I check my breathing and there is no need to slow it down from its already even pace. My hands are tucked in my lap like the little southern lady I am. My brain is playing tricks on me.

I make it through dinner without spontaneously combusting, or having an orgasm, which is a real feat so I do a mental pat on the back. Good girl. After dinner, we head to a local club. It's Thursday, so its college night, which means lots of college kids in a beach town. The place is packed when we arrived at 11. Jag offers me his hand when I exit the car, so I take it and remind myself not to place it between my legs. Public humiliation and all. When I emerge from the vehicle, he takes my hand and tucks it in his arm as we enter the club. Girls waiting to get in the club instantly take notice of the guys. Shit. Their security team has already flanked us. Koi, Kip, and Cam stop for autographs, but Jag keeps walking with my hand laced through his arm. His muscles feel fabulous. I bet he could pick my little ass up and throw me around a room for hours. Focus grasshopper. He leads me into the club in front of the waiting line, and I hear my name murmured as a question just as the door closes. Shit.

"Shouldn't you sign some stuff for your fans?" I ask him.

"No. I'm here with you tonight." He says eyes straight ahead.

Here with me? I just had a bunch of naughty thoughts. Ok, ok, ok, you're right I had more naughty thoughts. I should lay off the liquor tonight. I'm two things when I'm drinking liquor, honest and horny. Those two things don't mix with Jag. I let Jag lead me to a roped off area. The guys must have called and notified the owners in advance of their arrival. Jacksonville isn't like L.A. There aren't VIP sections in every club. Jag deposits me in a booth, and slides in next to me. He turns to face me, and plays with my long bangs I left loose when I pulled my hair up.

"You look so beautiful tonight. I love when you wear your hair like this." His eyes sear straight through me.

I will have to wear my hair like this more often. Wait, did he say love? Mmmm.

"Thank you," I manage to say.

Luckily, our server emerges, and she is eyeing Jag like he is a full course meal. I want to slap the bitch. Ok, hold up girl, he isn't yours. I get that, but he could be with me, right? We are sitting here alone, and she should take that into account before she starts eye fucking her customers. Just saying. Jag orders us beers and whiskey. The other guys appear behind her, and she eye fucks them too. Good, she is an equal opportunity eye fucker. They put in their drink orders as well and make their way to the edge of the roped off section to check out the club clientele. Let me rephrase that, they are looking for the hottest bed warmer in the building. Shit, I don't want to listen to my brother fuck a chick. Gag. I may have to get my own room tonight.

The server brings our drinks back, and Jag raises his glass to ours for a toast.

"To Henley. Please don't have sex with Kip."

We all fall in a fit of laughter, but Kip frowns and flips Jag the bird, but smiles his best panty-dropping smile at me right before he tosses back his shot. Jag asks for another round before the waitress has a chance to sashay off. Bitch.

Kip announces the time has come. "Ok, wing woman, it is that time. I fed your coffee addiction, and now…… Wow, I'm an enabler! That's kinda cool!"

Have I mentioned he has the attention span of a five-year-old child?

"Focus grasshopper," I say.

He snaps out of it and smiles. "I need my brunette now. I need to be able to look at what the sea has to offer tonight. I also need enough time to get her hammered enough so she will bring a friend back to my hotel room, and I can show them how impressive my erection is. So, two brunettes? I still can't make love to a blonde, Hen. It just brings back all those memories of our love."

Jag chuckles beside me.

"Ok, let's hit the dance floor." I pull out a menthol, and Jag offers me a light. I smile at him, grab my beer, and he lets me out of the booth. Two bodyguards follow us to the dance floor. I have to give it to them; they are really good at being inconspicuous. We find a place in the middle of the dance floor. Mike Will's "23" blares out over the speakers, and I dance my ass all over Kip while he grinds all over my ass. I haven't danced in years, but it is a lot like riding a bicycle... or having sex. And I haven't forgotten how to do either one of those. After the first song, I begin my wingman job.

It may sound counterproductive for me to grind all over Kip in an attempt to get him laid by someone else, or in this case 2 someone else's. The human brain is a funny thing though. When a woman sees a man as attractive as Kip dancing with another attractive woman, she wonders if she can get a piece of that for just one night. Jealousy is a hell of an emotion, and it makes us do strange things. I instantly look for brunettes and see one off to my left. She is undressing Kip with her eyes. I start to dance us over in that direction. Once we are in her vicinity, I whisper in Kip's ear what my plan is. I then give him the cue, and he bows to me in the overdramatic way that only Kip can. I leave the floor so he can make his move on her, but she will do all the work. Bitches be catty. I've said that before, right? The brunette will want to make him forget all about his previous dance partner, and she will work hard in doing so. The more attractive another woman is, the harder a chick is willing to show a man how good her own assets are.

I make my way to the ladies room and relieve myself. I wash my hands and check my hair and makeup in the mirror. The mirror is crowded with girls. Several of them are staring.

"Is it really you?" a cute blonde asks.

I smile, wink, and place my finger to my lips to ask for their silence. They giggle like school girls, and I giggle back. Cute blonde asks for my autograph and a picture, so I oblige. I forgot how much fun meeting new people can be.

"Are you here with Jagger Carlyle? I thought I saw you two walk in together. I'm sorry to say this but he is so hot!"

I look around to make sure phones are not recording me. Once I have made sure that isn't an issue, I give them what they want.

"No, we aren't together; we've been friends for a very long time. And yes, he is very hot. Man gorgeous!"

They giggle again. I wave good-bye, and when I open the door, I see the very same Jagger Carlyle waiting for me. God he really is gorgeous.

"You shouldn't go off by yourself Henley," he growls at me.

Keep growling daddy and see what happens when I lay it on a man. Shit, sorry, the sex gods are fucking with me again. I'm sure they have joined forces with the lush gods who are using the alcohol in my body to make me think very naught thoughts. Very!

"Did you just growl at me Mr. Carlyle?" I give him my best Scarlett O'Hara voice.

He steps closer to my face, and I look up into his crystal blue eyes.

"Ms. Hendrix, it really isn't safe for a woman of your stature to go out into the big world all by herself. I shudder at the thought of the things that can happen to you out here whilst you roam around all on your lonesome," he says in his best Rhett voice, and I giggle. "I love that sound."

There he goes with that damn love word again. He cups my face in his hand, and an involuntary shiver runs down my body. I pull my eyes from his when I hear girls giggling behind me. I turn and wink at them. They giggle again.

Still in his Rhett persona, "May I ask dear woman what all that nonsense is about?"

"You have fans my dear." I kiss him on his cheek, turn on my heel, and leave him to follow me.

I return to the table Koi and Cam are drinking at. I slide into the booth, but Jag doesn't follow. He finds a table in the corner of the small VIP section and opts to watch me. I know he is watching me, I can feel his gaze burning a hole in my body. Speak of holes in my body… damn you sex gods! I shoot another whiskey shot and light a cigarette. I'm buzzing from the whiskey and start to care a little less that Jag is staring at me. I visually search the dance floor and finally find Kip. He is living it up with the brunette I left him with. The man really makes me laugh. He has since we were kids.

Koi leaves the table in hot pursuit of something he found interest in. Cam sits and talks to me for a while. Cam is the quiet one of the crowd, and he has a heart of gold. Cam nervously brings up Caleb, but I quickly put him to ease. I didn't talk about my best friend for so long after his death, I find it refreshing that people miss him as much as I do. Cam and I are lost in conversation about the first time Caleb and I smoked pot. We got so incredibly high that we hid in the woods for hours so our parents wouldn't know. When my grandfather finally found us, the man in black himself was tagging along.

Johnny Cash simply looked to my grandfather and said, "These two have been smoking that wacky backy." He found absolute hilarity in our state. We, on the other hand, did not. Paranoia doesn't even begin to describe what we were going through.

At fourteen years old, I realized two very important things. One, my grandfather wasn't a rat. He never told our parents we were high as hell. Two, the man had smoked far more than his fair share of reefer. I couldn't wrap my head around the latter for many years. My grandfather could do no wrong in my mind and facing the fact that he was known to toke on a fatty didn't sit well with me. How did I discover the man smoked? His grand idea for sobering the two of us up, and helping calm down the paranoia, was to sit Caleb and me in his studio and identify Johnny Cash songs by the first chords. They kept a tally of who identified the song quickest. It helped to squelch the paranoia, but I watched my grandfather roll up previously referenced fatty, and smoke with Cash. Those two had entirely too much fun teaching us the unwritten rules of pot smoking. We were too scared to comment since we had already been caught fucked up as a soup sandwich. If I ever write a memoir, this story will be included since our friends love to hear it over and over again. Cam is currently laughing his ass off as we reminisce.

A few shots later, I brave looking at Jag as he stares at me ruthlessly in the corner. He drinks his beer and smokes on his pack of cigarettes. I ruthlessly try to ignore him. Try, being the key word here. Kip returns to the table with the brunette and introduces her as Rebecca. She sits and Kip pours shots down her throat. She seems nervous at first, being surrounded by rock stars and all. I try to ease her mind by asking her questions about herself. It seems to work, and she answers them. She is in nursing school. She seems really intelligent, which is a definite plus for her, but not so much for my friend. Kip may want to pour some more shots down her throat. Cam leaves to find some nighttime action when Koi returns with a girl. She is absolutely stunning. He introduces her as Carrie and gets her set up with shots as well. Jag continues to stare in the corner. I continue to smoke and drink, and the sex gods continue to fuck with me.

Cam returns shortly after with a blonde. She is the epitome of a Florida girl. She has long bleach blonde hair, tan skin, and a natural look about her. She is also stunning. Cam introduces her as Madison and sets her up with shots. These poor girls. Jag continues to stare. I continue to ignore, or so I tell myself. Screw you sex gods! I shake my mental fist at them.

Jag finally approaches the table and asks me to dance. What? I can't speak, so I light another cigarette, grab a beer, and put my hand in his. He leads me to the dance floor, and spins around. Prince's *Purple Rain* is playing. Great, just fucking great. He pulls me to his body, and his hand rests on my lower back. Easy tiger, a few inches and you will be grab- assing. Which I'm completely okay with. I'm so afraid to look at him. What if he kisses me? Shit. I want him to kiss me right? Fuck.

"Are you going to ignore me the entire song?" He asks.

"I'm not ignoring you, I'm dancing with you," I correct.

"You were ignoring me while I sat in the corner waiting for you."

"I wasn't ignoring you. I was having a good time. You chose to sit in the corner brooding, so I continued on with my night." Ok that is a bit of a lie.

"Brooding?" His head falls back with laughter. "To be one of the most intelligent women I know, you really are oblivious sometimes."

The whiskey has the fuse on my temper a bit short. "Oblivious? Oblivious to what Jag?"

"I was hoping just you and I could hang out tonight. I sat at a table away from everyone, and you didn't follow. When you didn't follow, I chose to look at the most gorgeous thing in the room, while I enjoyed my whiskey," he says.

"You were behind me when I left the ladies room. How was I supposed to know you wanted me to hang out with you? You couldn't simply say, 'Hey come over here and hang out with me. I want to catch up.' But you didn't, and you expected me to read your fucking mind somehow," I spit.

"Whoa there, firecracker, calm down. I wasn't trying to upset you. I promise."

His voice is soft, like velvet. Mmmm…. I like the way velvet feels. Shit, I forgot I wasn't supposed to drink liquor around Jag tonight. Thanks again lush gods. I'm so screwed.

"Just dance with me, okay?" He asks.

We dance for the remainder of the song, and the next one is slow too so we keep dancing. He is holding me in the most intimate way. My right hand rests on his heart, and my left on his shoulder. I didn't realize I was doing it until he stills under me, but I touch his neck with my fingernails. Fuck, he is so confusing. It's like my touch repulses him sometimes, and then other times he acts like he wants to show me his one eyed monster. Which, just in case you are wondering, I would not turn down a chance to see his wanker to if the opportunity were to arise. I like to live big and all, no regrets. Shit, I need more whiskey. When the song ends, the sex gods possess me, and I lean up and kiss Jag on the cheek. It is an out of body experience really. I don't remember telling my body to do that, but it did. Demonic possession is a plausible explanation. I mean, I'm from the south.

The shock of the kiss registers in Jag's eyes, so I do what I think is best. I'm at this point not possessed by a demon or sex god or the likes. That bitch would've had me tearing his clothes off in the middle of the club and screaming his name as he made me see fireworks. Dramatic much? A bit, perhaps. I walk away from him and head back to my savior, whiskey.

I enter the VIP section and grab the bottle of Crown Black sitting on the table. I pour everyone a shot, and we toss them back. The girls are each sitting in Kip, Koi, and Cam's laps. They are all inebriated. I pour us another shot. I don't feel tanked just yet, and I need to be to numb my sexual feelings for Jagger. Please don't play *Sexual Healing*, I think to myself.

Kip raises his glass. "To rock-n-roll!" We all second his toast and clink glasses.

Jag leans into my ear and whispers. "If I didn't know any better, I would think you are trying to get me drunk." I can hear the smile in his voice.

I turn around and whisper back in his ear full of liquid courage, "I didn't know I had to get you drunk."

He whispers back, "You don't. You only have to snap your fingers."

I think I gasp. I probably did because I can feel the vibration off Jag's chest. Asshole.

I whisper back, "Then stop confusing me Jag."

He pulls back from our close stance to look at my face with his brows drawn in a frown. "Confusing you?"

That just pisses me off, so I decide to confuse the hell out of him. It is much easier to show him that when you fuck with my libido you are fucking with my emotions. I grab his hand and take him out to the dance floor. I find a place in the corner of the club away from our own section, and away from most of the prying eyes. I pull a chair to face the corner, push Jag into it, and begin confusing him right back. I dance with the beat of the music. I grind my round ass all over his lap. I stand up straight, grab my ankles and perform the best ass clap I have managed in my entire life. Thank you, sex gods. I stand and continue to dance with my back side facing him. I grind on him again, and then lean back so when I do, I know he can see down the top of my dress. I can feel his heart beating fast. Yeah, I said confusing motherfucker. I can feel his hard dick under me. If it is any tell, I might actually be scared of Jag. Fuck it. I keep dancing, I mean confusing Jag.

The last of the whiskey shots kick in, and I throw all inhibition to the wind. Three songs later, I turn around to face Jag. I put my chest in his face, but he doesn't look. He looks me in the eye. Well fuck you too buddy. I have a nice rack. You and Kip both said so last night. I keep dancing and grinding all over his dick. His hands find their way to my waist and he pushes me down to grind harder on him. Ok, I need a new plan. He can't have control here. This is my show. I take his hands off my hips, and mouth no touching to him, and he flashes that damn panty-dropping smile. I warned you about that smile, didn't I? I take a quick peek to make sure my drawers aren't around my ankles. Check.

Security approaches and notifies us of our admirers nearby. Great, I didn't know how much longer I can keep that act up without shooting myself in the foot. Jag grabs my hand and quickly leads me to the VIP section. The guys are ready to go when we get there, and the girls are coming with us, so we pile in the two Escalades waiting for us outside.

Chapter 8

Jag climbs into the backseat with me. Let me clarify, he climbs into the third row seat with me, even though I had hopes of escaping him after my little performance. And to make matters worse, two security guards sit in the second row. The party is apparently in the other car. I really want to be in that car, and think seriously about stomping my feet and saying so, but hey that's not sexy. Jag asks the driver to turn the music up.

He says. "Loud."

Shit on a stick. I'm so screwed. Jag beats the back of the seat in front of him to the beat of a Chevelle song. I look at his fingers and think really bad thoughts. Dirty, naughty thoughts. Really, really naughty thoughts. Stop it! I chastise myself. The more I look at his fingers, the more I talk myself into it. It has been four long years since I last had my wig shook properly. Sex on a stick over here has his long fingers out on display as he drums to the beat. I feel like a kid in a candy shop. I want what's in that jar, and in that jar, and in that jar. I can try to meditate. Drunk meditation? I'm sure it breaks some unholy rule in Buddhism to mediate about sex while intoxicated. I should just add some coke and a few strippers in the mix to ensure I really will be reincarnated into a cockroach next time. Cock. That makes me giggle. Damn you whiskey. Jag notices my giggle.

His fiery eyes find me. Oh shit! Okay, take me now. I'm a weak human being. Ravage me right here, right now. I will regret it in the morning, but tonight I will gladly swivel my hips all over you. Wait, did I say that out loud? He still hasn't spoken, so I might be okay. Then his phone rings. The driver puts the sound system on mute and Jagger answers.

"What?" He answers. Oh someone isn't happy. Welcome to my world you little tease. He taps a button on his phone and Kips voice breaks through.

"I said don't you dare touch my future wife in there. I will tea bag you every day for the rest of my life if you touch her. We have a special kinda love. She lets me do shit to her you wouldn't do to a farm animal. That's a special kinda love!" Kip yells.

"Don't you have a brunette on your lap right now?" Jagger asks clearly frustrated.

"Well yeah. She is singing on Mr. Microphone right now if you know what I mean. Have I ever told you how much I love drunk college girls?" he asks.

We hear a female voice, but I can't make out what she says. "No love, I was talking to my mom when I said that, just go back to doing what you are doing," Kip instructs. Jesus.

I pipe in. "Kip, love, I love you dearly, but I do not want to talk to you while you get a blow job from that sweet little girl you picked up at the club."

"You are right my darling. I should not have been so disrespectful. I'm torturing myself here. I'm surrounded by two other blondes, but I have a brunette out of respect for you. It is just crushing my heart that I have to do this to you. Do you still love me?" he asks as he lets out a groan.

"Oh gross, Kip. Hang up the phone," I squeal.

I hear the phone drop, and Kip yells, "Hold on, I dropped the phone. Koi wants to talk to Jagger."

More groaning sounds. Gross.

"I swear to God Jagger Carlyle, if you fuck my little sister, I will cut your balls off and give them to Kip to play with," he says.

Then he groans. Gag.

"Dude you are on speaker phone, your sister is sitting right beside me, and she can hear you groaning as you are apparently getting your knob slobbered on. I'm going to hang up now," Jag says and ends the call.

I burst out laughing at the craziness that is my life. Jag joins me, and the security guards even joined in the chuckle fest.

"Well fellas, it looks like we are a lot of horny bastards who won't be getting laid tonight." Jag says.

"Don't forget the little lass back here," I add.

This makes Jag stop breathing. Literally he stops breathing.

"May I speak openly Ms. Hendrix?" John, the head security guy, asks.

"John, I'm not the President, you can speak however you wish to me, and you know it. We have known each other how long?" I ask.

"Eight years Ms. Hendrix. I mean Henley. I was just going to say, that you probably shouldn't say things like that about yourself in a car full of horny men unless you are willing to be the star of their fantasies tonight," he says with a chuckle.

"La la la la. You can't make me hear you!" I say with my fingers in my ear. All the men erupt in laughter.

We arrive at the hotel minutes later. Security jumps out first, then Jag, and he offers me his hand. I take it and step down. The other car is not exiting so gracefully. Kip falls out of the car with his pants still around his ankles. Koi is yelling expletives at him, and the brunette looks confused with bright red, swollen lips. Way to go Kip! Madison exits the car in a hurry and runs to a nearby bush to puke.

"Great. You had to pick one who can't handle her liquor." I say to Cam.

He looks terrified. I have seen this look before, and it means I'm going to be taking care of her tonight. I ask Jag to get some cold paper towels from the lobby restroom, so he runs in the hotel as I walk over to Madison. She has tears running down her face from vomiting. She is dry heaving by the time I get to her. I rub her back, and about the time she stops the violent heaves, Jag arrived with the wet towels. I smile at him, expecting him to book it, but he stands with me as I help her. I wipe Madison's face off and let her catch her breath. She looks exhausted. John the security guard shows up with a bottle of water, and she gladly drank it. I slow her down several times though to prevent her from getting sick again.

Eventually the parking lot is empty, and Jag and I are left to help Madison to a room. I'm so angry at Cam for bailing on her. When we get her into the elevator car, she sits in the corner and buries her head in her knees. I have been there before, and it hurts. I look up from the opposite corner from Madison, and catch Jag's intent gaze on me. I don't look away, he doesn't either. He crosses the elevator in one long step, and presses me against the wall. He cups my face in his hands and is about to kiss me when he stops an inch from my lips.

He is already breathing hard. "Tell me to stop Henley. Tell me this isn't what you want."

I can't form the words because they would be a lie. I'm too drunk to lie. He looks between my eyes and my lips. Men are such wimps, so I lean forward just a bit, and softly brush my lips against his. The kiss is soft. Our tongues softly meet, and the kiss continues at a slow pace. I can't believe we are kissing. He picks up the pace a little, and he is hungry. I want to rip his clothes off right now. I run my hands up his abs and feel all that spectacular muscle. He moans in my mouth, and I swear to the sex gods, I almost came right then and there. I guess the elevator ping is drowned out by all that damn passion… damn you passion, because the first thing I heard, is "Holy shit."

We both look up and see Cam standing there with a t-shirt in hand. Ok, maybe he didn't disappear on me. He was being sweet and getting Madison a t-shirt. The elevator door attempts to close and Jag put his foot in it to open it. Cam stands there still shell-shocked, his jaw literally open, while Madison is very much asleep in the corner of the elevator.

"Speak Cam." I order.

"I can't believe he finally did it." That is all he can muster up. Bless his heart.

Jag ignores him and bends down to see about Madison. I walk over to help, but Cam announces he will carry her. Jag and Cam help Madison to Cam and Kip's suite. I run to my suite to grab the complimentary toothbrush and toothpaste for her. When I arrive back at Cam's, I open the door and hear Madison vomiting in the toilet. Cam looks terrified again. Jag shakes his head at our friend. I open the door when the vomiting ceases and help her out of her clothes. I put a cold rag on her head, and ask Cam to order Alka-Seltzer, Advil, Tylenol, water, and toast from the concierge. I undress Madison and get her in a bath. I close the shower curtain on her to give her some privacy when I hear a knock at the door.

Jag stands at the door still looking gorgeous. When doesn't he? He hands me everything I asked for. When I take the plate of toast, he holds it for a moment until my eyes meet his. He smiles. Oh dear God, that kiss. I wasn't sure if I wanted to slap or kiss Madison for interrupting what could have been. I smile back, take the plate, and close the door. I get Madison to eat, drink, and take all of her meds. I bathe her, wash her hair, dry her body, and dress her. I brush her hair, and she manages to brush her teeth. I get her into Cam's bed. He lies down beside her, and thanks me as I turn off their light and close the door.

Jag is asleep on Cam's suite couch, so I grab an extra blanket and cover him. I take a few minutes to look at him, really look at him while he sleeps. He looks so peaceful. I crushed so hard on him when he was a boy. He was so quiet and mysterious to me. He was gorgeous even then. He was also an incredibly talented musician. I remember his small acts of kindness throughout the years. He always remembered the things I like and always bought the most thoughtful presents. What am I afraid of? I'm living life again, right? I climb under the covers with him. Here goes nothing.

He wakes when he registers me. He stands up from the inside of the couch.

"Inside. I won't have you falling off," he says.

I move to the inside of the couch, and he lies back down beside me. He brushes some stray hairs behind my ear and then strokes my face. He licks his lips, and I know he is going to kiss me again. He softly kisses me as though he would break me. He deepens the kiss, but kept it gentle. I have no idea how long this kiss lasts, but I'm about ready to pick up speed when he pulls away. He kisses the tip of my nose, and then holds a long kiss on my forehead.

"Sleep." He orders.

So Jagger Carlyle is a gentleman. I would've been more disappointed that this isn't going further, but I'm drained, both physically and emotionally.

"Can I play kickball with you?" I ask the little boy with dark brown hair and honey brown eyes.

"No! You are a girl, and girls are gross!" He exclaims, and all the rest of the boys join in on the teasing.

"I may be a girl, but my granddaddy says I can do anything a boy can!" I yell back at him.

"You can't pee outside!" He says.

"I sure can!" I scream.

"You can't pee standing up!" He screams back.

"Well that's the only thing I can't do! You are just scared you will get beat by a girl!"

He gets nose to nose with me. "Girls aren't allowed to play with us. We have a secret club, and no girls are ever allowed! Especially in kickball!"

"I'm telling my brother, and he is going to beat you up!" I yell back.

"I'm not afraid of your brother." He growls and then he pulls my long hair.

I instantly punch the boy in the nose, just like my daddy taught me. He should have just let me play kickball. Now he has a bloody nose, and a girl gave it to him. My daddy will be so proud. The little boy charges after me and pulls me to the ground. Before he can land a punch, our teachers are pulling us apart.

"Little girls don't fight Henley!" Ms. Randolph says.

"He started it! He pulled my hair!" I defend myself.

"Is that true, Caleb?" Ms. Terry asks.

"She wanted to play kickball, and no girls are allowed! It's in the club rules!" He shouts.

"It's not nice to leave someone out, Caleb." Ms. Randolph says.

"But no girls are allowed, EVER!" He says again.

"I will tell you how we will fix this. Caleb and Henley, you will spend the recess of morning recess, sitting with one another and holding hands. You will do the same at lunch when you are not actually eating. You will repeat this during afternoon recess. Until you two apologize to each other and become friends, you will do this each day you are at school." Ms. Randolph says with a smile.

"I can't hold a girls hand! It's against club rules! My friends will laugh at me." Caleb says.

"I guess your friends need to learn how to get along with girls too, or they will be holding someone's hand as well." Ms. Terry says.

We all march to a bench near the entrance of our school and told to sit. Caleb offers me his hand with sheer disgust all over his face. I won't take it though. He pulled my hair and it really hurt. He should apologize, not me. I quietly refuse to hold his hand. My teachers attempt to coerce me into this whole ridiculous handholding, but I'm not budging. Ms. Randolph says she is going to call my parents, which is fine by me. He pulled my hair, and I punched him in the nose. That's what my daddy taught me to do.

We are allowed to enter class after recess, but at lunch my mother and father sit at a lunch table that has been designated specifically for Caleb and me. There are two other old people there, so they must be the idiot's parents. Stupid boys. I look down at the table and refuse to meet any of the adult's eyes.

"Henley." My father says.

"Yes sir?" I pout.

"It wasn't nice to punch Caleb in the nose." He advises.

"Daddy! He pulled my hair because he was scared he was going to get beat by a girl in kickball. They wouldn't let me play!"

"I was not scared of being beat by a girl!" Caleb shouts!

"Was too."

"Was not."

"Was too."

"Was not."

"Was…"

"Enough." The lady at the table says.

"Caleb, you must play nice with everyone. You can't exclude girls. How would you feel if she was playing kickball and wouldn't allow you to play?" his mother asks.

"I wouldn't want to play kickball with her because she is a girl!" he answers.

"I see we have two stubborn children on our hands," my mom says, and I glare at her. She is supposed to be on my side. This isn't fair.

"I guess you two will have to eat lunch together, miss recess, and hold hands until you become friends. If you do not hold his hand or do anything your teacher asks you to, I'm taking away your guitar," my mom says.

"What?!!" We both yell.

"Y'all have a nice lunch," Caleb's dad says.

Each of the parents leave the table and speak to our teachers on their way out. I'm so mad at my mommy and daddy. I eat lunch in silence, and with the threat of my new guitar being taken from me, I place my hand palm side up on the table. Caleb takes my hand and we both wear a scowl that could rival any villain. After lunch, we are made to walk down the hall to class holding hands. I roll my eyes the entire way. I don't like this boy. He is mean and stupid!

At recess, we sit on the bench and hold hands again. I make sure Ms. Randolph can see so she will tell my mommy, and I won't have my guitar taken away.

"You have a guitar?" Caleb asks.

I nod my head.

"Do you know how to play it?"

"Better than a boy can!" I snap.

"I don't know how to play the guitar. I didn't know girls could play guitars."

"I told you girls can do anything that boys can do."

"Except pee standing up," he giggles.

"Okay, fine, except pee standing up."

"How did you get a guitar?"

"My granddaddy bought it for me. He plays guitars with all of his friends, and they make these really cool faces when they do. My granddaddy says it is called a guitar face, and I had to learn how to play the guitar so I could have a really cool one too. I'm still working on my guitar face though. It's really hard because sometimes I still have to look at the guitar while I play."

"I want to learn how to play too. Maybe my mom will buy me one if I become friends with you."

"That would be cool," I say.

"You should bring your guitar to show-and-tell on Friday. I really want to see it. What color is it?" he asks.

"Brown."

"At least it isn't pink."

"Why would it be pink?"

"Because girls like pink," he says.

"I don't. My favorite color is blue."

"Mine too!" He says.

Ms. Randolph approaches us. *"It looks like you too are having fun."*

"Ms. Randolph, Henley has a guitar and knows how to play it. She is going to bring it to show-and-tell Friday so I can see it. Her favorite color is blue like mine!" Caleb says.

My reverie is disturbed by a gruff voice, but I try to fight my way back to it. I want to go back to first grade with Caleb.

"I'm going to kill him." I hear my brother's voice.

Light is shining in from somewhere. I just need a few more hours sleep. I feel something shift beside me, and I let out a hung over groan. Wait, something shifted beside me? My eyes pop open, and I see Jag. He really is a gorgeous man. He winks at me, and the night's events come back to me. We kissed… twice. It was amazing.

He whispers, "I think we are in trouble."

"I know you fuckers are awake," my brother says.

Shit, I'm so not ready to deal with an overprotective brother and all the man rules that accompany kissing your best friend's sister.

"I'm so hurt Henley. I really thought what we had was beautiful. I sacrificed so much for you last night. I went for a brunette out of mad respect for you. You are my everything!" Kip says.

Jag and I chuckle.

Jag stands from the couch and then offers me his hand to help me. I decide I can't make it upright just yet, so I only manage to sit up. He sits back down by me. Kip jumps on my other side and pulls me to him with both arms.

"She is mine, and you can't have her Jagger Carlyle. Do you know where his penis has been?" he asks.

I didn't want to think about that.

"No, I don't Kip. But I know where your penis was last night," I reply.

"Shit. You have a very valid point." He releases me. "I will need to think of a million more reasons why you should be with me and not him," he says.

I laugh at the ridiculousness that is Kip.

"You ready for this?" Koi asks.

He flips on the TV in the suite living room, and the E Channel blasts through TV's surround sound.

It appears Henley Hendrix has reemerged after a four year sabbatical, and what better way to reappear than on the arm of Jagger Carlyle? The two were spotted at a Jacksonville nightclub last night entering arm in arm. Onlookers report he was very protective and fond of her. Once inside the bar, the pictures tell a pretty telling tale. This particular picture shows Carlyle and Hendrix holding each other on the dance floor. It is reported the two danced to Purple Rain. Are you trying to tell us something? More pictures emerged from club goers who captured the two in the corner of the club. It appears the Guitar Goddess is giving rock-n-roll's bad boy a run for his money. The pictures are a bit grainy, but it shows Carlyle in a chair, and Hendrix straddling him. I'm not sure who I'm more jealous of.

Kip turns the television off. "I can't take this. I'm dying with jealousy over here. You never straddled me in public, pumpkin."

Jagger throws a pillow at him. I burst out laughing. I stop long enough to see the look on Koi's face, and then I laugh some more. I laugh so hard and for so long, tears run down my face. No one else in the room is laughing or smiling. They look a bit concerned.

"Is she losing it?" Koi asks with concern in his voice.

I keep laughing. He wants to know if I'm losing it. Funny.

"Maybe we should get her a doctor," Kip suggests.

"Just give her a minute." Jag orders.

I keep laughing. I try several times to stop, but I found their hypocrisy to be too much.

Cam enters the room from his bedroom. "Is she okay?" he asks.

I laugh some more.

"What did you do to her last night?" Koi asks Jag.

"What did *I* do? Why is this *my* fault?" he asks.

"You broke man code. First, you are sleeping with Koi's sister on the couch. Secondly, you are trying to steal the love of my life. You don't bone your bro's sister, and you don't steal another bro's girl," Kip says.

"Don't forget he kissed her in the elevator," Cam says. "I can't believe he finally did it. I mean who has balls enough to kiss *her*?"

"You kissed my sister?" Koi asks.

"You kissed my Henley?" Kip asks.

"Jesus Christ," Jagger says.

"Why is she laughing like that?" Cam asks.

"We were photographed dancing at the club last night. E! News already has the story," Jag says.

"I wouldn't call the last set of pictures dancing," Koi says gruffly.

"Now you two will get the combo name. I already had ours picked out. We were going to be Kipley. You stole all my glory! Now you two will be Jagley," Kip says, and it only makes me laugh more.

Jagley. It is as ridiculous as *Kipley*.

"She needs coffee," Jag says.

"Got it," Cam says with concern in his voice. He thinks I'm leaving here in a strait jacket. I finally stopped laughing and sit up from my slouched position.

"Koi, I bet you are wondering why I'm sleeping in here, instead of in my room. Frankly, I didn't want to listen to you screw your company all night. I had to listen to you and Kip both receive blow jobs last night, and frankly it was just a little much for me. Yes, Jagger kissed me. It was amazing. So, I was being kissed by a man who behaved like a gentleman the entire night, while you two were anything but. It couldn't go any further if we wanted it to, because I was up taking care of Cam's date. He was too terrified to do so. Jag was already asleep on the couch after I helped Madison to bed, so I crawled in with him to avoid hearing you moan all night. Now, E News has this breaking story of us two together and the entire world thinks we ended the night with rough, raw rock star sex. We are some of the only ones who weren't fucking. I also find it quite hilarious that I haven't been seen in four years, and the only thing anyone cares about is me being on Jagger's arm. Nobody gives a shit why I went off the grid for four years, or where I have been. The world is so shallow; they only want to know how many inches I took last night. And here I was, all worried the whole Caleb thing would come up." I let out another laugh.

Koi stares at me for a beat. "So you two…. didn't?"

How old is he?

"What? Fuck, knock boots, shag, bang, bump uglies, screw, do the deed, make whoopee, get dirty, get it on, pork, bone, smash guts, play hide the salami, ride the bologna pony, hanky panky, or get ball's deep?" I ask.

"Jesus Christ, that was impressive," Koi says.

"To answer your question, no, we did none of the above. Not that it is any of your business. You don't get to play man code here. I have been friends with him just as long as you have. Man code is a moot point," I say.

"That is sacrilegious. You just totally dissed man code. If we don't have man code, the world will fall apart," Kip says hysterically.

"Man code still stands in 99.9% of situations, Kip. Just not in this one. Your universe is still aligned," I assure.

"Thank fuck for that," he sighs.

"I'm going to shower in my room. Koi, when I'm done, you and I are going out for breakfast. Be ready." I leave the room and meet the concierge at the door with my Starbucks in hand. I take it from him, kiss him on the cheek, and leave him blushing.

Chapter 9

The hot shower hits the spot. I'm finishing my makeup when Koi emerges in my bathroom. He watches me with careful eyes and a hint of a smile on his face. Even if the rest of his face isn't smiling, his eyes always give him away. I have the same tell.

"I like the happy you. I really miss you like this," he says.

"I just needed some time, Koi, and apparently a little interference from Jagger. It all seems like such a blur now. The time just flew by. I was so wrapped up in my own thoughts and grief. Everything around me reminded me of Caleb. Thoughts of Caleb always lead to memories of the car flipping. Then I have to remember trying to revive him. I couldn't bring him back, and that makes me feel like I failed him. Maybe I didn't perform CPR correctly, ya' know? Then I remember me screaming at the paramedics to help him, and the look on their faces told me everything I needed to know. It felt like a bad dream."

"Henley, what happened, what you went through was enough to crush anyone. We all lost him, and we all grieved, but you were his best friend since the first grade."

"I had a dream last night about the day I punched him in the nose," I laugh.

He laughs too. "I remember mom took your guitar so you pouted for weeks. I snuck you my guitar in hopes you would teach me how to play better, but you thought I felt sorry for you."

"Oh so your motives were self-serving, yeah?"

"Hell, I couldn't let my little sister play guitar better than me, so I thought if you taught me I would get better. You were always better at it than me though."

"Koi, you are a hell of a guitar player. You wouldn't have gotten this far in this crazy industry if you weren't."

Koi smiles, and the conversation turns to last night.

"So, you and Jag?" he asks, sounding resigned to the idea.

"Yeah, I guess maybe something is going on there," I say.

He lets out a belly laugh. "Maybe something, my ass. The two of you have had it bad for each other since you were in middle school."

"You knew?" I ask, genuinely surprised.

"Yeah, and I'm okay with it. I don't know how far it will go between you two, but don't hurt each other. I said the same thing to him. I can't watch two people I love hurt each other. We have already had enough hurt for a lifetime," he says with a sigh.

"I don't know why you freak out so much about me and men. I'm not exactly a virgin bro," I say.

He looks disgusted for a half a second, and then realization struck him. "Yacht man?"

I know exactly who he is referring to. "Yup."

"Damn. I'm actually impressed. I think I can talk to you about your sex life now. Did you get him to talk in the pirate voice?" he asks clearly interested.

This is…. different.

"You know I did," I say with a mischievous smile.

"Wait, and Irish boy with the temper? We drank like fish that night," he says.

"Yup."

"Damn. Impressed again. What about vampire man? You were in Africa on the environmental thing, yeah?" He rubs his jaw, clearly running through all the men I have been photographed with in the media.

Let's be honest, there aren't many, and they are always publicity photos, where we both happen to be in the same place at the same time. The photographs are usually promoting a charity or something of the sort. It's hard to get laid when you are famous if you don't want the entire world knowing. He may have to think awhile.

"Yup. Him too. He is very… attentive. Not to mention well equipped," I answer.

"Shit. He is kinda pretty, with those blue eyes and all," he says with a laugh, and I laugh along with him.

"Dave? The whole music project? And he was married to…. God, she graced my walls during my puberty years. I loved Baywatch, and she was on my favorite issue of Playboy. You kinda had sex with her too since you had sex with him. I'm feeling a bit jealous. Can I touch you?" He pokes his fingertip into my arm.

"Feel better?" I ask.

"Yup. So what happened with all of them?" he asks.

"I was looking for a good time. They fell in love. Sometimes, I think it is more the idea of who I'm, then it is really who I am, if that makes sense. You know, beyond all the Guitar Goddess bullshit. I went into those relationships with clear expectations. You can't help when your feelings grow for someone. It's human nature. At the first sign of trouble, I got the fuck out of dodge. I put space between us, and eventually they moved on."

"Conversation over. I have been outdone by you already. Shit." He smiles.

I hug my brother. "Let's go eat some breakfast."

***

After breakfast, Koi heads to the hotel gym. Jagger pulls me into his room as I attempt to make my way past. He scares the hell out of me. He picks me up as I wrap my legs around him and closes the door with his foot. We stand there for an eternity. This man always meant the world to me, and I'm both scared and excited about where this could lead.

"What's wrong Henley?" he whispers as he strokes my cheek.

"I'm just scared and excited about this. We can hurt a great deal of people if it ends badly, Jag."

He pulls back from my face to look me in the eye. "Hey, we don't worry about the unknown. I won't ever hurt you intentionally, and I know you won't hurt me. We will be conscious of the people in our lives. If for some unforeseen event drives us apart, then we act like adults, and figure it out. No worries, gorgeous."

He dips down and kisses my lips, but the kiss isn't as soft as it was last night. He tastes so good. His tongue moves in and out of my mouth with such expertise. It makes a girl wonder what he could do with that tongue below the belt if ya' get what I'm saying. Someone clears their throat nearby, and it interrupts our make out session.

"I'm truly sorry to interrupt, but I have an appointment at the venue, and there is no other exit," Randy says.

Jag pulls back from me, his eyes searching mine, and then we look over at Randy who is looking at his shoes. Awkward. Jag put me down on the floor, and I straighten myself out.

Jag clears his throat. "Sorry about that Randy, I didn't mean to block you in," he says.

Randy looks up and smiles at us. "I always knew you two would end up together. It's about damn time." He exits the room whistling.

Once Randy exited the room, Jag turns to me. He cupped my face with his hand. He searches my eyes as though he is looking for the right words to say. "I can't rush into shit with you. I don't want this to be some sort of fling. I've wanted to be with you for a long time, Hen. I can do flings, but not with you. Our lives have been connected for a long time, and if we ended it would indeed be bad for a lot of people. I want to tear your clothes off every time I see you, but you, and us, means way more to me than that. It will take every sliver of will power I have to be good, but this is important to me," he finally says all breathy. Screw him for turning me on when he is all breathy.

"So what you are saying is, you won't be tearing my clothes off any time soon?" I deadpan.

He growls, and kisses me again. So not fair. "You aren't going to make this easy on me, are you?"

I reach down and grab the impressive hard on he is sporting through his pants. "Now, where is the fun in that?" I leave him to find my brother, and he follows while adjusting his pants.

***

We decide to eat lunch a few hours later in the dining room of our hotel. Somehow the guys have rid themselves of their evening company. I will never know how they do it so smoothly. I have seen girls pitch fits, cry, and act like fools when the morning rolls around.

Jag holds my hand the entire time. It gives me butterflies. I feel like a kid again. My brief affairs with men over the years, are just that: brief. I never had feelings for other men beyond genuine care, respect, and sexual attraction. Jagger makes me feel things I've never felt before. His touch is enough to send shocks through my body. After lunch, we load into the Escalade for a radio interview. I'm accompanying them since I don't have shit else to do. The concert is tomorrow in Jacksonville, and I'm really stoked about photographing the entire thing.

Once we arrive at the radio station, Jag offers his hand to me, and I smile as I exit the Escalade. He holds my hand the entire way into the building, and I have to say, a girl could get used to this. The building isn't large like they would be in L.A. or New York, but it is big enough. The staff takes notice of us right away. They care way more about Jag holding my hand, then Broken Access standing in front of them. A man in his late forties with long hair and tattoos greets us and shakes each of our hands. He leads us into the studio where each of the guys will speak with the D.J. I decide to sit outside the glass where I can watch and listen from there. Jag leans down and gives me a peck on my lips, then on my cheek, and follows his band mates to a stool in front of four mikes.

After a brief rundown of what the interview will entail, the On Air light lights up.

Thank you for listening to X-1-0-2-9, Jacksonville's alternative to rock. Today I have the guys from Broken Access here. Ladies keep your panties on. These guys are rocking the stage at the arena tomorrow night on the Face Off tour. Guys, say hello to our audience today. Hello. Hello Jacksonville. Sup. What's going on...? So your last album dropped three months ago, and you have been touring for the last four. What is different about this tour as compared to the others you have been a part of?

"I think the amazing line up on the bill has a great deal to do with the difference. We really have the most amazing bands in rock on the tour. We are lucky that each band that joined us was free. I mean where else do you get to see Randolph Cane, Resin, Carbon Copy, and Succubus in the same night?" Koi asks.

"I would like to ask about a song written on the album. The ballad Hands Down has been a fan favorite, and there has been a great deal of speculation that the song is in reference to Caleb King's death. Is there any truth to that, or would you like to add to it?" the DJ asks.

Surprisingly, it doesn't hurt so much to hear Caleb's name. I'm glad people haven't forgotten him. I haven't heard Hands Down so I need to take time to listen to Broken Access's last two albums since I missed out on them.

There is a pause, and the guys all look at each other. Jag and Koi look at me through the glass, and I nod. Tell the truth.

"I wrote the song about my personal experience with Caleb and Henley when he died. The song is only partly a reference to his death. I have written so many songs as tribute to him, but I haven't been able to put them out there just yet." Jag says.

"Jagger, is it difficult to bare your soul like that? You lost a childhood friend? Is that what is keeping you from recording his tribute?" the DJ asks.

"The lyrics are very personal for obvious reasons, and it is definitely difficult to bare your soul to the masses, but not necessarily in this case. I haven't recorded the tribute yet because there is a list of people who need to be ok with it first." Jagger replies. Oh my sweet Jagger.

"Speaking of Henley, stories broke around the world this morning about the two of you getting cozy in a nightclub in our city last night. Is this another set of pictures taken out of context, or are you two an item?" This bastard is nosey as hell.

Jag looks at me with a frown. He doesn't know what to say. I nod a yes to him. I refused to lie to my fans back in the day. These guys shouldn't either. He smiles.

"The pictures are not taken out of context. We are dating. I have known Henley a very long time, and I'm very lucky she decided to give me a shot. I'm the luckiest man on earth."

He winks at me. I wink back with a massive grin on my face.

The interview went on for thirty more minutes. Luckily, it got back to the music, and not Jagley. I spend the rest of the interview texting my mom. I want to break the news before she found out from the media. As expected, she is ecstatic we are together. I let her know we are taking it slow, and she is happy about that too. We text more about my grandparents and my dad. I like to make sure their health is okay.

***

That night at the show, the guys open with their song *Reckless*. It is off the new album, and the only way I know that is because Koi announced it. The song is hard, raw, and the guitar riffs are scratchy. It gets the crowd moving. When the song is over, the lights dim to just Jag. His roadie hands him an acoustic guitar.

"I've never sung this song live, and I wasn't sure if I ever would. Tonight, I want to sing this song so I'm the first one she heard it from. This is for you Caleb. This is *Hands Down*." Jagger says into the mike. Koi and Kip are by my side, both holding my hands. He strums a beautiful, but simple melody on the guitar.

When I found you, you were gone.

She tried so hard to keep her hands down.

You never had a chance though,

But she kept pushing down.

She pushes down until she can bring you back.

Her heart willing yours to beat.

I'm taken aback.

Please don't let your fates meet.

I wiped her tears away.

She kept her hands down.

I tried to keep her from giving way.

Her screams are the only sound.

I kept my hands on hers.

I sat there for an eternity as she struggled with letting you go.

Her tears blurred,

She misses you so much, just so you know.

The hours turn into days

And the days turn into weeks

She now lives in a world of grey.

I can't help her, I feel so weak.

Please bring her back to me.

I'm down on my knees,

Begging to see her smile.

I just want to hold her for a while.

I wipe my tears away.

I will keep my hands down.

I won't give way.

Please give her back her crown.

I need her hands on mine.

I can't seem to let her go.

Where has she gone this time?

I miss you so much, just so you know.

She tries to smile through the pain now.

I know better, I know she feels the loss.

But she is beginning to come around.

Maybe one day she won't bear this cross.

Her eyes still light up when she smiles.

Man, you should see her strength.

Sometimes it means she keeps me at arm's length.

But, I know she will only be gone for a little while.

I will wipe your tears away.

We still keep our hands down.

I wish you could've stayed.

Your music is the only sound.

I miss you every day.

You were so full of life.

I will never forget that day in May.

Friend, I will see you on the other side.

Jag stops playing and sighs into the mike, his head looking down. The lights go out completely. The only illumination comes from the thousands of lighters in the crowd. They softly chanted Caleb's name. Mad respect. I see flashlights and Koi and Kip wiping their tears away, so I begin wiping my own. Jag is face-to- face with me in a matter of moments.

He is panicking. "I just realized, I should have told you. I should have prepared you first."

He kisses my forehead and hugged me. We shared the firsthand experience of Caleb's death. The experience is one of the many ties that bind us together. He pulls away and wipes my tears. The band pulls me into a group hug while the crowd continues to chant Caleb's name, and I love that they haven't forgotten him. I think for so long I tried to because it hurt so much.

"Caleb would have loved it. Thank you for that gift," I say, and Jag softly kisses my cheek.

"That song isn't just for Caleb, Henley," he says, his forehead pressed to mine.

I smile a sad little smile. "I know." I touch his beautiful face with my hand.

The song is about me losing my way because Caleb left. It is about how this beautiful man in front of me waited for me to come home both physically and emotionally. He was waiting for me. How could I not see him in front of me all this time? I saw Jag in a physical way, but how did I not see I hold his heart in my hands? I won't soon forget.

"Go play for your fans. It is my turn to wait." I smile. He kisses me again softly and takes his place on stage.

Chapter 10

Jag and I spend hours curled up on a couch on the bus watching television. We doze for a few hours and then watched some more TV. Eventually, we climbed into his bunk since he also sleeps on the bottom bunk. It feels so good to be held by him. I enjoy every second of it.

I awake sometime early in the morning to the sounds of passion. What the fuck is that?

"Oh yeah girl, show 'em to daddy," Kip says. A female voice loudly moaning is persistently filling my head. "Shit girl, I didn't know you could bend like that. I think I want to marry you."

I feel Jag chuckle beside me. "He is watching porn. He likes to wake us up this way. The sad thing is that he isn't even rubbing one out. He is just fucking with us."

"Maybe we should give him a run for his money?" I ask with a wink.

"This is going to end so badly for me," Jagger answers with a sigh.

I begin moaning and softly calling Jagger's name. I throw in lots of "OH's" and "right there's." Jagger pretends to tell me to be quieter several times, and then he groans.

"Shit Henley, you are so tight." I have to hold back my giggles because during all of this we are both lying on our backs staring at the top of the bunk.

"Jag, your dick is so big. Yeah right there." Kip's porn stops.

"Oh baby, I knew you were a squirter," Jag says.

"Hold the fuck up, Kip says. I hear his bunk curtain open. "You're a squirter, and you never told me, pumpkin?"

Everyone on the bus bursts into laughter, except Kip.

"Thank fuck someone finally one upped his morning bullshit. Even if I had to hear Jag pretend to fuck my sister, it is worth ending that screaming whore. How do you find ridiculous porn at eight in the morning?" Koi asks, and we all chuckle.

"So you aren't really a squirter?" Kip asks.

"Oh banana bread, I'm capable of squirting so much I can cover the faces of an entire army in my love juice," I answer.

"Nice comeback Hen," Cam says.

Jag looks at me and whispers, "Are you really a squirter?"

"Not so far." I wink.

"Yup it ended badly," Jag says, and I giggle. Poor guy.

***

We are in Birmingham now. The guys have a show tomorrow night, so we have the day off. I get up and cook breakfast for the boys, and we take our time lounging around the bus. I read a book, and the guys play Xbox. The banter between them always cracks me up.

Later in the morning, Koi sits at the booth table writing a song. He throws his pen down in frustration and lets out a few expletives.

"What's wrong bubba?" I ask.

"I can't finish it. It has holes all in the damn thing. I'm ready to throw it away," he says.

"Let me see it."

He hands me the paper. I read over the song, and it did have holes, but it is a great song. I move to the table and pick up his pen. He sits beside me. I've done this a hundred times with Koi, and I realize how much I miss it.

"What if you put something like, 'And it takes all I had', right here. Then you can use the line again here and put it in the chorus. It fills up a lot of the holes and rounds out the meaning of it."

"That's fucking genius," he says.

"Have you thought about what sound you are going for?"

"The song is about living on the road, and seeing face after face, and not finding anyone who truly gets it. Everyone wants a piece of me, wants to touch me, wants to fuck me, but no one truly wants to know me," he says.

"Ah, the curse of the rich and famous. We become the industry's whore." I know all too well the feelings he describes.

"So, the song should be soft and sweet to begin with to show your love affair with music, and then it should get dirty and angry to show the love affair the world has with you. The angry shows you want no part of it," I say.

"Acoustic opening?" he asks.

"Yeah it can work. You can bring in a slow drum beat after the first two lines, then drop the bass line in it, and have Jag pick a blues number until you get to the first chorus. Then the drums should explode, the bass should dig in, and Jag should scream with the guitar to mimic you screaming at the world."

Koi picks up the phone. "Find me a studio in Birmingham," he orders.

***

We end up at a house studio outside of Birmingham within the hour. The guys are amped and ready to lay down the track. I work with each of them when they ask for help. It feels great to write and make music again. We are there for six hours before it is done. It turns out exactly how I had imagined it would.

I take a cat nap when we get back to the bus, and I'm awoken by the most horrible sound a musician can ever wake up to. Someone is attempting to play an acoustic guitar, and it hurts to hear the sounds coming out of it. I make my way to the back of the bus where the sounds are flowing from. Kip is attempting to play the damn thing. I instantly take pity on him.

"What are you doing?" I ask.

"I'm serenading you sweetheart," Kip says. "The way I figure it, you like those idiots who play guitars, so I figure I will learn how to play so I can seduce you. Jagger will understand. I mean he can't play drums for shit, so you will have no choice but to fall madly in love with my guitar *and* drum playing skills." He grins like a child.

"Good thinking," I say. "At the rate you are going, though, I will be eighty before you pick a decent lick on the poor thing. You are hurting its feelings right now."

"Yeah, but I will practice every waking moment until I have written and played you the most epic love song of the century," he says while wiggling his eyebrows.

"Epic, yeah? We need to work on your guitar lessons right now. You have to set small goals and work from one up to the next," I advise.

"Show me, oh great one!" he laughs.

Kip and I sit in the back of the bus for two hours. I show him some basic chords, and he gets them down quickly. We hand the guitar back and forth, and he mimics me. I give him several goals to work towards, and he accomplishes a couple during the lesson. I set up a practice schedule for him so that he can maintain what he has learned today. He is very serious during the entire lesson, and the world is only ever graced with that side of him when it comes to music.

I look up to see Jagger standing in the door. "You are teaching him to play guitar?"

"Yes, and we are bonding over the experience. I will take her from you Jagger Carlyle. She will be mine. She will not be able to resist me once I have become a better guitar player than you, which let's be honest won't take much," he says, and I giggle.

Jag is one of the most amazing guitar players I have ever seen. He has always had a natural ear for music, and Kip knows it.

"Kip, if you are the only man I ever have to worry about taking her from me, I will have it made," he says.

"One day sir, you will break my sweet Henley's heart, and I will be there to pick up the pieces."

Jagger stills for a second, and the strangest look passes his face. Just as quickly as it appears, it leaves. Maybe I imagined it.

"I will pick up this guitar, and I will play her a love song to mend her broken heart, and then my friend you will only be a fleeting thought. Shit, I should write a song about a fleeting thought, it makes me sound smart and shit." I grin at the thought of Kip writing a song.

"And then you will wake her the next morning with horrible Euro porn," Jag says with a laugh.

"My bumble bee appreciates my porn. Tell him Henley," Kip says.

I laugh and Jag orders Kip out of the room. He closes the door, locks it, and turns his heated eyes on me. Oh daddy! He crosses the room and kneels in front of where I sit.

"You look so hot with a guitar in your hands. It is all I can do not to rip it away from you and tear your clothes off," he says.

I think my breathing has stopped. I almost raise my hand and say, "Oh me, me, me, me. Pick me."

He pushes my long blonde hair behind my ear, and kisses me. The kiss quickly grows into something wild and hungry. I think my clothes just melt off. I run my hands up and down his strong arms, and he runs his down my sides. He gently pushes me down on the couch and climbs on top of me. Then he kisses that spot between my neck and shoulder, and OH MY GOD! His hands begin to descend my body to the hot zone. Mayday! Mayday! He runs his finger tip along the top of my jeans and teases me.

Do I have to shove your hands down there? He releases my button and opens my zipper slowly. He kisses me on my mouth again, slowly lapping his tongue against mine. He pulls back a hair, smiles at me, and places both hands on either side of my jeans. He yanks them down, and it startles me. He kisses my stomach and gets almost to that spot. You know that spot, the spot that if shown proper attention can make you see God, the angels, and the heavens above.

He pulls his body back over mine. What are you doing? Go back sparky. In the name of all that is holy, go back! He shoves his hands between my legs, and plays on the outside of my honey pot. I moan in his mouth, and he growls in response. Oh what a marvelous sound. He pushes a finger inside of me, and proceeds to play me like his fucking Les Paul. Let me pause here, and stress to men out there, the art of fingering does not lie in you sticking a finger or fingers inside of a woman and doing the whole in and out thing. No, you see you can do things with your fingers you can't do with your dick. You feel for the spot that makes her moan and you keep massaging it until she comes all over your fucking hand. That makes you the man. Where was I? Oh yeah, in heaven with Jagger Carlyle.

He is breathing heavy in my ear. Obviously he is as turned on as I am. I arch my back as he hits a spot that almost makes me go blind. Because he is Jag, he instantly takes notice and focuses on that one spot. I have never felt anything so marvelous in my entire twenty-six years on this earth. I think I let out at a "Don't ever stop doing that." I mean it too. If he stops I will become temporarily insane, blinded by my love for that finger inside of me. His chest vibrated with silent laughter. Then I moan and he growls again, and I arch my back more as he strokes my fun hole. Then the sensation hits me, I'm going to piss on myself. No, no, no, not now. I still and Jagger leans up to see what has stopped my dive over that cliff of ecstasy.

"I'm going to piss on myself," I say, a bit embarrassed.

He laughs. "No, you aren't. I found your g-spot love, and you are going to come. You say you aren't a squirter yet, so we are taking care of that."

"You are going to make me squirt?" Shouldn't you tell someone you are doing that to them before it happens?

"Lie back Henley. Let me make you come." His voice is covered in honey and his eyes hooded. How do you say no to that?

"It's going to feel like you have to pee, you won't though. Just relax through it and let it find you," he says, and he keeps hitting that glorious spot.

I'm sure that's what the 'G' stands for. I feel like I have to pee again, and I tense up.

"Let go Henley. Come for me." He leans down further to my ear. "I want to feel you come all over my hand. I'm going to lick up every last drop when you do."

I'm still trying to let go. The talking dirty shit is working, that's how I like it. I push his shirt up with my hands and dig my fingernails in his back. He moans, and that does it. I come harder than I have ever come in my life. I didn't even know that was possible. I think I cry out. There is no telling what I said. I see fireworks. They are amazing. I talk to angels and can see the future and crazy shit like that. When my spirit enters my body again, I open my eyes and Jag is staring at me with biggest shit-eating grin I've ever seen.

"That is the most beautiful thing I have ever seen. We should record that in the name of art. Shit, I almost came on myself just watching you," he says.

I'm mute. Words escape me. He must've fried my brain. I stutter and can't make coherent words come out of my mouth. He throws his head back and laughs at me. I don't care. He lies down on the side of me, and brushes my hair away from my face. He looks at me with adoring eyes, and at that very moment all is right in the world.

"So you squirted," he says with a proud look on his face.

I sit up and look around the room for evidence of the event, and after I find nothing, I look back at him with confusion clearly written all over my face.

"Where?"

"Not every woman can projectile squirt across the room. Most of it ended up on my hand. I licked it off. You don't remember?" he asks.

"Perhaps I was still in an alternate universe at that moment?" I offer.

I can feel his erection on my leg. I guess I should return the favor. I lift my ass, pull my pants up, and straddle him. "Stand up," I order, and he complies.

I pop the button on his jeans and slide his zipper down. I yank his pants and boxers down to his ankles, and his dick springs free. Holy mother of God, talk about a work of art.

"Henley, you don't have…," he begins.

"Shut up Jagger," I order, and he smiles.

I slide my mouth over his cock and slowly suck. I lick and suck all the way up and down his length. He moans and softly says my name. His dick starts to jump, and I know he is close. The head begins to swell even more, and I cup his balls in my hand and gently massage them.

"Fuck," he growls.

Oh the power of a blow job.

"I'm going to come. Just use your hand."

Not hardly, hoss. I keep going.

"Henley, I'm not kidding," he manages through gritted teeth.

I keep going. His dick swells even more, and then the salty goodness shoots into my mouth.

"Fuck. Jesus Christ. Motherfucker. That's it. Oh God. Suck it. Hard. Fuck. Fuck. Fuck. Fuck."

I swallow every last drop, sit back on my knees, and pull his boxers and jeans back up. He stares down at me like I just bought him a fucking Ferrari.

"You could suck the rust off a bumper," he finally manages.

"Thank you. That is so romantic. You are good at this compliment thing," I say with heavy sarcasm.

"Oh that is most definitely one of the best compliments a woman can receive after giving head. Blow jobs aren't meant to be romantic, love. If you want romance, I will give you romance."

This is the second time he called me love. It makes me giddy. Stupid grade school giddy.

"I was being sarcastic Jag," I said.

He pulls me up to him from the floor. He hugs me tightly and smoothes my hair down in the back.

"Yeah, but you will still get romance." He types out a text message and then turns to me. "You have an hour to shower or change or do hair and makeup. We are going on our first date." He kisses my forehead. "I will be back in an hour to get you."

Chapter 11

I shower and dress in a pinup style dress. It's a halter dress in a gorgeous shade of periwinkle blue with a high-waist black belt. I add some cute bracelets, a necklace, and some dangly diamond earrings Koi gave me last Christmas. I step into my black peep-toe Christian Louboutin stilettos with an asymmetrical strap that sweeps across the top of my foot. I do the whole smoky eye thing and straighten my hair. I'm spraying some perfume when Koi knocks and opens the door.

He looks up towards the heavens. "Why does my sister have to be beautiful? Is it too much to ask for an ugly sister?" he asks.

"Does that mean I look stunning?" I ask.

Kip shoves himself between Koi and the door. "Gorgeous, darling. Just gorgeous," he says in his best Joan Rivers voice. "Go away Koi, we need to make mad, passionate love right now."

Koi rolls his eyes.

Cam walks in the room. "And where do you think you are going dressed all sexy? You are not leaving my house dressed like that. Koi tell her she is grounded," he says, and we all laugh.

Cam hugs me. "You look beautiful."

"Keep your paws to yourself," Jag says from the door.

I spin around to see him dressed in jeans, chucks, a white collared shirt, and a dress jacket. He's holding a bouquet of flowers. Wow, he really is doing romance.

"May I take my girlfriend out on a date, or are you three going to stare at her all night?" Girlfriend? I like the sound of that.

I smile, and he hands me the flowers; they smell wonderful. He kisses me on the cheek and turns to offer me his arm. I take it and beam up at him like a fifteen year-old girl.

"Have her home by 9:00 dick weed," Kip says.

"It's 8:30 asshole," Jagger fires back.

"Exactly. Anymore time and you will deflower my sweet princess," Kip says.

"Can we not talk about deflowering my little sister?" Koi asks with a sigh.

"Kip, I'm not a virgin," I say.

Why am I having this talk again? Do people really think I'm such a prude?

"You close your mouth wench. I refuse to listen to such lies. Shame on you for feeding me such deceit." He sits on the couch and pats his lap. "Come here so daddy can give you a spanking for being a bad girl."

"Do you ever shut up?" Jagger asks.

Kip seems to ponder this for a bit. "Nope. I say what I think," he says, shit-eating grin in place.

"You ready love?" Jagger asks, and I nod with a smile.

Jagger walks me down the bus, and outside to a limo waiting for us. I have been in limos for most of my life, but I've never been in one on a date. I want to jump up and down and squeal like a little girl. I manage to hold it together. It wouldn't be attractive. He opens the door for me and holds my hand while I climb in. He follows suit, and once he is situated, hands me a glass of wine. I take a quick sniff and know immediately he is handing me Roscato. My smile is so big it hurts.

He holds his wine glass up for a toast. "To romance."

I clink glasses with him and take a sip. He is romancing me. I have never seen this side of him, but I like it. Yes sir, I do. The ride is short, and once the limo stops, Jag opens the door, and holds out his hand for me. I take it once again and climb out after him. He holds my hand and leads me into a restaurant called Chez Fonfon. I'm assuming it is French from the name. The maître d' is waiting for us at the host stand.

"Mr. Carlyle, we are pleased to see you. We've set up a private table for you in the courtyard at your request. Please follow me."

We follow the older gentleman. Jag's hand remains on the small of my back the entire way. The other diners instantly notice us as we pass through. I hear our names pass as whispers across their lips, gasps, and even a few cell phone cameras taking photos. Something I learned early in this industry is to look straight ahead, so I do. I won't let star struck diners ruin our first date. Regardless of how famous either one of us are, we are both on our first date. We have these growing feelings between us, and we want to enjoy them as any other human being would.

We follow the gentleman through a door to a courtyard lit by white Christmas lights. The courtyard is cut out of a massive garden that smells like honeysuckle. It is incredibly beautiful. Jag pulls my chair out for me, so I sit and shoot him a smile. He walks around the square wooden table lit by candles and sits across from me.

"Ms. Hendrix, we are equally pleased to see you. Would you like for me to pour your wine?" the older gentleman asks.

"Yes, please."

He pours us each a glass, and we thank him. We might be rich and famous, but we were raised in the South, and dammit, we have manners.

"I asked the chef to make something off the menu. I know you love duck, so he is making Magret de Canard. You will enjoy it." Jag seems a bit nervous.

I guess I'm a little nervous myself. The conversation finally starts flowing, both of our nerves a little apparent, but it is interrupted by a handsome gentleman who appears to be in his early forties.

"Good evening Mr. Carlyle and Ms. Hendrix. I'm Paul; I own the restaurant and will personally take care of you tonight. Are you two ready for your salads and bread?" he asks.

We nod. He leaves, and our conversation turns to Kip picking up the guitar. I tell him about the lesson and how quickly he is picking it up. We also talk about our parents and how things are back home since I have been in Macon more than he has in the last few years. He speaks about my grandfather and how legendary he is. He is 70 and still walking around with the health of a 20 year-old. We enjoy our salads, and our main course. Most of our conversation revolves around our childhood, and the early years in rock-n-roll. We have several good laughs at some of the idiocy we were involved with along the way. We drink wine throughout dinner and enjoy sitting in this beautiful courtyard. Thirty minutes after the main course, Jag asks me to dance with his hand held out.

We step close to a pond with a waterfall and begin dancing to a soft French jazz song. The music is beautiful.

"Thank you for tonight. It is perfect. I never knew you were such a hopeless romantic," I tease.

His crystal blue eyes look back into my dark blues, and he says nothing for a beat.

"I've never had romantic notions about anyone but you. I've always wanted to give you everything. When your birthdays came around, I had already thought about the perfect gift for months. It had to be perfect for you. I have listened to everything you ever said, Hen. For you, I would do anything. I would give you anything, all to make you smile and make you happy."

"You make me happy Jagger. Thank you. I had a crush on you too, you know?" I finally just spit it out.

"No you didn't!" he exclaims.

"Oh, yeah! I had it bad. The long-haired, pierced, teenage, bad boy Jagger Carlyle was the star of my teenage fantasies. You have a lot to live up to," I answer.

"Don't toy with my emotions like this," he says sarcastically.

"Oh, I wouldn't dare. The only time I deviated from you as the star of my fantasies is when I saw you with another girl. I was green with envy, so I punished you. I guess it isn't really punishment if you didn't know," I say.

"Oh, it is punishment now. The only reason I ever brought girls around you was to impress you. I thought if you saw how cool they thought I was, you would think I was cool too," he laughs.

He spins me around as we continue to dance.

"I thought you were the coolest guy in the whole world. You had this edge to you. You were so mysterious to me. When you started up the band with Koi, I was excited. I hoped I would get to know you more, but instead you broke out the guitar and the girls came out of the woodwork. I was pissed off most of the time I was around you," I laugh.

"You want to know how bad I had it for you?" Jag asks, and I nod. "I never saw any of those girls. What I did see, I instantly compared to you. Their eyes weren't yours. They don't laugh like you do, or have anywhere near the sense of humor you do. Hell, most of them couldn't stomach Kip, much less love him. They weren't confident or sure of themselves. They didn't know shit about my music or music in general. You always got it. There hasn't been one woman in my life that hasn't been compared to you. Why do you think I'm still single?"

"That makes two of us. I found a means to an end, companionship for a time I guess you could say. I never wanted it to last. There was always something missing. They weren't the bad boy of rock-n-roll," I say and look down at his chest a bit surprised by my revelation.

I suppose I always compared the other men in my life to Jagger. It wasn't their fault they didn't make the cut. I briefly think back to our teenage years when Jagger's quiet nature and acts of kindness pulled me under his spell. When he became a young man, he shed his shy skin, and the limelight pushed him into being more open and social. This side of Jagger piqued my interest just as much as the mysterious teenager did. Jagger is now all man, and the one thing I will never forget is the time he spent with me as I tried to revive my best friend. Sure, he was devastated by Caleb's death, but his main focus in those long moments of attempted resuscitation was me. I'm not sure how I didn't see it then, but I do now. He loves me, and he has all along. My fear of rejection prevented me from seeing what right in front of my face was always. Better late than never I suppose.

He lifts my face up to his with a gentle pull of my chin, and kisses me. The kiss is full of all the emotions we now know we've held onto for far too many years. The kiss is slow, but eager. I feel everything he feels for me through that kiss, and I hope he feels everything I have to give through mine. I don't know how long the kiss lasts, but it is interrupted by the sound of a closing door. The kiss is broken, and Paul is staring down at his shoes out of respect for our private moment.

"Paul, dinner was amazing. Thank you for everything you did for us tonight," Jagger compliments.

"It has been my pleasure Mr. Carlyle. I do have one small favor to ask before you depart," he says.

"Sure," Jag answers.

"Ms. Hendrix, the favor has actually been requested of you," Paul says as he directs his attention to me.

"Okay," I say, unsure of what lies ahead.

"You may of course decline. I understand this is your time together, and I will understand if you are unable to oblige. A young gentleman by the name of Noah is one of our guests this evening, and his parents are regular customers. He has endured chemotherapy and surgeries for the last eighteen months of his life due to a tumor in his spinal column. I know you must hear this all the time, but he is indeed your biggest fan. He is also your grandfather's biggest fan. He is quite an old soul for a ten year-old boy. He has requested you to play a song for him before you leave this evening," Paul says very nervously.

I've imagined this day so many times. The day someone is brave enough to ask me to play. The world doesn't know I stopped playing altogether. My imagination always visualizes an überpanicked Henley. I don't feel panicked at all though. I only think of the little boy in the restaurant who spent the last eighteen months of his life fighting to stay alive while I selfishly didn't live at all. I'm healthy, and I don't deserve to be after the way I've behaved over the last four years. I would give him my health if I could. Will I play him a song? "I would love to play for him. Does he have something in mind?" I ask.

"Yes. I believe he has chosen *Angel from Montgomery*. He has informed me you would know the song," Paul says with a massive grin on his face.

"Can you give me fifteen minutes?" I ask.

"Sure. I will advise Noah you will be in shortly."

"Will you call Koi and ask him to bring me a guitar?" I ask.

Jag leans down and kisses me. "I will do anything for you, Henley."

I shiver with genuine excitement from his kiss and words as he dials Koi and requests a guitar.

I take a moment to go over the lyrics in my head. I've sung the song hundreds of time. It is one of the first I actually sang and played on the guitar at the same **time** when I was a child. The song is written by John Prine, and it is about an old woman who regrets some of her choices because she hasn't lived her life to the fullest. Damn, is this kid trying to tell me something? Well, good for him if he is.

I take Jag's hand when he ends the call, and we enter the dining room. Paul waits on the other side of the door. He nods and starts towards a corner on the opposite side of the dining room. We follow. The only little boy at the table sits in a wheelchair and has no hair on his head. Despite this, he smiles from ear to ear when he sees Jag and me. The table is surrounded by adults who obviously adore this little boy. The dining room is virtually empty with only a few other diners remaining in addition to Noah's party.

"You must be Noah," I say with my biggest smile.

A woman who looks similar to Noah stands to greet me. "I'm Noah's mom, Carol. Please have a seat."

I sit with Noah, and Noah's dad leaves the seat on the other side of him for Jagger to join us. We talk about music. The kid loves music, and he reminds me so much of myself when I was his age. He even has the same taste in music.

"So favorite Led Zeppelin song?" I ask.

"That's easy. *Black Dog*, hands down. Yours?" he asks.

"I have never been able to pick between *Thank You* and their remake of *Since I've Been Loving You*."

"Favorite Allman Brothers song?" He asks.

"*Please Call Home*. Yours?" I enjoy the back-and-forth.

"*Whipping Post*," he answers.

"Favorite Beatles' song?" he asks.

"That's a conversation you should have with Jagger. He's the Beatles fan."

"That's easy," Jag says, imitating Noah. "*While my Guitar Gently Weeps*."

"Good one. Mine is *Hey Jude*." This kid is amazing. "Oh my God," he says and covers his mouth.

The front door opens, and Kip, Koi, and Cam stroll through carrying guitars, a bass guitar, and a drum kit. I know them, and when Jag told them about Noah they wanted to pay their respects to the little fighter. I laugh at Noah's reaction to Broken Access. The rest of the adults at the table vacate their seats and motion for the three additional men to sit down. They all instantly take to Noah, and more banter about music goes around the table. Noah's family finds a great deal of humor in our conversation. I have no idea what time it is or how long has passed, but I have nowhere to be. I'm sincerely enjoying talking to this little guy.

"You play any instruments?" Kip asks.

"No, but when I get better, mom says I can start guitar lessons," Noah answers.

"I actually started my guitar lessons today. Henley is teaching me," Kip says.

"You are a drummer. Why do you want to play the guitar?" Noah asks.

"Well Noah, I want to steal Henley from Jagger. She tends to like boys who play guitars, so I thought what better way to steal her by writing her an epic love song played on the guitar? Plus, it makes me the better man if I can play two instruments," Kip deadpans.

"I don't know if you can steal Henley, Mr. Kip. She is the prettiest girl I have ever seen, and by the time you learn to play the guitar, she and Jagger are going to be married," he says.

Marriage? I've actually never thought of marriage with anyone. If I were to marry, I guess I would want it to be to Jagger.

Kip puts on his serious face and leans closer to Noah. "How do I stop her from marrying him, oh wise one?"

Noah leans his head closer to Kip's. "Girls like it when you give them candy. My mom even likes chocolate. It makes her really happy, but any candy will do. You have to buy her awesome candy! If that doesn't work, buy her a puppy."

Oh don't say that, Noah. I will have a house full of dogs.

"Great advice. I will have to start on that immediately," Kip says.

"Will you play me a song now?" Noah is impatient now.

"I would love to." I lean down and kiss his forehead.

"Kip, I don't think you have a chance now. She is so totally into me!" Noah exclaims and the entire room bursts into laughter.

"I will take you down little man," Kip warns with a smile on his face.

I play the blues opening to *Angel from Montgomery* on Jag's electric. I sing my heart out in the first verse, and the guys join in on their instruments. Koi adds the harmonica to the sound, and it sounds perfect. I pick up the guitar tempo and pour the blues out of my soul after the second verse. The guys keep up with me. We have small amps, no mics, and it is a simple and uncomplicated type of beautiful. It's like the old days when we were kids. When the song reaches the end everyone claps, but we decided to do one more for Noah. I open up Susan Tedeschi's *Rock Me Right*, and my friends jump right in. Jag and I play against each other in the middle of the song to see who can keep up. He loses and I snicker.

When the song is over, we put down our instruments. Security comes in quickly to retrieve the instruments, but Jagger tells them to leave his electric guitar. We spend a few more minutes with Noah and his massive family. When we finally begin our farewells Noah pouts, but Koi jumps in to save the day.

"Hey, little man, why do you look sad? This isn't goodbye. We were expecting to see you at our show tomorrow."

Noah's eyes light up, and a smile stretches across his face. "I'm coming to your show?"

"Oh I didn't mention that before? I thought your mom was your tour manager, so I asked her if you had an opening on your schedule, and she said you just happen to have some time between all those girlfriends you have and the gigs you play. I'm so honored that you can watch us play tomorrow night. Guys, a legend will be among us tomorrow night!" Koi yells and all the musicians hoop, holler, and high-five each other.

Koi pulls tickets out of his back pocket and hands them to Noah. "I understand if you are too busy to make it with you being a big rock star and all, but we would really appreciate if you can try your best. I scraped together twenty tickets for the front row and twenty back stage passes for you and all your favorite people." Noah throws his arms around Koi's neck in affection.

"Thank you. This is going to be so awesome! Tomorrow is my 11th birthday!" he says.

It all shocks us for a moment. His birthday will be amazing if we have anything to do with it.

Jagger speaks up. "I would like to give you my guitar for your first birthday present. I will also leave the practice amp, case, some extra strings, and some picks."

My heart is swelling again.

"Dude!" Noah is so excited. "Can all of you sign it for me?" The guys surround the little man and dote on him. They sign the guitar for him with heartfelt messages.

I step back to speak with his mom about a few ideas I have for his birthday, and I ask if there are any health issues we need to plan for. I want his experience to be amazing without having to remind him of how sick he is. Carol and Noah's father Rick hug my neck and thank me. I make sure to get their contact information for tomorrow.

"Henley? Will you sign my guitar too?" Noah asks. His eyes are so hopeful.

"Of course I will, handsome," I say. Kip is sitting beside him. "Kip, move so I can say good night to my boyfriend," I demand.

"You wound me! I have been replaced by an almost 11 year-old," Kip pouts dramatically.

"Dude, I told you she is into me," Noah says. Once again, the room erupts into a roar.

As we exit the restaurant, Jagger grabs my hand. "I had something else planned if you aren't too tired."

I smile and nod. "I'm never too tired for you."

We enter the limo, and Jag immediately attacks me with kisses.

"I haven't heard you sing in so long, I forgot how horny it made me." He doesn't let me get my giggle completely out before he attacks me again.

We arrive at Oak Mountain State Park. Its pitch black outside, so I begin to wonder what we are going to do at a park. The limo rounds a corner, and I can see the lake is filled with floating lanterns. Jagger is already out of the car and offering his hand to me. I exit the limo and follow his lead to a dock where a small boat sits. Inside the boat are two acoustic guitars. I look back out at the lake. No one is in sight. It is beautiful.

"Did you do this?" I ask.

"Yes, baby. I wanted to give you romance. Eating dinner was just a cover for the guys to have long enough to set this up," he says.

Baby? Mmm, say it again.

"I don't think I'm the only one who wanted romance," I tease.

Jagger feigns shock. "I have a reputation to uphold as the bad boy of rock. Don't go around tearing it down."

I tease back. "I know it takes a great deal of women, bottles of booze, and hotel damage bills to build up that reputation. Hard work, yeah?" He doesn't laugh or crack a smile.

"I never started that stupid shit until Caleb died. It got worse when you were in Europe and Africa. When I saw you this past Christmas, it stopped. But once you are stuck with a reputation in this business, it isn't easily shaken off. I stopped partying when I saw you smile at Christmas."

"What?" I'm so confused.

"I numbed the hell out of myself. I couldn't have you, love you, or see you. The truth is… I pined for you Henley. I worried about you constantly. The only way I could forget how much it all hurt… Caleb… you… you not being here… was to drink it away. Sometimes I would fuck it away. I didn't sleep with most of the women I was photographed with. If I had an ounce of inhibition left in me, I found something wrong with each one of them. This past Christmas, I showed up on your doorstep unannounced, and the smile on your face when you opened that door melted me on the spot. You threw your arms around me and hugged me tight. I still think my heart stopped beating for just a moment. I had only seen you twice since the Christmas before, and you seemed so preoccupied. That was the first time it felt like the real you was back. We drank beer on the front porch and played Rummy into the morning because I couldn't bear to leave you. All it took was you smiling at me, and I didn't need any of that shit anymore."

Tears pierce his eyes, and I feel like the biggest idiot on planet earth. How did I not know that my actions affected him so much? How did I not know he only needed to see that I was still whole? I remember opening the door to him at Christmas and feeling like this man's presence made everything seem alright in my world. I knew then that I wanted Jagger, but my selfish fear of rejection prevented me from letting him see how I really felt.

"I'm so sorry. I'm just so sorry. I had no idea my absence affected you like that, or I would've tried harder to be around. Why didn't you say anything?" I ask.

"You don't get to be sorry Henley. You dealt with it the only way you knew how, and I felt like we all reminded you of Caleb and the music. Just promise me you will lean on me when you hurt. I need to know that I can be that person for you."

He bends down and picks me up by my ass, and I wrap my legs around his waist. His mouth crashes into mine, and all the pain, longing, sorrow, sadness, and love passes across our lips. I find it is how Jagger and I communicate the deepest of emotions. No matter what words pass between us, our bodies can convey far more than the English language can. In this moment, I realize what has held me back from handing my heart over to a man. Sure, I always compared every man to Jagger, but what really averted me from a true connection was trust. When you are a celebrity, there is a fear that takes precedence in relationships. No matter how another human being makes you feel, it's all overshadowed by the possibility of exposure. Every news media outlet in this country splashes relationship failures, and the reasons that led to the demise of each one are spread across the front pages for all to see. People who will never know you personally are privy to your weaknesses, failures, heartaches, and personality flaws. How do you trust someone with your heart when they may not only break it, but parade the most intimate of moments in front of the world? My misgivings about men has always been somewhat dictated by the lack of faith I have in a man to protect my heart entirely. There has never been a moment in time when I haven't trusted Jagger entirely.

"If you don't stop seducing me, woman, I'm going to tear your clothes off, and you will end up with ticks in all sorts of places," he says.

He puts me down, helps me in the boat, and rows us out into the middle of the small lake. We spend the next several hours playing our guitars, singing, laughing, and reminiscing.

Chapter 12

From where I stand on the side of the stage, in the depths of total darkness, I can hear the fans scream. My nerves are catapulting around my body, and the result is a trembling that my body can't shake. Anxiety about stepping on this stage is overtaking my entire being. The fans can't see me as I wait for the house lights to go down, but I can see and feel their energy. Stage fright. I have stage fright, and I'm going to make a damn fool of myself. I'm Red Newman's granddaughter, and the headlines will be savage if I don't pull this off. Fans are unrelenting in their pursuit of a perfect live show. They will not take their disappointment kindly.

In the blackness, someone grabs my hand, and I know the instantaneous calmness that has disseminated over me can only come from Caleb.

"Don't let it get to you doll," he says.

"I think I will be fine when I get out there."

"Remember you can't see past the first three rows when the house lights come down. If you feel nervous, find me or Griffin, and we will play music together. You don't have to play for anyone but yourself Hen."

"Okay," I softly agree.

At that moment, the house lights go down. I'm about to play my first major venue, Madison Square Garden, at just sixteen years old. I've waited for this moment for a very long time. I knew it was coming, and yet, here I am with a classic case of stage fright. Caleb pulls me up on stage with him, and I stand at my mic with guitar in hand. When the first riffs come through my monitor, it is all over with. I'm in a different place, and I couldn't care less how many thousands of people watch. I'm a slave to my guitar, and I play it with the same devotion and intensity that I have since I was a small child. During the chorus of this first song, I look over at Caleb to see him smiling back. The first song ends with thousands of fans screaming. The sound is exhilarating. I realize I don't remember which song comes next in the set list. I look over to Caleb, but he isn't there. I look to the other side of the stage and then to the back. Griffin and Rhys are gone too. The fans begin to boo at us. As I search the stage again, the Porsche is sitting upside down, battered. Where is Caleb? I scream for him. I can save him this time. I have to get out of the car quicker this time. I scream for him again as I walk across the stage to the Porsche. I look in, but I can't see me. Where did I go? The fans are jeering at me, but I don't know where Caleb is. We were in a car accident. Can't they see that? Tears pour down my face, and I scream for Caleb again. Where is he? I need him to tell me so I can help him. I can save him this time!

"Henley! Wake up! Henley!"

"Caleb!" I scream over and over again. "Where are you?"

Jagger and Kip are directly in front of my face, and I'm drenched in my own sweat.

"We have to find him! We have to save him this time! Help me!" I scream.

"Henley, you are asleep, baby. Wake up. You are having a bad dream. Wake up," Kip pleads.

"Where is Caleb?" I ask, still confused.

"Henley, you have to wake up," Koi says.

Koi pulls me to him, and it takes a moment for the fog of the nightmare to lift. Then, like a fist to my gut, realization dawns on me. It was a dream. The concert was real in my past, but the accident didn't happen that night. My need to save Caleb, to bring him back, haunts my dreams. Freud believes the unconscious mind drives our dreams, that our mind uses dreams to fulfill our unconscious urges and needs subconsciously. My urges and needs surround Caleb's death. I feel the bile rising in my throat. I pull away from Koi and make it to the small bathroom just in time. I vomit all the fucking urges and needs into that toilet. I hate myself when I feel so weak. No one, aside from my friends Jessica, Samantha, and Stephanie, have ever seen the result of my dreams.

I lie on the floor, against the wall, when there is nothing else left. I work to control my ragged breathe. There's a quick knock at the door, and my sweet brother steps in. He wets a small towel and slides down the door next to me. We are cramped in this tiny space, but I can't bear to tell him to leave. He is worried and will only worry more if I send him away. He wipes my face for me, and he looks me over with gentle, concerned eyes.

"Do you want to talk about it?"

"There's not much to talk about. They always end the same way. I search for Caleb, and he isn't there. I try to find him quicker than I did that night so I can save him… keep him here with me… but I can't ever find him. Hysteria always sets in when I can't find him."

"Sounds like there is more to talk about than you think."

"It won't change a damn thing. When he died, a part of me died too. I can't fix that. We are all shaped by the events in our lives, and his death shaped so much of who I am now. I won't ever be the carefree girl I was before," I offer.

"Death does that to us. It takes so much more than a person's life. It claims everything it can in the process. Loss doesn't allow us much control in the ordeal, but we do have a little. It took me a long time to accept that he was really gone. I picked up the phone to call or text him more times than I can count. I guess I never had closure, because in some morbid way, we all need to see a lifeless body to start accepting what fate has dealt us. Your lack of closure stems from not being able to revive him, and that's natural. Death can be a leech on us if we allow it. I think you put up walls for close to four years to try to avoid letting us see how much his death affects your everyday life. Walls don't help you process baby girl."

"I guess you're right. I feel so weak because I can't control the dreams."

"Look, I know you have always been strong as hell, but you are human and breakable. Don't let your need for control and strength prevent you from healing. I'm going to tell you something that stays between you and me. After he died, this band barely spoke on most days. We were all so wrapped up in our individual grief that we couldn't do much more than sleep and play music for six months. When the anger phase began, Jagger tried to fight every asshole he could find in a bar. Kip cussed out every single human being that mentioned his name, and Camden tried to drown it all in a bottle. I lashed out at every female I brought home and treated them like fucking lepers. I've never treated women like that, but I couldn't take it out on anyone I loved. I think most nights I searched those women out specifically to have an outlet. It wasn't healthy, and I feel like shit for the way I treated them, but we all deal with our shit differently. Griffin didn't leave his house for seven months. He tore the damn place apart more than a handful of times. Rhys spent his time on social media and writing articles about the asshole that killed him. It would've been the healthiest of all our choices if he didn't suffer from insomnia and forget to eat. The point I'm trying to make is that we all suffered, and we all handled it in our own ways. Not one of us should ever be ashamed of hurting. You couldn't save him Henley. No matter how much earlier you found him, he was already gone. His spinal cord snapped on impact, and that can't be fixed. You have to find a way to accept that so that you can find a way to let go of the guilt for not reviving him. Okay?"

"Okay."

"Let's get you back to bed," Koi says. "I think Jagger wants you with him."

I crawl into Jagger's bunk, and he pulls me tight to him. I wish he never saw me like that, but I can't take it back now. He kisses the top of my head, and when I hear his sniffles, my own dam breaks loose. The tears stream down my face, and we hold each other as we cry ourselves to sleep.

I wake later that morning in Jagger's bunk, but he isn't there. I can smell bacon cooking. Is that also coffee I smell? Someone loves me. I rise out of the bunk and make my way to the restroom. When I emerge with my eyes only half open from exhaustion, my nose follows the smell. Someone grabs my face, and plants a kiss on my forehead. I hold my hand out for a coffee cup, and I hear Jagger laugh. A few moments later, a coffee cup is in my hand. I slide down the cabinets behind me to the floor. I sit with two hands on my precious little cup of coffee, and sip. Once I can open my eyes, I look up to see Jag standing in front of me.

"Are you alive now?" he asks with a smile on his face.

He cuts the burner on the stove off, slides down across from me, hands me a cigarette, and places an ashtray between us. He lights my cigarette and I inhale. I should quit smoking, but I really do enjoy it. He lights his own cigarette, and we sit there for several minutes staring at each other. The silence is surprisingly comfortable. I realize something paramount in this moment… he sees me. Jagger Carlyle has always seen me. He doesn't see me as the Guitar Goddess, or the rock star, or even the poor girl who lost her best friend. He sees *me*. The real me who encompasses all of those things and so much more. I don't need to explain my nightmares to him or how I feel. He was there, and even if he wasn't, he would still get it because he sees me. The fact that he sees me for everything I am, -good, bad, or indifferent - summons an epiphany in me. I have always been in love with Jagger, and he is the only man I will ever love.

"I am *now*. It only takes a little nicotine and coffee to jump start my heart in the mornings." I wink.

"How are you this morning?" he asks, giving me the chance to decide whether I want to talk about my dream.

"I'm okay, Jag. Promise."

"I had fun on our first date last night. Thank you for going with me," he says.

"You can take me on a date anytime. I had fun as well. Thank you for this morning… when I was upset."

He runs his hands through his hair. He does this when he is frustrated.

"I… just hope… the music and you being on tour didn't cause the dream. I… hope I didn't cause it. I would never hurt you baby."

I scoot closer to him and touch the stubble on his face. I lean over and give him a small kiss.

"You didn't cause anything. The dreams have been recurring for four years. Koi and I had a long talk last night, and I think I know why I still have them. So, I'm going to try to deal with that. Please don't ever think you helping me heal causes me harm."

He takes my hand from his face and kisses it. "Will you help me cook breakfast for our small army?"

"I would love to."

We cook bacon, sausage, eggs, and biscuits, and I'm put in charge of the pancakes since Jagger refuses to try making them. Our conversation focuses on Noah and all the ideas we have for his birthday.

"You want to know my favorite part of last night?" he asks. "I loved spending time with Noah and playing with the whole crew there. It felt like old times, and Noah reminds me of how much our music touches people. That little boy has been through hell for the past eighteen months, and all he wanted was to hear you sing."

"That really put shit in perspective for me. I thought the first time someone asked me to play that I would freeze up or have a panic attack. Luckily, it was Noah who asked. I never thought twice about saying yes. He is such an amazing kid who has been dealt a shit hand of cards. I think we often forget what we can do with the platform we've been given. We did something wonderful last night, but Noah did something even more amazing for me. He restored my love of music," I say.

He smiles a sad little smile. "I was so nervous about the two guitars in the boat. I didn't know how you would react."

"If it hadn't been for Noah, I don't know how I would have either. I owe him the world, and he doesn't even know it. That little boy will always be the reason I quit running from who I am and what I love. Don't think I don't know what you guys did for me as well. Koi played frustrated with an amazingly written song to draw me in. You played that song you wrote for Caleb, and then you threw two guitars in a boat. Kip pretended to want to serenade me, so he asked me to teach him to play the guitar. Cam acted like he completely forgot how to play the bass when you guys recorded yesterday," I say.

"Are we that transparent?" he asks nervously.

"Not at all. It took me a while to piece it all together, but I finally did. I'm very thankful for what all of you did. No one else on this earth could've known how to bring me back to music, other than Noah. Was helping me find my way back the reason you pushed so hard for me to tour?"

"Are you crazy? I brought you out here to sweep you off your feet lady," he answers.

"Mission accomplished."

***

After breakfast, I have a huge day to plan. Noah gave me the greatest gift I've ever been given in my life, and I don't plan on forgetting that anytime soon. Last night, before the dream, I thought about calling my band mates, Griffin and Rhys, to talk about recording a new album. I will spend my days thanking Noah for bringing me back. He is too young to understand, so for now I can only spoil him.

I call my attorney and ask him to dig up some information on Noah's parents. I give him their contact information. I really want to know if they are financially stable since health care costs can drain a family. I also want to ensure Noah is receiving the best care money can buy. Next, I phone to Randy and ask him to coordinate with the other bands because I want Noah to meet them all. I make plans for a local bakery to make a huge cake in the shape of a guitar and deliver it backstage for him. I text his mom and ask about his favorite foods. I then put in a huge pizza order at the local Pizza Hut for later tonight.

I quickly shower so we can shop for presents. By the end of our shopping excursion, Noah has guitars, amps, drums (Kip), a Play station 4, a Xbox One, every game and accessory the kid can want for either system, a laptop, an iPad, an iPod, and an iPhone. His parents might kill us. We finally find guitar theme decorations for the party, and Kip rants on and on about how companies don't ever put drums on party accessories. By the end of the rant, Kip came to the conclusion the lack of attention drummers get is one gigantic government conspiracy against drummers. According to Kip, drummers are the most intellectual and artistic type of people. Those types of people scare the government. We just nod and smile like we usually do.

I want to make sure that not only Noah is taken care of, but his parents as well. They have endured eighteen months of emotional agony. It can't be easy to watch your perfectly healthy child be diagnosed with cancer and then lose his hair, vomit constantly, and end up in a wheel chair. They need a break. I buy them each a massage at a local spa for the next twelve months. I book a three-day trip to Hawaii, since I don't think they would want to be away from their son any longer, and I cover all outstanding medical costs. All of his doctors have been informed to forward any other outstanding costs to my accountant.

Apparently, Noah's mom had no choice but to quit her job when Noah was diagnosed. So his dad works two jobs and very rarely sees either of them. They were forced to empty all stocks, retirements, and savings to make ends meet. I pay off their mortgage, cars, and credit cards. I don't do this last part alone. Each of the four guys asks me to total up the debt, and we split it five ways. Now both of his parents can spend time with him and not worry about losing their home.

As I put the last touches on my makeup, I hear Jagger excitedly call little man's name, so I knew he has arrived at the venue. Koi comes to the back to let me know they are giving him and his guests a tour of the venue. I will meet them there as soon as I'm finished.

When I arrive on the side of the stage, most of the musicians from the tour are standing around Noah showing him how to shred a guitar. I can hear Noah's giggles over the music. He is an easy kid to adore. His mom approaches me as I stand back from the crowd watching my boys.

"Was it you?" she asks.

"I'm sorry?" I say in confusion.

"Last night my parents had to pay for our dinner because we couldn't afford it. They wanted to take Noah out for his birthday while he was feeling well, and by this afternoon, I didn't have a financial care in the world. Did you do that for my family?" she asks with tears in her eyes.

"It wasn't just me. Koi, Kip, Cam, and Jagger also helped. I had someone get your family's story so I could make sure y'all didn't need or want for anything."

I remember the envelope holding their vacation and massages. "Here, please take this. Promise me you won't open it until you leave tonight."

"Why? Don't get me wrong, I'm thankful, but people don't wake up and take care of every worry someone has because a little boy is sick," she says.

"I didn't do it because Noah is sick. Four years ago, my best friend of seventeen years was killed by a drunk driver. I spent the first year after his death trying to figure out why I was still alive. I couldn't function, much less play music. The second year I tried to keep busy. The third, I backpacked in Europe and stayed with Buddhist monks. The fourth, I spent trying to become human again in the real world. I never once thought I would play or sing again, and I had no desire to. Those four men over there are slowly but surely trying to get me there. But when a little boy fighting for his life asks you to sing for him, you don't say no. Your son gave me back music. You have a pretty awesome kid. I will never forget what he did for me even if he is too young to understand. It's these types of gifts that put life into perspective."

She hugs me so tightly. "Thank you so much. He *is* such a great boy. I haven't seen him smile like that in months. You put the spark back in his eye."

"I didn't do it alone." I look towards some of my favorite men who are still doting on Noah.

"No. I guess not. I will make sure I let them know how much I appreciate them," she says.

"Tonight, you have no worries. You and your husband sit back, have a few beers, and enjoy being alive. I will help see about Noah."

She hugs me again, and I watch the guys with little man. Jag is so great with him. He is such a kind person. If the world only knew how beautiful the bad boy of rock really is, they would give the title to someone else. He catches me looking at him, does a double take, and holds my gaze. A smile crosses both our faces. I'm in trouble here. My heart feels like it wants to burst.

***

The night is amazing. Noah is able to meet every musician on tour. They all do more than just meet him though. He plays their instruments, and gets more free band gear than I think his closet can hold. Koi calls him out on stage, and the guys hand him an unplugged guitar. He doesn't know it is unplugged, and he rocks out with Broken Access. I capture the entire evening on my camera.

The after party is free of groupies, fans, drugs, and drunken musicians. Everyone gathers round and sings *Happy Birthday*, eats cake, and takes pictures in the photo booth. The gift table is overflowing. The other bands decided to spoil him further when they heard he would be here tonight. I think his parents' hearts stop beating a few times when they see all the instruments and electronics. Noah is a happy kid. When we show him his phone, we show him our numbers are in it. We ask his mom to keep us up to date on his health and to call if she needs anything. Noah is asleep when his parents load him into the limo, so I kiss him good night on the cheek. I know I will be seeing this little guy again.

***

After Noah leaves, I sneak around the corner to make a phone call that I have been thinking about all day. It rings four times, and I think it is about to go to voicemail. If it does, then I know I shouldn't go down this path.

"Hen?" Griffin asks.

"Yeah. It's me."

I knew he would be surprised to hear from me. I just hope it is a good surprise. Griffin is the bassist in our band, Abandoned Shadow.

"You okay?"

"Yeah." I can't find the words.

"Henley. You are starting to worry me," he says.

I can't say these words over the phone. "If I send you a plane ticket, will you meet me in Memphis on Saturday?"

"Yeah, I would love to," Griff says and my nerves settle. "Hen, I saw you on the news with Jag. I think it's great. You look so happy. Your voice… it sounds more like you. I miss you girl."

Sadness tugs at my soul because I miss him too. "Thanks Griff. I feel more like myself now. Jag and I… well, we are seeing what happens."

"You never know until you put yourself out there. He looked rough the last time I saw him. It was right before Christmas. All he… we talked about was you. Glad you are back. See you next Saturday." We disconnect shortly after.

Thoughts of Christmas overtake me. I remember how happy I was to see Jagger. I remember how much I missed him on a daily basis, but I couldn't figure out where I fit in any of their lives since I left rock-n-roll. I didn't realize exactly how much I missed him, though, until I laid my eyes on him that day. I think we both stayed up all night because neither of us could bear to say good night.

I make my second call. It picks up on the second ring.

"Woman! I miss yo' face!" Rhys says.

Ever the partier, I can hear music blaring in the background.

"Hey hold on, Hen. Let me step out." I hear the sounds change as he walks through a room, a door opens and closes, and then it is quiet. "Alright, I can hear now. Fucking strippers. They know white trash with cash when they see it. So… Jagger fucking Carlyle! The man finally grew a pair, yeah? You look happy Hen. When am I going to see your amazing face again?"

"I was hoping we could meet in Memphis on the 9th," I say.

"Fucking A I can! We gotta tie one on girl. Been way too damn long. Wait, you and Carlyle aren't going to force me to watch you get all hot and heavy are you? I mean, you have always been quiet with your shit, so I have never had to watch a motherfucker maul you. I woulda caught a charge fo' sho'," Rhys says.

"Always quiet with my shit?" I ask.

"Look, I'm a playboy, and it takes one to know when a girl is discreetly getting her lady parts serviced. Feel me?"

I burst out laughing. "Yeah, I get it kid."

He makes goat sounds… I call everyone kid, but Rhys always makes goat sounds when I do.

"Seriously, Hen… miss yo' face."

"I miss yo' face too," I say getting all teary-eyed again.

"See you in Memphis. If I don't make it, make sure the authorities know a stripper who goes by the very exotic name Indigo, is responsible for my disappearance. I can feel her trying to swallow my soul through that dark hole also referred to as her snatch," he says.

"Will do."

We disconnect. I have a band meeting scheduled, Noah and his family are taken care of, and Jagger and I are doing really well. I'm falling in love. Life is good.

Chapter 13

I wake again in typical Broken Access style.

"What the fuck is on your back Carlyle?" I hear Kip ask sternly from the front of the bus.

"Dude, really? Has it been that long?" Jag asks.

"I'm sitting right here, fuckers." Koi says.

"Oh, this is going to be fun," Cam the quiet one says.

"Do you see this shit, Koi? These are defensive wounds. Something very horrible was forced onto Henley, and she had to defend herself from that behemoth over there. I can't believe you are just sitting there. We are talking about your sister jackleg!" Kip yells.

"I'm not talking about this," Koi says.

"Defending herself?" Jagger asks.

He is egging Kip on. We enjoy his entertainment.

"Dude, rape is so not cool. When a girl says, 'No, don't touch me there, that's my no-no square,' she means no you sexual predator!" Kip says.

I'm already laughing. I emerge from the bunks, and Kip immediately sets his sights on me.

"Darling, why didn't you tell me how this asshole traumatized you? I would have beaten the shit out of him for you."

I hold my hand up and Kip shuts up. Good he understands my sign language. I relieve myself, exit the restroom, and Jagger hands me a cup of coffee. Didn't I say I'm falling in love with him? Kip attempts to speak again, and I put my hand up once more. He pipes down. I slide down the cabinets again, and Jag joins me, placing the ashtray between us and a cigarette between my lips. Luckily, he never lights them for me. It's the first hit I enjoy most. Maybe he gets it. He lights my cigarette, and I inhale a menthol cloud. Ah… much better. I look up at Kip and motion for him to continue, and he wastes no time. Everyone chuckles.

"I was just saying to you, my little sweet roll, that it is not okay to think you are the victim here. Rape is bad," he says.

"Ya' think?" I mumble and take another sip of coffee.

"Look at her Koi. She is so traumatized she can barely speak. Why aren't *you* kicking his ass yet?" Kip stands with his hands on his hips.

Koi sighs. "Because, as much as it pains me to say this, I don't believe she was raped."

Kip immediately throws his hand to his chest as though he is having a heart attack. His voice reaches a very feminine, shrill level. "Say what?!!"

Cam jumps in. "What Koi is trying to say without having to think very much about it is, Henley did not have to defend herself against Jagger. Those are marks of passion, my friend."

Kip repeats himself. "Say what?!!"

"Kip, Jagger found my G-spot for the first time in my life. He made me squirt. I second what Cam says," I say.

Kip feigns outrage. "You cheated on me pumpkin?" He tries to sound sad.

"No. It isn't sex, so it isn't cheating," I say.

"Then how did he…Never mind I most certainly do not want to know. I forgot I was talking about my sister. Got it, loud and fucking clear!" Koi says and retreats to the back of the bus, which makes us all laugh.

"Oh, so he hasn't stuck the beaver basher in yet?" Kip asks.

Beaver basher?

"Well, not in my beaver," I offer, and wink at Jagger who almost pisses himself.

Kip pretends to have a panic attack and loads himself onto the bench seat at the table breathing loudly and jaggedly. He stands suddenly and points to Jagger.

In his best Antebellum southern voice he yells at Jag, "You sir, have defiled my innocent sweetheart. How dare you! This is war!"

"Kip we agreed that you would sleep with brunettes while I sowed my wild oats," I say.

"So, this Jagger thing is just a wild oat?" he asks.

"No, you asshole, I'm not a wild oat. But you can tell yourself that if it helps you sleep at night," Jagger adds.

He stands and helps me to my feet. He bends down and plants a kiss on my lips, then dives in with the tongue. Good morning to you too, sparky.

I feel Kip and Cam walk past us to the back. That finally ends Kip's morning outburst.

Jagger pulls away and smacks my ass before he turns back to breakfast on the stove. It looks like he is attempting pancakes this morning. A domesticated rock star.

"Where are we sexy?" I ask him.

"Sexy, huh?" Oh, the smile on his face makes me want to devour every last inch of him. "We are in the Big Easy. One of your favorite places on earth if I remember correctly. We have five days off here. We are playing a smaller venue, so we play a Friday and Saturday night show."

***

We hit the French Quarter to find lunch a few hours later. I love this city. Anything goes here, the food is to die for, and the music makes me feel so nostalgic. We hit my favorite bar, Fritzel's, after lunch and drink beer for several hours. We tour the art district after Fritzel's, and we all buy some amazing art and have it shipped to our homes. I find a shop that specializes in antiques, and try to talk the owner down on his price for a gorgeous sapphire necklace, earring, and bracelet set. He even has two hair pins to match. The sapphires are set in old silver and made in the 1920's. I thank the man when we can't agree on a price, and we march on through the rest of the shops.

Kip wants to go to the Voodoo temple on the outskirts of the quarter, so we join him. Jagger holds my hand everywhere we go and kisses the top of my head often. I enjoy his affections so much. Once we are at the temple, Kip tries to talk the High Priestess into letting him hold the snake. Even though she attempts to tell him Voodoo is not what Hollywood has made it out to be, he is very persistent in attempting to procure a hex spell. I have no idea who Kip would put a hex on, but the idea that he would probably do it for shits and giggles is frightening.

We head back to the bus to unpack and check in at The W. When Randy hands us our room keys, he nervously glances between Jagger and me.

"I wasn't really sure if you two were sharing a room, so I tentatively gave Henley the second room in Koi's suite."

"She is staying in my room," Koi quickly says.

"Yes, she is," Jagger says, and I frown. "Baby, I'm only human. I can sleep with you on a bus full of men who include your brother and hold it together, but I won't have any will power if we share a room."

He kisses me on my forehead. When he puts it like that, I guess I'm okay with it.

Jag helps me with my luggage, and I settle into my room while he finds his own room and does the same. I lay down to read a book, and doze off.

I wake to Jagger talking on the phone. "Yeah, mom we are good. We are really happy." He pauses. "I know. Me too. I've wanted that woman since I was a kid." He pauses again and then laughs. "I think that is rushing things a bit, don't you?" Pause. "Tell dad he has to keep his paws to himself. He is a dirty old man. Henley looks at him as such. Make sure you tell him that." Pause. "Yeah, mom I do. I've loved her since the first day of sixth grade. It's different now that we are older, and now we've been through Caleb's death together. I like this love. I'm so comfortable with her, and she makes me laugh. She sang and played my guitar the other night for this little boy. He has cancer, and he knew we were in the restaurant. He asked her to play and she didn't hesitate to make his dreams come true. It's probably the first time she's sung in four years." He loves me? Pause. "Hearing Henley sing and play is always like hearing her for the first time. I have never been so mesmerized with another musician's ability like I am with hers." Pause. "Yeah, yeah, we are indeed a little partial." Pause. "Look mom, I'm going to wake Henley from her nap so I can take her to dinner. Can I call you in a few days?" Pause. "I love you too."

I pretend to be asleep since the conversation was not meant for me to hear. I'm still stuck on 'He loves me?' I can't hear his footsteps on the carpet, but I feel the bed dip when he sits on the edge. He tucks my hair behind my ear like he always does, and then he softly speaks my name. I let him speak it a few more times before I slowly open my eyes. He smiles when I do.

"There you are, sleepy head. You want to grab a bite to eat?" he asks.

I smile back at him. "How long have I been asleep?"

"A couple of hours. You looked tired most of the afternoon. Touring wears a body out quick."

"Let me throw some jeans on and we will go."

He takes me to The House of Blues for dinner. We walk the entire way hand in hand, and to onlookers, we surely look like a seasoned couple. The comfort that surrounds us would give almost anyone that impression. A few people notice us, but no one bothers our date. Dinner is great, and we actually have dessert this time. He insists on taking a carriage ride after dinner where we snuggle into each other. The ride is peaceful, and very little conversation passes between us. We just enjoy being in each other's company. We steal several kisses, and every time that man sticks his tongue in my mouth, I think of many creative ways to bend his will power.

We ride around the entire French Quarter in the carriage. It takes us close to an hour and half to see all of it. We avoid the less romantic places like Bourbon St., and when the driver is close to our hotel, Jag asks him to drop us there. As the carriage pulls up to the curb, Kip is standing outside and catches sight of us.

"Thanks for bringing pumpkin back, jackleg."

He jumps into the carriage and scares the shit out of the old man driving it. He pushes himself between Jagger and me and hugs me tight.

"Kip, I can't breathe," I squeak.

He loosens his grip on me and runs the palm of his hand down the side of my face in a really awkward fashion. He smoothes my hair. "Shh. It's ok, daddy has you now."

"Jesus Christ," Jagger mutters.

"Get off me, and out of the carriage, Kip," I order.

He smiles, but lets me go. "I love it when you are bossy. It makes me want to be your submissive. It can be like *Fifty Shades*, except I'm the bitch."

Koi and Cam join us in front of the hotel.

"What's up?" Jag asks.

"Strip club," Koi says. "You love birds down?"

"Fuck yeah!" I say excited.

"I'm not going to survive this," Jag growls.

We visit several strip clubs before we find a decent Sunday night lineup. I'm more entertained by Kip's interaction with the dancers than I am with the naked women. The funny thing about strippers is that they can smell cash a mile away. They know who they are dealing with when these rock stars walk through the door, and they are extra attentive to them. Each time a dancer attempts to dance on Jagger, he politely pushes her away. He doesn't seem to be having fun.

I ask him to walk outside with me for a smoke. He leads us out of the club, and we lean against the sidewalk to smoke for a beat.

"You can enjoy the women Jagger. I went to a strip club with you. I expect you to behave like a man."

"Say again?" he asks with his eyebrows raised.

"You look miserable in there. At least try to enjoy yourself. I'm not saying I want you fucking or really even touching any of them, but you can watch and allow the girls to dance for you. Somebody has to put them through college," I say.

He turns from my right side to face me. He cradles my face in his hands and tilts my head up to him.

"You are the most amazing woman I know. I didn't know how you felt about the girls. If you want them to dance on me, you will have to buy the lap dances baby. I have no desire to touch or fuck anyone else, Hen. I have already told you that I have compared every woman I've ever laid eyes on to you my entire life. They don't even come close." He kisses me.

I pull his hand and tow him towards the door.

"Come on. I have lap dances to buy."

I walk Jagger over to the VIP section, and I find a girl sitting on a couch. She is a beautiful brunette. She has long brown hair, tan skin, and a curvy body. I'm almost jealous. I have curves, but I'm such a petite woman. I leave Jagger at the VIP bar and approach the girl. When she sees me, she spits her drink out.

"You are gorgeous!" She says.

"Thank you. You are also very beautiful. My boyfriend and I are wondering if you would join us in a VIP room." She tells me how much she charges, and I assure her it won't be a problem. I retrieve Jagger from the bar, and we follow the girl into the room. She begins dancing for us as soon as we are seated. It is really erotic to have a naked woman dance for you when you are with your man. Jagger doesn't seem the least bit interested, so I ask her to dance on me. Now *that* catches his attention. I watch her dance and appreciate her body. I don't know that I could ever do it. She has a beautiful body, and I'm comfortable enough with my sexuality to watch a naked woman dance. If Jag's hold on my waist is any indication, he enjoys me watching.

When our three songs are over, we exit the room and find the guys in the main room. We stay another hour, and I'm ready to go. The boys aren't ready to call it a night yet, so I decide to walk back to the hotel. I try to get Jag to stay and hang out with the guys, but he isn't letting me walk through New Orleans by myself, and he swears he doesn't want to stay.

We walk back hand in hand and talk, the conversation moving freely. We decide to lie down and watch a movie in my room, but he wants to grab some shorts and his cell charger from his room. I walk with him, and he goes directly into the bedroom and takes his shirt off. Oh, Dear Lord Baby Jesus! Don't look Henley. Look away and back out of his room quickly.

"You see something you like?" he asks.

Self-control, do not fail me now. "Put your clothes on Jag."

"What's wrong baby? Will power giving way?" he asks.

"Jagger Nicholas Carlyle, if you do not put your clothes back on my head is going to spin around like the fucking exorcist, and I assure you it won't be pretty. They always projectile vomit bugs, just to ensure it's not pretty," I warn.

He grabs a shirt and throws it on. He takes my warning seriously. Good boy. He approaches me, and as he gets closer, I step back. He looks like a fucking predator on the hunt, and it did things to my girly bits. They are on fucking fire! I finally run out of room in my retreat when my back hits the wall. He reaches to my right and closes the bedroom door and quickly looks back down at me. He tenderly touches his lips to mine and kisses me so sweetly. My heart skips a fucking beat. I have fallen so hard for him.

He picks up the pace of the kiss, and his hands run down my body. I run my hands under his shirt across his abs and chest and feel all that delicious tight muscle. He growls in my mouth, then picks me up by my ass and jacks me up against the wall. He begins kissing my neck and leads a trail down to my chest. Jagger grabs the left side of my bra and pulls my breast out. He slowly licks and sucks on my nipple. Where is baby Jesus when I need him? His dick is pulsing through his jeans, and he begins to grind it into me. He finds my mouth again, and between kisses, he begs me.

"Tell me to stop. Tell me to wait." He kisses me again.

I ain't telling you shit, sparky. You can continue doing exactly what you are doing.

He begs again. "Henley, you have to tell me to stop if you don't want this. If we go any further, I won't be able to stop."

"Shut up, Jagger." I kiss him with everything I have.

He carries me to his bed and gently lays me down. He slows down the pace for whatever reason, so I go with it. There isn't an inch of my body he doesn't touch or kiss. I think we are both overdressed for the occasion, so I pull his shirt off. I push him on his back and begin licking, kissing, and sucking on his chest and abs. I get all the way to his belly button and follow his happy trail down. While I kiss, I unbutton his jeans, and unzip his fly. I can feel him bulging through his jeans. I yank at his pants and boxers, and he lifts his ass so I can pull them down. I put him in my mouth and suck slowly. I don't want him to come yet. He watches me. I must say… hot!

He pulls me back up to him and rolls me on my back. He takes my shirt and pants off. He slowly unhooks my bra and removes it. He shows my girls some slow, naughty attention. I never knew my nipples could feel so damn good. As he licks his way down my stomach, he reaches down and rips my panties off. Seriously, I read that men do that shit all the time in books, but he really did it. It is *way* fucking hotter in person. Before he gets to the bottom of my abs, he begins pushing on my inner thighs so they fall open for him and boy, do they. I swear they have a mind of their own. He begins on the inside of my right knee and slowly kisses all the way down until he hit my… oh God, his tongue is the most amazing thing I have ever felt. He licks and teases and even grazes his teeth on my lips. Moans escape me and my back arches in response, which only makes him even more anxious. He pulls his face out of my apex and reaches for his jeans. He pulls out a foil wrapper and rolls it on his length.

He lays down on top of me, touching his hand to my cheek. He looks into my eyes, and I know right then I'm the only thing in his world.

"Hen," he says, struggling to find his words. "Hen, I can't do this without telling you what it means. I can't do this…"

I cut him off. "Jagger, just say whatever it is, baby."

He sighs. "I love you Henley. I'm in love with you."

My heart literally stops. He said it. He feels it too.

I say the only thing I can. "I love you too."

He smiles, a little shocked. "Yeah?"

"Yeah."

He leans down and begins a slow assault of kisses. He takes his sweet time, and then finally, I feel him reach down and guide himself into me. He takes his time here too. He feels so good inside me. He reaches up and pushes my hands above my head and holds each one with his own hands. Our breathing becomes ragged, but he never speeds up. He keeps the same gentle pace the entire time. I get so close and so frustrated. I fear I won't be able to make it over the edge. I push against our hands that are still interlocked, and I roll him over on the bed. I mount him and began a slow grind. I miss kissing him, so I pull him up to me. While he sits up in the bed, I continue grinding on him. We rarely break the kiss. I lean back to get more traction, and he kisses my chest and sucks on my nipples. It gets me even closer. I pull my body back up to his and kiss him.

I whisper in his mouth. "Please come inside of me."

He growls again, and the pace is picked up just enough to give me the friction I need. With his hands guiding my hips, it only takes a few minutes before I find an earth shattering orgasm. I call out his name and moan through the oblivion that finds me. He comes right after I do, and he whispers my name through his growls. He jerks a few times as ecstasy tears through him, and it extends my own release.

I collapse on his shoulder, and together, we fall back on the bed. A combination of touring, my raw emotion for Jagger, and my slow journey back to music leaves me in an exhausted heap. I fall asleep on top of him.

Chapter 14

My mornings are always a comedy show. I wake to hot, tan, god-like muscle draped over me. I'm cocooned in Jagger. The night's events hit me like a bitch slap in the face. I panic for a minute, and then I remember he told me he loves me. I returned the endearment. That calms me down. Jagger loves me, and I love him right back. The sex was amazing, and it is hands down the best I have ever experienced. Don't get me wrong, I've had plenty of amazing lovers. But Jag quickly took the number one position last night.

There is banging on the bedroom door. Randy has his own room this go round, so who the hell can it be? I will give you three guesses, and the first two don't count. The banging continues. Go away! Then the hotel phone rang. Jagger grunts and turns over to his side of the bed to answer the phone.

"Yeah?" he says, his voice all sexy and raspy.

I can hear Koi through the receiver. "Hen with you?"

"Yeah. She stayed with me last night," Jag answers. Uh oh.

"Fuck. Well, alright. She okay?" He is clearly struggling with this.

"Yeah man. She's good," Jag says.

"You might want to deal with our maniac drummer. He came back looking for her last night. He wanted guitar lessons after he had enough alcohol to kill three large men. You know how he is when he gets something in his head. He slept on the couch in my suite last night, but he's gone now." Koi's voice is interrupted by the incessant knocking at the door.

"I think he is at the door," Jag says and laughs.

"I will leave you to it," Koi says with a chuckle.

"My sweet precious cinnamon roll, it is time for our guitar lessons. I need you! I should write a song about that," Kip says.

"Fuck off, Kip!" Jag yells.

"Is she naked?" Kip asks.

Jagger smiles at me. "Yup."

"Can I see a boob? Just one? Just a little nip?" Kip begs.

"Fuck off, Kip!" I yell.

"I like it when the sailor comes out in you. It gives me wood," Kip says.

"We better get dressed babe. He won't stop until we open that door."

"Fuck that. If there isn't coffee on the other side of the door, he can wait," I reply

"Did you bring her coffee jackleg?" Jagger asks.

There is a pause. "Shit. No. I will be back." I hear the suite door open and close and Kip is gone.

"How did he get in your suite?" I ask.

"He probably flashed those dimples at housekeeping and gave them some ridiculous story that only Kip can make up, and boom he has access," Jag answers.

"That's scary."

"Indeed."

Jagger and I jump in the shower, and soap each other up, to clean all the dirty off from last night…..and the subsequent shower fuck session this morning. He is such an amazing lay. I'm washing the conditioner out of my hair when the bathroom door opens.

"I brought you a coffee pumpkin," Kip says.

Through the frosted glass, I can see Kip sit down on the toilet seat. You have to be fucking kidding me. He has no boundaries.

"What are you doing Kip?"

"Well, my blueberry muffin, I got you a coffee. When I returned, you didn't answer the bedroom door, so I opened it, and heard the shower. I knew it would make you happy if I handed you the cup as soon as you exited the shower. I even have you a cigarette, lighter, and ashtray," Kip says.

"That's my thing," Jag says defensively.

"Don't start getting all jealous on us now," Kip says.

Jag exits the shower and grabs a towel from the rack.

"Jesus Christ! Your dick should have its own zip code," Kip exclaims.

"Turn around, freak," Jagger says. Kip must've hesitated. "Henley is getting out in a sec, and you are not going to eye fuck her. You *will* turn around and face the door, so you can't see her in the mirror either. Understand?"

"Geez. You are so serious in the morning. I will just wait on the bed for her. She will know where to find me," he says.

I hear the bathroom door open and close, so I turn the shower off. Jagger hands me a towel. I dry my hair with the crappy hotel blow dryer while he retrieves my luggage from Koi's suite. When he returns, I dress in shorts and a tube top. I twist my hair up and emerge for my morning coffee.

Kip is waiting impatiently on the other side of the door when I open it. "I had to microwave it so it is still hot. Who's the man?" he asks.

I kiss him on the cheek and go to the balcony for my morning cigarette where Jagger is waiting for me. Kip follows, and we all light up and enjoy the morning sun. New Orleans is blistering hot and humid in the summer, but I love it. I've lived in the Deep South my entire life, and I prefer the hot weather over the cold. I put my cigarette out and find my makeup bag so I can apply my war paint.

I hear a knock on the suite door followed by excited voices. I apply mascara and saunter into the living room suite to check things out. When I enter the living room, Griffin, Rhys, Samantha, Jessica, Stephanie, Meghan, and Kathrine are hugging Kip and Jagger. Holy shit! My people are here! My band mates and my best girlfriends are here! I throw myself into their hugs.

"What the hell?" I ask. No one said a word about coming to New Orleans.

Jagger wraps his arms around me from behind. "It is tradition for us to dress up 1920's style and unleash debauchery onto New Orleans. We can't do it right, if they aren't here love," he says.

I see the looks on my girl's faces. Yup, they are adjusting to seeing us together, and if their faces are any indication, I detect a wee bit of jealousy.

"Me and the fellas are going to find Koi and Cam. It will give you girls a chance to catch up," Jag says.

He kisses me on the lips and leaves.

"I'm not sitting in the middle of a sausage fest. I'm staying here with all the beautiful ladies," Kip winks.

"Get your ass moving," Jagger says.

Once the door closes, the squealing begins.

"How big is it, bitch?" Stephanie asks.

"Jesus! I missed you too." I pause for a bit and look at the impatient faces around me. "Let's just say he is a shower, not a grower," I say, and they squeal again. Apparently, I didn't let them down with that knowledge.

"His ass is so fine. I can't believe you finally fucked Jagger Carlyle. I need details. What does daddy like?" Jessica asks.

"I don't want to hear about straight sex," Samantha says, ever the token lesbian in the room.

I catch up with my girls. The guys are gone for about an hour, and I know Jag is letting me catch up. I appreciate how thoughtful he is. We talk about the tour, the shows, Noah, playing again, and itching to record. I grew up with each of these girls. We are quite the six some. We grew up in a very conservative city where liberalism isn't always the norm. I feel as though my beautiful city is behind in the times. We are all tattooed, strong, independent women who could give a shit what anyone else thinks.

Jessica is my personal assistant. She never gave up the position after we lost Caleb; she did an amazing job of protecting me from all the media bullshit after he died. She's had more time at home these last four years, but I know she misses traveling the world. Samantha is my publicist. I hired her after she finished college with a public relations degree. I gave her the money to start up her own firm, and she represents Koi and the guys as well. She also represents my grandfather and several other high profile names. She has offices in Atlanta and Los Angeles, mainly dealing with the rich and famous. Stephanie is a tattoo artist in Macon at Redemption Ink, and she and her partner Chris do all of my work. Their work is phenomenal! Kathrine runs my grandfather's foundation. She is always planning charity events to raise money for music in our city and surrounding counties. She raises the money and then liaisons with school districts to implement music programs for the students. The foundation provides instruments, accessories, and sheet music. She has recently implemented a free after school program for students to receive music lessons from local musicians. It is highly successful. Meghan is an attorney. Her work is also based in both Atlanta and Los Angeles. Her parents are best friends with my parents, and we grew up together since we are so close in age. She is the one who suggested I backpack through Europe as therapy. She knew what I needed better than I did.

When the suite door opens, Koi walks through pushing a cart full of food. Jag, Kip, Cam, Griffin, and Rhys follow behind, each with a cart of food. Hotel staff follows with folding chairs. I'm pretty sure it was Jagger and Koi's idea to bring us breakfast. They always spoil us girls. Each one lights a candle in the middle of the cart, pours us a mimosa and asks us to sit. I sit with Jag, Jessica with Koi, Stephanie with Rhys, Kathrine with Cam, Meghan with Griffin, and Samantha with Kip.

We sit in the small space and enjoy our friends. Rhys gives Kip a run for his money in the funny man department. The comic relief with this group is almost more than a person can bear. After breakfast, our large group spends the day in the French Quarter. We shop, eat, and drink. At six, Koi suggests we head back to the hotel and get ready for the night. The girls take over Jag's suite while the guys dress in Koi's.

This particular group of rock stars always looks hot when it dresses up. The 1920's tradition began in our late teen years, and these guys go all out. Their suits are complimented with a vest, white button up shirt, a tie, and either a derby hat or a fedora.

Girls have so many options for the flapper look. Stephanie and Samantha do our makeup. I opt for finger waves and a cloche hat. My dress has a black rushing over a grey solid slip, and black sequins are sown into designs on the sleeveless number. It has a scoop neckline, a drop waistline, and a deep V cut in the back. My girls look amazing! We all found dresses during today's shopping expedition. Once the women are all dolled up, a knock comes at the door. I open it to see six men who look as though they walked straight out of the Great Gatsby. Sexy men!

Jagger leans into the door frame and smiles that big smile that drips with sex. Let me lick that up for you, sir. I look down to my ankles to make sure my panties aren't on the floor. He grabs my hand as he walks through the door, and I follow him to the extra bedroom, where he closes the door behind us.

"I thought this would be perfect with your dress," he says, and pulls several jewelry boxes from his pockets. He opens the boxes to reveal the sapphire and silver pieces I looked at the day before. He even bought the hair pins.

"Oh my God," I say and cover my mouth in typical shock fashion.

I know what the merchant wanted for the jewelry, and while I may be rich, I was not willing to spend that much on these pieces. I hope Jagger didn't either. I don't mention it though. The smile on his face tells me how much thought he put into this gift and bringing my favorite people to New Orleans. He really does listen to everything I say.

"They are gorgeous Jagger."

"May I?" he asks, and I nodded permission.

He places the bracelet on my arm and the necklace around me. He removes my earrings and places the antique pair in.

"I would put these in, but I would mess your hair up," he says holding the hair pins out to me.

I face the mirror to put the pins in and take a long look in the mirror and appreciate the true beauty of the jewelry and the man standing behind me. I turn to him and lean into a thank you kiss. He kisses me back roughly and picks me up by my ass to place me on the dresser behind us. He deepens the kiss, and I begin to think our friends will be going out without us. I place my hand on his abs and run them up and down, taking in every inch of spectacular muscle.

The door opens suddenly, and Jessica and Samantha come through unaware we are occupying it. The chatter stops between them.

"Oh dear God, I want one," Jessica says.

"I'm gay, and I even have to admit that is pretty fucking hot," Samantha adds.

"Sorry, girls. I'm taken," Jagger says after he breaks our kiss.

"The passion is so thick in here, this entire hotel floor was just turned on," Jessica fans herself.

"I got serious lady wood," Sam says.

"Stop smiling like that Jagger Carlyle, or I will bend you over my knee, and whip you like the bad, bad boy you are," Jessica winks.

Stephanie enters the room. "You wouldn't know where to begin spanking a man like that, girl. Come to mama Jag," she orders.

"It's like having an entire room full of female Kips," Jagger says, and we all burst into fits of laughter.

"You ready to go love?" Jagger says with a look of adoration. The girls and I all exhale in a collective sigh.

"I really do want one," Jessica says.

Chapter 15

We enter the lobby and heads turn as the beautiful people in my group stride through. Samantha asks one of the staff members to take our picture with her camera, and we all gather in front of the 1920's era hotel bar. Some of us sit on the bar, some on bar stools, and the guys either stand or kneel. The pose turns out amazing. I can't wait to convert it to black and white to give it a more 1920's vibe.

Jagger holds my hand as we walk down Bourbon Street, which is enough to make my heart skip a beat. We crowd into Fritzel's and order shots and beer.

Rhys holds his shot glass out for a toast. "Inny Minny Miny Moe. May these shots reveal the ho!"

We all cheer and clink glasses. Didn't I say Rhys would give Kip a run for his money? We drink at Fritzel's for a couple of hours and then walk to Maison Bourbon, which is my second favorite bar in New Orleans.

Jazz is flowing out of the doors when we arrive. The bouncer checks our IDs and gives me and our group a second look.

"THE Henley Hendrix?" he asks. I smile and nod. "I see a great deal of celebrities here - and this will be a first - but can I take a picture with you?"

Stephanie takes the picture on the bouncer's cell. I kiss his cheek, and we enter the bar. I dance the night away with Jagger and my girls. Koi finally asks me to dance, and we spin around the dance area like we did when we were kids. A slower number comes on, and we keep dancing.

"You look so happy, Henley."

"I am Bubba."

"Happy looks good on you. I have a feeling Carlyle has something to do with it."

"He does," I smile.

I kiss Koi on the cheek and head to the back of the bar where an outside area holds a ladies room. When I emerge, a man with tattoos crawling up the side of his neck smiles at me. I smile back, but goose bumps travel up the back of my neck. As I turn towards the bar, he grabs me by my elbow and spins me around, pulling me flush against his body. The man smells like cheap gin and cigarettes. He is a little older than me and would've been attractive if he wasn't being a douche. He looks with his dark brown eyes into mine.

"A girl shouldn't be out alone in this city dressed the way you are," he says.

"I'm not alone. Now, if you will kindly let go of my arm, I will be on my way back to my friends," I say through clenched teeth.

"I think we should take a trip into the bathroom. I'm going to show you what happens to pretty girls who dress like you do," he says as he leans down and kisses my neck.

It takes a lot, but the fuse on my temper is getting pretty fucking short. I hate when men think they can be so incredibly rude, handsy, and degrading to women because they are dressed up. My essential parts are covered, and flappers didn't dress like hookers, so he is completely out of line. Even if my ass *was* hanging out of my dress, he has no right to touch me. He begins to push me towards the restroom. I can't get my arm free, and I'm standing too close to punch him with any force. He has gotten me right inside the restroom door with a push, but I keep digging my heels in. You have to step up into the small room, so he is standing a little further away, and at the perfect level. I swing my foot up and connect with his balls. He instantly leans over and shouts at me.

"You fucking whore!"

Someone picks him up by his hair, and drags him out of my view, and the sounds of a man getting his ass kicked quickly follow. I step out of the restroom and close the door. Koi, Rhys, and Jagger are beating the shit out of him.

Kip runs to me. "You okay?"

I nod my head. He has his serious face on, which is a rarity. A few guys step into the courtyard with us and start arguing with Griffin and Cam. All of my girlfriends follow behind the two newcomers, and I realize this douche bag is their friend. Great! One of them is really large and before I know it, he punches Griffin in the face. Griffin stumbles back. Once he regains his senses, he lunges at the guy. He quickly takes him down and beats the shit out of him. The second guy pushes Cam. He's not quite as ballsy as his friend was. Cam utters a warning to him, but before the guy can take a swing, Jessica jumps on his back like a fucking ninja and Stephanie punches him in the throat. The guy Griffin is fighting knocks his feet out from under him and stands over Griffin kicking him. I run across the courtyard, and as Kathrine pushes the guy off of Griffin, I throw a gut punch. Samantha kicks the back of his knees, bringing him to the ground, and Kathrine kicks him in the balls. Griffin lands the last punch that knocks his ass out cold. I turn around to see the guy Stephanie is fighting duck and attempt a punch. She steps out of it, lands the most incredible undercut you've ever seen, and knocks his ass out. She looked really hot doing it too.

I feel a push and almost lose my balance. The smaller man of the three grabs me by the throat, and I lose all sanity. I bring my knee up to his balls, and he releases my throat. I punch him in his own throat and then land the hardest punch I can to the gut. Samantha kicks his knees out from under him, and I kick him backwards where he lands. I jump on top of the little shit and punch him over and over again. His face is covered in blood.

Someone attempts to pull me off him from under my arms, and I pull free and punch the asshole some more. I feel several hands go around me, and I'm subsequently lifted off the bastard. I kick my feet trying to get free, and someone grabs those too.

I'm put down moments later, and Jag wraps his arms around me tightly. "Stop fighting me, Henley."

"Fuck you," I say. Okay, that wasn't nice, and the fight leaves me.

Kip bursts out laughing. "She weighs like a buck fifteen, and it took five of you to pull her off. That is great. Can we do it again?"

Jag loosens his grip, and the scene in the courtyard unfolds in front of me. Several of my guys are bleeding, but the four guys who fought our group are lying on the ground. Two are knocked out cold, and the other two are rolling around groaning in pain. We all burst into laughter. This isn't our first rodeo.

A big burly middle-aged man steps into the courtyard. "All of you out! Now!"

Koi steps in his face. "Fuck you! That motherfucker was pushing my sister into a bathroom trying to rape her. We pulled him off her only after she kicked him in the balls. These other three motherfuckers started with my friends. They threw the first punches. You want us out… fine!"

Koi steps towards the bar when burly man stopped him. "Dude. I didn't know. I will have them thrown out. You're Koi Hendrix, right?"

"Yes, I'm Koi fucking Hendrix, but that doesn't have a goddamn thing to do with this. Did you not hear me? He was pushing her into a bathroom. Why don't you have security back here? This is a breeding ground for motherfuckers like this to hurt women."

"Mr. Hendrix, I apologize for this. I will have security here from now on. Are you injured Ms. Hendrix?" he asks. I give a shake of my head. "I will call the authorities. Please enjoy the rest of your night on the house."

The cops show up, and we all give our statements. The four men are arrested, and I know this will more than likely hit the media. Stephanie cleans up Rhys' cuts while Kathrine cleans up Cam's, and both of the men look like they might be in love, or lust, whichever. Kip is attempting to persuade Jagger to punch him so I will clean up his wounds. When the cops leave, we take the burly man up on his offer. We drink like fish.

Kip takes over the next toast. "May women with stubble, at least have big bubbles!"

We dance the night away without any further harassment. I notice Cam is cozying up to Kathrine, and Rhys is following Stephanie around like a lost puppy dog. It makes me smile. Cam had his heart broken six years ago by his high school sweetheart, and I haven't seen him date anyone since. I don't know why I never thought to put those two together. Cam is perfect for Kathrine. Both are incredibly artistic, quiet, and huge Saints fans. Stephanie is a gorgeous, take no prisoners tattoo artist, and Rhys is covered in more tattoos than anyone I know. Both of them love to draw, and Rhys loves a woman who won't put up with his shit.

"I can see the wheels turning baby. Are you planning their weddings yet?" Jagger asks as we dance.

"Not quite, but I probably should. I can't figure out why I didn't set those couples up sooner. Do you think they would be opposed to a double wedding?" I ask.

"Because you have been really busy being a rock goddess and making the world fall in love with you," he says. "Speaking of, have I told you how beautiful you are tonight, or how much I love you?"

"No. You haven't," I smile.

"You, my love, are the most beautiful woman on earth. You look good enough to eat tonight, and I love you so much."

"I love you too baby. You also look good enough to eat. Have I ever told you what it does to me when you wear a suit?"

"No, but you should."

"Do you remember when Clay and Becca married in February?"

"Yeah, I do. It took me an hour to work up the nerve to ask you to dance at the reception," he confesses.

"You wore a pinstriped suit with a baby blue tie that matched your beautiful eyes. Stephanie and I sat at our table discussing the naughty things we would do to you if ever given the chance. I was so worked up by the time you asked me to dance. I wanted to take every piece of clothing off of you, except for that blue tie," I spill.

"What sort of naughty things? What does the tie have to do with that?"

"Control. I can lead you around by the tie and direct you when needed," I say.

"Continue. I like dominant Henley." He beams down at me with those crystal blue eyes and a panty-dropping smile.

Quick, check to make sure my panties aren't around my feet.

Before I can continue, the bar announces last call. We settle tabs and management apologizes for the earlier events once again. The group takes our loud, drunk, obnoxious selves back to The W. I jump on Jag's back, and he carries me into the lobby.

As we enter the elevator, I whisper in his ear, "Please tell me you don't have whiskey dick."

The car is crowded with our friends, but he barks an order. "Out! Everybody get the fuck out right now!"

They all groan and exit the car. As soon as the door closes, he jacks me against the wall and runs his hands up my dress. He kisses me so hard, my lips hurt. I'm too drunk to care though. He grinds into me, and when the elevator pings to signal we have reached our destination, he grabs me by the hips as I wrap my legs tightly around him. We fumble to his room with his mouth never leaving mine. He somehow manages to pull the key card out and open the door. He shoves it open so forcefully, it loudly hits the wall behind it. He carries me through the threshold and uses his foot to slam the door shut. We go through the living room and into his room. He slams the door closed with his foot again, and my back is against it in a nanosecond. He reaches under my dress, pulls my panties down, and then rips them off, leaving them hanging on one leg by a thread. I hear him dig a foil out of his pants, and then the beautiful sound of his zipper making its way down fills the air. His mouth never leaves mine, and he thrusts into me without notice and proceeds to fuck me hard. I moan into his mouth, and he growls back. Let me note here, Jagger Carlyle definitely does not have whiskey dick.

My arms hold on to his neck, and he pounds into me, the door bouncing against the frame each time he thrusts.

"Henley, you feel so good."

I moan against his whisper. He stops kissing me and looks into my eyes as he continues to fuck me, and I look back into his. He grunts through his pleasure, and I feel like I'm queen of the entire fucking world in this moment. He puts his hands on my back and lifts me from the door. We fall onto the bed, but he pulls out. No, no, no, put it back!

"Over," he demands.

Yes sir! I flip over, he grabs me by the hips, and pulls my ass into the air. He thrusts into me again, and fucks me doggy style. He fucks me like it's his job. He continues to pound into me mercilessly. He can't get enough, and neither can I. I moan his name, and he says some really naughty things in my ear. He says I'm a bad girl. I guess I will have to be bad more often. He reaches down and grabs a hand full of hair, which brings my upper body up just enough for him to hit that spot. Oh, he knows what he is doing.

"I want to feel you come on my cock," he growls.

That did it. I erupt around him, and I'm pretty sure I scream. When I come down from my blissful high, he is still pounding into me. I reach between my legs and cup his balls. It does the trick. His dick jumps, and then he calls out my name. Well, more like screams, but hey who's pointing out the difference?

He pulls out of me, and I collapse facedown into the bed, still fully clothed. Who needs to take their clothes off for sex? We don't have time for that shit.

***

I must have dozed off not long after my face hit the bed. I feel Jagger moving my body.

"Come on baby, we have to get you out of these clothes." I just groan. I'm fine in my clothes. I'm drunk and have just been fucked senseless.

"Come on baby, help me out here."

I open my eyes, and he smiles when I do. "You are kinda grumpy when you're sleepy," he says.

"I've never claimed to be a morning person," I say.

I lift my hands up so he can take my dress off. He removes my shoes, and the torn underwear from my leg, and he dresses me in panties and cute little boxers. He takes my bra off and throws a Broken Access t-shirt over my head.

"You really need to try to eat before you sleep again. We also need to get some water and Advil in you. Come on, I have some food on the balcony."

I follow him to the balcony in a drunken, sleepy daze. He hands me a glass of water when I sit and opens the plate of food for me. Eggs, bacon, waffles, and fruit stare back at me, and I devour them. I try not to sleep on an empty, alcohol-filled belly, and I'm thankful he knows me so well. He hands me Advil and another glass of water when I clean my plate. Jag climbs behind me on the lounger, and I lie back on his chest. We smoke several cigarettes in silence.

"Did I hurt you?" he asks with sadness in his voice.

"No Jagger, you didn't hurt me. I don't break easily."

"You sure?"

"Jagger that is the hottest sex I have ever had in my life, and we were both fully clothed. I'm very sure."

The balcony door opens and Jessica emerges. The woman can smell bacon from a mile away.

"You ate it all?" she asks.

"Yeah, but I will order you more. What else do you want?" Jagger asks.

I love when he takes care of my friends. He always has, even before we dated.

"I want eggs, bacon, waffles, French toast, fruit, mimosa, water, coffee, and ham if they have it," she says wiping her sleepy eyes.

"Jesus Christ, where do you put it all?" Jagger asks.

"I'm a black girl. My gorgeous ass, of course!" she exclaims, and we chuckle.

The room service arrives about twenty minutes after Jagger ordered it. The three of us haven't spoken much. Jag and I smoke and enjoyed the night air. Jagger did say it is five in the morning, so I must've fallen asleep for a couple of hours before he woke me. We arrived at the hotel around two, so we apparently went at it for damn near an hour.

Jessica pushes her food away when she is done, and Samantha joins us on the balcony.

"Food," she grumbles. Jagger picks up the phone and orders more room service.

"Let me explain something to you two. I'm gay, and I do not want to hear hot and steamy heterosexual sounds coming from that room for the remainder of my stay," Samantha says, scrunching her nose in disgust.

"She's just mad because she got all hot and bothered, and I wouldn't have sex with her. I rather enjoyed hearing it. I mean I kept thinking, 'How much longer can he possibly go?' but you just kept fucking and fucking. Then I got jealous. I've never been fucked like that, and it depresses me. Woe is me, and my vagina," Jessica says.

"Thank you, I think," Jag says.

"Oh, it is a compliment buddy. I just want to bottle up some that stamina and pour it down the throats of all the men I knock boots with from here on out," she laughs.

"What is your deal with heterosexual lovin', Sam?" Jagger asks. Uh oh. I know where this conversation is going.

"There are two heterosexuals who once did that nasty deed, and I was the result of the encounter. I'm perfectly okay with that particular instance of straight sex. It produced me. However, there is never any need for it to happen again," Samantha deadpans.

"If straight people quit having sex, there would be no hot women for you," he points out.

"Very valid point. And it is so incredibly insightful, that I have changed the error of my ways. I'm okay with any straight sex that produces hot ass women."

"If all straight sex produces hot women, then there are no boys to make more hot women," Jagger continues.

"Damn you Jagger Carlyle, and your room service, and your reason! I feel like I don't even know who I am anymore," she says. "Will you hold me Jessica?" She feigns a cry.

Jessica holds up her fork. "Bitch, you are a damn fine woman, but you can't do anything for my girly parts. I like to put things in it."

"I have a massive strap on."

Jessica thinks for a beat. "Define massive."

"I'm going to bed. You two enjoy the food," I say.

Chapter 16

The rest of the stay in New Orleans is entertaining and lively. All twelve of us have a spa day the following morning to nurse our hangovers. Jagger and I stay in that evening and watch movies. The rest of the days are filled with shopping and food. Broken Access has several interviews in the city. The fight at the bar is all over the media, so Samantha and Jessica spend some time cleaning that up. The guy who started the altercation is charged with attempted rape, assault and battery, and violation of probation. He has already served jail time for rape in years prior. That piece of knowledge makes me realize how lucky I am. His buddies are charged with accessory in addition to assault and battery.

The manager from Maison Bourbon issued a statement to the public citing the four men began the altercation as a result of the man assaulting me. The media spun all the guys from the two bands as the knights of rock-n-roll who saved a damsel in distress, and it did nothing for Jagger's reputation. Women across the globe shared just how turned on they were by the rockers fighting in a bar. The fact that they came to a damsel in distress's aid only made it worse. Kip and Rhys are thoroughly enjoying the attention.

Cam and Kathrine spend a great deal of time together. He is so attentive to her and treats her well. When the girls say goodbye on Saturday night in New Orleans, they both look equally sad. I catch Koi looking at Jessica several times and find she is oblivious to it, which is unlike her. He continually places himself directly by her every moment he can. Griffin is spending time with Meghan, and I have a feeling those two saw some action. Rhys is still following Stephanie around like a lost puppy dog, and it's really cute. Rhys is the epitome of a rock star. He can have any damn woman he wants, and he exercises that right frequently. It's quite entertaining to see him chasing after Stephanie, and my bitch doesn't pull punches. She gives it to you straight up. Kip attempts to talk Samantha into trying a man for a change. That doesn't end well for him if the permanent marker penis on his face is any indication. Rhys and Griffin are still meeting me in Memphis on the 9th, and it will be here before I know it.

Saturday night after the show, we board the bus and head to Little Rock, Arkansas. Jagger and I eat on the bus and then crash in his bunk. He brings his iPod with us, and we play different songs that remind us of our childhood. I really like that being with him is so easy.

"Will you listen to something for me?"

"Sure. What is it?" I ask.

"It's a song I wrote about you. It's on our last album. I think the guys knew it was about you, but it's never been announced."

I get all teary-eyed, and I wish I could tell him how many of the songs I wrote are about him. I don't want to seem obsessed though, so I don't tell him. How long have I really been in love with this man? Maybe since we were kids?

"Hey, why the crocodile tears?" He wipes one that spills over.

"You are just so perfect. I don't know what I did to deserve you," I say, and he kisses me softly.

"No, you are perfect. I thank my lucky stars every day that you are in my life. You have no idea how good it feels to be able to tell you I love you," he says.

"I'm far from perfect. I was a broken mess for a long time. That is hardly perfect."

"Do you know that I was intimidated by you for so long? I still am sometimes. It takes balls to step away from your grandfather's shadow and break out on your own without his help. I know he respected you for it. Hell, the entire world did. It takes strength to throw yourself out there and make it on your own. Then you had even bigger balls when you named the band Abandoned Shadow. That shit isn't lost on anybody. You abandoned the shadow you and Koi lived under for so long and said 'Fuck it, I'm doing this my way.' When you were criticized for some of your lyrics because some found you too abrasive or unladylike, you found a shorter dress, higher heels, and said 'fuck' as many times as you wanted to. You never apologized for being you, and that is so incredibly sexy. When other musicians find out I grew up with you, they have this idea of you in their head. They ask a million questions about what you're really like. They want to know if you are as amazing as the stories are. Prior to Caleb, I told them how amazing you are. You truly are the most amazing human being I have ever met. After Caleb, I told them the same damn thing, but I added how you are just a human being like the rest of us. You hurt, cry, bleed, laugh, get angry, and most of all you love. You aren't broken baby. You are being human."

I kiss him with everything I have in me. At that moment, I stop looking at myself as broken. I'm strong, and I made it through losing the person who understood me on every level.

"Are you going to let me hear my song?" I ask. He smiles and turns the iPod on.

A piano opens up, and it is a sweet, gentle sound. Then an electric guitar vibrates and adds a sound quite contradicting to the piano. Jagger begins to sing, and the drums pick up pace after the first stanza. When the bass enters, the piano is almost drowned out. It's a ballad with dark undertones, and it conveys a man who struggles with a longing in his heart so deep, it consumes him. It also offers insight into a man's heart, a heart that beats for the chance to love one woman.

You are standing there all alone
And they are screaming your name
But, they don't know the girl from home
They only know the fame.

The first time I saw you, your eyes shined so bright
I never wanted to look away
I watched you grow and rise
Wonder if you know I wait.

I wonder if you know
You own the heart in my chest
I wonder if you know
I was yours from the time we met.
I wonder what you would do
If I kissed your lips.
I wonder what you would do
If you knew I wanted more than this friendship.

They only know the fame,
But I know it's not the same.
Your heart beats for the song,

I hope it beats for me erelong.

I want to give you the world,
And protect you from it too.
Let me love you for everything I'm worth.
We can live the dream, just us two.

I wonder if you know
You own the heart in my chest
I wonder if you know
I was yours from the time we met.
I wonder what you would do
If I kissed your lips.
I wonder what you would do
If you knew I wanted more than this friendship.

One day I'll tell how I feel
I will lay my heart out for you to see.
You will see my love is real.
I need you to set me free.

Free my heart from this longing.
Kiss my lips, so I can finally breathe.
Let me hold your heart, I will so carefully.
All I need is for you to love me.

I wonder if you know
You own the heart in my chest
I wonder if you know
I was yours from the time we met.
I wonder what you would do

If I kissed your lips.

I wonder what you would do

If you knew I wanted more than this friendship.

Tears run down my face as I listen to him pour his heart out, and Jagger wipes them away.

"I love you. You have my heart, Jagger. You always have." He climbs on top of me and shows me how much he loves me.

***

Broken Access plays Little Rock, and then St. Louis. When we arrive in St. Louis, fans are outside the hotel. Sweet Baby Jesus, there are so many of them. Randy calls security, but there are only so many staff members that can get us in. The bus parks as close to the hotel door as physically possible, and we quickly tear through the crowd. I almost made it to the door when someone grabs me by my hair. The guys don't notice right away since their security is between most of us.

A girl launches into a scream, "He's mine you stupid bitch. You can't have him. Jagger loves me! You wait and see. Once he lays eyes on me, you will be old news."

She tugs and tugs, but I can't turn around to get my hands on her. The guys rush back out of the lobby, and the crowd erupts in screams, pushing and pushing. The girl who has me by the hair must have been pushed because she throws her body into mine, and her weight causes me to fall. She lands on top of me, and when she realizes it is me beneath her, she rears back to throw a punch. Security grabs her fist before she can connect, though, and hauls the crazy bitch off me.

I can hear Koi and Jagger screaming for me, and once security helps me up, they wave the guys over. Jagger rushes to me, scoops me up, and runs into the lobby with me. He places me in a chair and begins to frantically look me over.

"I'm fine. Just tell me she didn't actually pull my hair out because it hurts like a bitch."

Koi checks my hair, "No, baby girl, it's all there. But your scalp is bright red."

"Go get a medic," Kip orders to someone I can't see.

"It's fine," I say. I'm just a little beat up.

"Henley, you aren't fine," Jagger says, and he looks at me as though I've been shot.

The guys are giving each other worried looks. I look back and forth between them and decide to show them how fine I really am. They really are being overdramatic. I stand, but the room spins. I try to sit back down, but everything goes dark.

***

I heard a beeping sound, and the damn thing is screaming. What the hell is that noise, and would somebody shut it the fuck up? I can hear people shouting, and the urgency in their voices is clear. Jagger is shouting my name. I wish he would stop. My head is killing me. Koi is screaming at someone, but I can't make it out. It all goes black again. Along with the black comes quiet.

The next thing I hear is a man yelling. He is asking for someone to pass him something. I open my eyes, but all I can see is a blurry white light. I hear voices that I don't recognize shouting my name. Jagger starts shouting my name, and a woman yells at him to get back. Jagger? Where are you? Blackness comes again.

I can hear people whispering. Thank fuck they stopped shouting. I can't make out who it is or what they are saying. I pry my eyes open and can't register the surrounding things. My vision is blurry.

"Welcome back, Ms. Hendrix. You gave us quite a scare," a chipper female voice says.

"I can't see well."

"That's normal sweetheart. You took a pretty nasty hit to the back of your head, and a small bruise formed on your brain. It's called a cerebral contusion. It's not causing a great deal of swelling, but you will need to be monitored closely until the bruise subsides."

"How long have I been out?" I ask.

"You have been in and out of consciousness for about eight hours," she says.

"Is that bad?" I ask.

"It's pretty normal with the impact you took. I'm Mary, your nurse. I'm going to let the doctor know you are awake. Do you need anything?" she asks.

"Is there a group of men here anywhere? They may have come in with me."

"You mean those tattooed, mouth-watering rock stars who we forced to go find food about twenty minutes ago?" she giggles.

"That would be my boys."

"Henley, they haven't left your side until I set Nurse Sally on them. She is about sixty, and she pulled Kip out by his ear for some inappropriate language. She threatened to take him over her knee."

I laugh the smallest laugh I can muster, "Please tell me someone captured that on video.

Mary leaves me, and a doctor returns with her shortly.

"Ms. Hendrix, I'm Doctor Vaughn. It's good to see your eyes open."

He performs a few tests with lights in my eyes and asks me to push and pull with my limbs.

"You have a small bruise on the back of your brain. We need to watch the swelling on your brain since that can cause all sorts of life-threatening issues. I would like to keep you for at least a couple of days for observation."

"I understand."

"Are you in any pain?"

"My head is pounding," I confess.

"That is pretty par for the course with a head injury. I'm going to write an order for pain meds, and you let the nurse know if they aren't working. I want to keep you as comfortable as possible," he says.

Shortly after the doctor exits, Jagger, Kip, Cam, and Koi enter my room. Their eyes are full of concern.

"I'm all right," I assure them.

They surround my bed, and my assurance did nothing to alleviate the concern in their eyes.

"How are you feeling?" Jagger asks.

"My head hurts, and my vision is blurry, but I don't feel as bad as I thought I would. What I want to know is how is Kip's ear feeling?"

The group chuckles and recounts the entire incident with vivid detail. Mary returns with pain medication and gives me something for my headache. She asks my friends to let me rest, and they all settle in on the couch and chairs in my room. Jagger remains by my side and holds my hand.

It isn't long before Koi and my friends are lightly snoring. Jagger is holding my hand, and I look down at him when he rubs his facial scruff on top of my hand.

"I was so scared, Hen. You were talking and not making any sense. Your eyes were unfocused, and breathing was crazy. When you passed out and didn't wake up for so long, I was terrified. I'm so sorry I let them hurt you baby."

"Jag, it wasn't your fault. I know as well as anyone how crazy fans can get. The security team pushed us apart by accident, and I got lost in the crowd. I'm going to be fine, love."

He lightly brushes his lips against mine, smoothes my hair down, and watches my eyes get a little heavier by the second.

He laughs. "Your eyes are the size of a pinhole right now, and you have this glazy look in your eyes. You must feel pretty damn good."

"Mmm," is all I can muster before I can no longer fight impending sleep.

When I wake several hours later, my head is throbbing, and my boys are all fast asleep sporadically around the room. My vision is a bit better, but I still can't see one hundred percent. I fumble for a button on the rail of my bed, just hoping a call button is somewhere on the damn thing. Jagger shifts beside me and notices I'm awake.

"What do you need baby?"

"My head hurts really bad. I need medicine. Please, find my nurse." I feel the tears in my eyes about to spill over. The pain is dreadful.

Jagger must've found a call button because a voice comes over an intercom, and he informs the voice that I'm awake and in a great deal of pain. After the call, he crawls onto my bed and envelopes me in his arms. He runs his hand through my hair and kisses my forehead. He doesn't know how else to help me so he showers me with affection and love. The nurse looks disapprovingly at Jagger when she enters the room until she sees the tears in my eyes, and she smiles a sympathetic smile. She inserts a syringe into my IV line, and within moments, I feel the numbness wash over me.

When I wake again, my parents are sitting beside my bed, and I see instant relief when my eyes open. I'm told throughout the day that touring is not an option for the next thirty days. I will need to consult with a local Georgia doctor as soon as I arrive home so that he may keep an eye on the bruise and swelling. I'm also ordered to stay with my parents or someone who can observe me for the first week. As long as my brain continues to show no swelling, I will be released tomorrow and board the first flight back to Atlanta.

Broken Access must board the bus tonight in order to reach their next show by tomorrow. Koi and Jagger attempt to cancel a few shows and follow me home, but I won't have it. I'm hugging each of them goodbye, and Jagger pouts as they each exit the room to give us a few moments alone.

"It doesn't feel right to leave you and tour," he says.

"I would feel the same way if it was you, but you would also tell me to go. Cancelled shows mean angry fans, and potential lawsuits from the venues. I will stay home for a month and then meet up with you on the road. We will talk every day. We can text, Facetime, email, and talk on the phone. I will be fine, love."

He crawls into the bed with me, scoops me into his big arms, and holds me tightly.

"I just got you back, baby."

"And you still have me Jagger. The doctor just wants me to be close to a hospital at all times, and I can't do that on tour," I run my fingers through his short hair in an attempt to comfort him.

He pulls back and kisses me softly on my lips, and then on my cheek.

"I love you. Promise me you will get better fast," he says.

"I love you too, and I will heal quickly and be back before you know it."

He kisses me softly again and manages to force himself to exit the room.

I sleep most of the evening and wake to a text at midnight.

Jagger: I miss you already. The bus is boring without you, and the guys are all depressed too. I love you.

Me: I love you too baby. Tell the boys I will be back soon. Enjoy the music, and it will fly by before you know it.

Chapter 17

Rhys is waiting for me at my parent's home when I arrive.

"I'm going to be the hottest nurse you have ever had!" he says.

"You as a nurse, frankly, scares me," I say.

"Fo' sho."

Rhys stays with me almost every day during my recovery. He takes me out to eat several times a week for lunch. We often hit the Rookery in downtown Macon, which is one of our favorite places to eat. Anyone who lives in Macon, Georgia, has a favorite Rookery burger. My personal favorite is the Johnny Jenkins burger. It's smeared with pimento cheese and topped with bread and butter pickles. It's served with battered fries that are to die for. We also often eat at Roasted or Ingleside Village Pizza when we visit Redemption Ink Tattoo Parlour, also in downtown Macon. Chris, Stephanie, and Trey have the most amazing courtyard behind their shop. We often shoot the shit while lounging under the Christmas lights.

After a few weeks home, I decide it is finally time to get another tattoo. This one will be for Caleb. For many years, I have thought about the perfect tattoo to remember him with. I finally decide on a Pikorua. It is a fern found in New Zealand and has a twist that entangles itself so tightly, there is no way to decipher a beginning or an end in the twist. It symbolizes friendship and two interwoven lives, much like mine and Caleb's lives. Chris draws the Pikorua and lays it on my rib cage under my heart. I decide to include the last part of Jagger's *Hands Down* song under the Pikorua so that it runs the length of my right side and stomach.

I will wipe your tears away.

We still keep our hands down.

I wish you could've stayed.

Your music is the only sound.

I miss you every day.

You were so full of life.

I will never forget that day in May.

Friend, I will see you on the other side.

Chris does not hide the fact that he does not care to tattoo all those words on me. "Why don't you just carry a damn book around with you?"

"Because it has to go with the tattoo."

"Why don't we just tattoo the entire fucking Library of Congress down your side?" he asks.

"Aren't you a ray of sunshine on this lovely day?"

"Aren't you an overachiever?" he retorts. "Why don't I write it out really pretty for you on a piece of paper, then you can just tape it to your side when you really want it there?"

I sigh at Chris. Fucking artists. "Because I would like it to permanently be on my body, hence my body sitting in your chair in your tattoo shop."

I catch a slight hint of a smile as he turns his head to dip the needle into ink. He runs the ink through and then presses the needle into my skin. The first few moments of a tattoo are always the worst. After a while, the incessant burn becomes more of an aggravation than pain. As he scripts the words closer to my stomach, and away from my ribs, I regret the long ass verse for a little while. Fuck that really hurts! Stephanie shows up to work and sits to talk with me. It takes my mind off the needle a little, and I watch Rhys watch her. I think my boy has it bad. Stephanie hasn't made much eye contact or engaged in much conversation with him, and I know her all too well to know her end game. She is playing coy because she is normally a social butterfly. I quickly wonder if these two have done the nasty.

After my tattoo is done, Rhys takes a picture and sends it to our friends. I purposely leave my wallet in Stephanie's station out of sight, so Rhys will have to retrieve it for me later. I know, I know, I'm playing matchmaker, but I'm curious how long it will take Rhys to return. I will wait until close to the end of Stephanie's shift to discover I left it.

I have been home a little over three weeks and am seriously itching to go on tour. I want to stop by my Grandfather's foundation to work with some kids before I leave again. Kathrine does amazing things here, and I've made a point to spend more time with the children she supports.

The after school kids greet me as soon as I walk in. Kathrine waves from across the room, and I settle right into playing with the kids. I show them some chords on one of my acoustic guitars, and we practice those for over an hour. Kathrine's phone rings, and her smile drops when she answers the phone, which makes me worry. I hope things are alright with her and Cam. She and my grandfather have recently worked on her schedule. So she works seven days one week and then takes the next seven off. Red knows what the lifestyle is like and is so supportive of their relationship. She pulls so many hours in a week. My grandfather has asked her to take more time for herself for the last two years, and I think he is happy to see her finally doing just that. She flies out to see Cam often, and they are doing so well.

I finish up with the kids a couple of hours later, and as the parents are picking them up, I make my way to Kathrine's office to use her restroom. I take care of business, wash my hands, and when I emerge, I'm hit in the face with the rotating news on her home page. I think have an out-of-body experience because this can't be real. I don't know what to do or say. In big bold print the headline reads: JAGGER CARLYLE CAUGHT RED-HANDED LAST NIGHT WITH STRIPPER IN SEATTLE.

This can't be happening. Jagger wouldn't do that to me. Is the distance too much? It's only been a month, but we talk all day long. We text, Skype, email, and phone. He is constantly letting me know he is thinking of me. I finally got brave enough to click on the headline. The article stated he was at Toy Box, a gentleman's club, after his show last night in Seattle. Patrons of the club state he spent all evening with one girl. She is either at his table, on his lap, or in a VIP booth with him. He showers her with attention, alcohol, and money. The pictures embedded in the article clearly show it is indeed Jagger. The tattoos give him away. She is on his lap or her chest is in his face, and it makes me physically ill. He smiles at her the way he does at me. Or is it "did"? The last two pictures open the dam on my tears, and my heart shatters into a million pieces. The first shows Jag leaving the club, and she is on his arm. The second is taken down at eye level, and Jag is climbing into a black BMW. She is in the passenger seat smiling for the camera.

Kathrine walks into the office as I sit staring at the photographs that just tore my world apart.

"No. It's not what it looks like Hen. Don't you close down on me!" I hear her, but I can't respond.

There is no way it can be anything else. It looks just like what it is. It hurts so badly. Kathrine begs me to talk to her, and honestly, I barely hear a word she says.

Her cell phone rings. "Now is not a good time Jagger."

No, it certainly is not. I wonder if he feels guilty. Has he done this before now? Why? Why does he say the things he does to me when he clearly doesn't really feel that way at all? Am I some kind of prize for him? Did he finally get his hooks in the Guitar Goddess and get bored? I feel like such a damn fool.

"Because she's not fucking talking at all! She is not speaking at all Jagger! She shut down! I don't even know if she can hear half of what I'm saying to her!" she screams at him. "Fine!"

She throws her phone on the table. She looks at me and smiles a sweet smile. She doesn't even try to talk to me. She picks up her phone she just discarded on the desk and speaks to someone.

"Phone isn't going to work. You are going to have to come here." Pause. "No, she is in shock." Pause. "See you then. Hurry." She makes a second call. "Can you get your ass down here? I need help. No it isn't that. Call Samantha on your way over here."

I grab my car keys and slip out the door while Kathrine is in the restroom. I just need some air. I can't breathe in here. Once I turn the ignition over, I realize I don't know where in the hell I'm going, so I drive with no destination in mind. I try to rationalize all the scenarios that can be one thing, but look like another. I can't come up with anything that makes sense. My heart aches in my chest. A broken heart is a bitch. There isn't a damn thing you can do to make it better. There are no medications and no therapies. Only time heals the wounds. Hopefully, with enough time, you don't end up with a bunch of fucked up scars. I don't think I can ever be okay after this. How am I supposed to trust anyone after this? I have known Jagger most of my life and look what he has done to me. I drive around Macon for about an hour before I realize I left my purse in Kathrine's office. I need something strong to drink and a carton of cigarettes.

Kathrine's car is still in the lot when I return, so I let myself in. I immediately see her pacing.

"You are okay," she says with a big sigh.

I simply nod because I don't trust myself to speak. I might start crying, and once that dam opens, all hell might break loose.

"I would've taken you wherever you wanted to go. You didn't have to be alone," she says with genuine concern.

I nod again, and she closes the distance between us and wraps me in her arms. I can't cry though. I won't let the world watch me fall apart. I hug Kathrine back and wonder if Cam would ever do this to her. Cam is such a kind person. I can't imagine him hurting a fly, much less sweet Kathrine.

Kathrine talks me into a cup of coffee, and I sit at her desk and try to take my mind off of my broken heart. I'm still sitting at Kathrine's desk when Stephanie walks through the office door. I look up at her and right back down to the pictures of Jagger on the computer screen. I'm trying to talk myself into believing they had been photo shopped, but I don't have much luck. I gaze out of the office window, my eyes tired of looking at the screen. The images are burned into my brain by now.

Stephanie hands me a bottle of Crown with the cap already screwed off. "Drink, bitch."

I follow her orders and turn the bottle up. "Come on, let's go smoke."

I follow her and Kathrine outside. The back door leads to a concrete stoop in an alleyway.

I sit down on the stoop and light a cigarette. Stephanie and Kathrine follow suit.

"Jagger wouldn't do that to you. That man is infatuated with you. Of course most of the male population on earth is, but that man loves the shit out of you," Stephanie says.

I don't know what to say to her, the pictures are contradictory to what she says.

The back door opens, and Samantha strides through in all her grace. She has these big beautiful eyes that can look straight through you. She wastes no time.

"I crushed that story a year ago, Hen," Samantha says.

"What are you saying?" I ask.

"I'm saying it didn't happen last night. It happened over a year ago when they played Seattle."

"Why is the story coming out now?" I ask.

I'm not entirely sure my brain can stop, turn around, and head in another direction so quickly. I want to believe, and Samantha has never lied to me before, but my heart is still checked in Heartbreak Hotel.

"I don't know. I know those photos aren't easy to see. The article isn't easy to read even if it happened a year ago. I would never lie to you. I do work for the band, but I wouldn't lie to you about this. The next headline you would've seen is: PUBLICIST KILLS JAGGER CARLYLE."

"It... I don't know." Words escape me.

"Look babe, you read the article, you saw the pictures, your heart broke, and you are trying to figure out how to wrap your head around what you thought was the truth. Look at me please." I meet her eyes.

"Jagger did not cheat on you. When the story broke, Kathrine and I attempted to shelter you from it until Jagger could get here. He and I are going to sit down and explain to you what happened a year ago and show you proof that it was indeed over a year ago. We didn't mean for you to find out this way."

"Why didn't you tell me over the phone?" I ask.

"If he told you over the phone, you would've seen them and not known that I buried it last year. You would have doubted him, and anybody would have in your shoes. Look, you need to call your brother. I think that will make you feel better. He's been blowing up your phone for two hours," Samantha says.

"I think I left my phone in the car," I say.

"I will get it," Kathrine says.

I sit in an alley in downtown Macon drinking whiskey and trying to figure out what in the hell is going on. Kathrine returns with my phone, and when I click the home screen, I see that I have 56 missed calls, 33 text messages, and 14 voice mails. Samantha, Koi, Jagger, Kip, and Rhys have all called. I scroll through the messages.

Koi:

Henley, please pick up your phone.

I need you to pick up the phone.

Look, I know this looks bad, but it isn't exactly accurate.

Shit, that sounded bad. I need you to call me so I can tell you it isn't true.

Jagger loves you Hen. He didn't do this to you.

Henley, I'm begging you, please call me back.

At least let me know you are ok.

Jag is coming to MAC. I will be there too if you need me. I love you baby girl.

Samantha:

Please pick up your phone.

This is not what it looks like.

I'm on my way from Atlanta. Everything will be okay.

Kip:

Henley, please call Koi.

If you don't want to talk to anyone, please call me.

Hen, Jagger is flying to Georgia. Please call me.

Jagger has booked a private flight straight into Macon. Please call us and tell us everything is ok.

Rhys:

You ok?

Jagger called hysterical. I need to know you are ok.

Look, Hen, I'm here if you need me. I called Samantha, and she says she is straightening this shit out. She swore to me Jag didn't cheat on you.

Jagger:

Baby, I love you. Please call me back.

I know this looks bad Henley, but I did not cheat on you.

Henley, I'm begging you to call me.

I love you. You have to know that. I would never do this to you.

Henley, I'm flying to Georgia if you don't call me back in the next 15 minutes.

Henley, please.

I'm booking a flight. I will be there as soon as I can. I love you.

If you won't talk to me, please talk to Koi. I need to know you are okay.

Please call Samantha. She knows what's going on.

Henley, I love you so much. I can't bear to live without you. Please don't leave me.

I'm so worried baby. Please let someone know you are okay.

I'm on my way to the airport. My flight leaves in an hour. I love you Henley.

I'm waiting to board. I just wanted you to know I'm really coming. I will be there soon. I love you so much.

I can't imagine what you are going through right now. I imagine the heartache you feel is crushing. I don't know if I could stomach seeing you with another man. It would crush me. I wasn't at a strip club last night. I didn't cheat on you baby. I'm dying here. I need to hear your voice. I need to hear you are okay. I need to hear you believe me.

The plane is taking off in a few. I will see you in Georgia. I hope Sam has time to get this sorted out. I want to spend what little time I have, showing you how much I love you. I love you so much. I always have. It's only ever been you.

I call Koi after I read through the text messages. "You okay?" he asks full of worry.

"I don't know. Samantha just got here and told me this happened over a year ago. She buried the story then."

"It's the truth. Jagger was with me all night. We hit the bus right after the show. We were tired as hell. We didn't even sign autographs last night. The bus pulled out of Seattle at one this morning. That's only an hour after we came off stage. We played Xbox until six this morning. We lost track of time and went to bed exhausted. Jag and I didn't wake until five your time. The story broke as soon as we turned on the TV."

I sigh. My nerves are starting to calm, and my heart is returning to a normal rate.

"Hen, we haven't been out one night since you were hurt in St. Louis. We usually stay on the bus. We don't even stay in hotels much anymore."

"I don't care if you guys go out," I say defensively.

"I know you don't. We just haven't felt like it. All I'm saying is nobody on this bus has been anywhere to meet any women this entire leg of the tour," Koi explains.

"Okay. Thank you for telling me. I'm sorry I didn't answer my phone. I'm at the foundation, and I left the damn thing in my car."

"S'okay. You and Jag will be fine, Hen. He really does love you. He wasted little time booking a flight when you wouldn't answer his texts and calls. He cares. Go pick him up from the airport. If this was me, my girl's face would be the first damn thing I would want to see when I stepped off that plane."

"Yeah. I will go get him. Thank you Bubba. Love you."

Samantha and Kathrine wait. "Koi told me everything."

"Do you want to see the proof?" Samantha asks.

"What proof?"

"I have letters, emails, monetary demands, and the whole attempted black mail thing if you want to see," she says.

"Nah. I'm good." I smile.

I hug them both and thank them for sticking by my side. Kathrine offers to drive my car to the airport on the South side of the county since I've been drinking, and Stephanie will follow to bring her back to her own car. Kathrine and I don't talk much. She turns the music up, and I keep drinking. My heart had a scare, and it's still raw.

Sam says Jag's flight left Portland over three hours ago. I would have to wait an hour or so for him. I hug them, and they left me to my own devices. I decide to listen to the voice mails. Surprisingly, most of them are from Koi and Samantha. They beg me to call them over and over again.

Jagger left one. "I don't even know where to begin. Since you won't answer my texts or calls, I'm assuming you've seen the story. I hoped to get Samantha to you before you found out. It wasn't the way you should've found out. The stripper broke the story fourteen months ago. I was with her that night, but I didn't sleep with her. I told you Hen, I could always find something wrong with them. I wasn't nearly drunk enough to go through with it that night. I had a hotel limo take her home. She was so angry at me because she felt rejected. I told her that my heart belonged to someone else, so she slapped me in the face and took off in the limo. Two days later, Sam calls and says the girl has pictures of us in the club and then of us leaving together. She wanted money. Sam did what only she can do and buried the story. I spoke to Samantha off and on all afternoon today. She still doesn't know why the story was dug up after all this time, but she is trying to get to the bottom of it. Anyhow, my plane is about to take off. I'm coming to you Henley. I'm dying right now, not knowing if you are okay, if we are okay…" He sighs and remains silent for a while, only his breath audible. "I don't know how to live without you. Please don't leave me. I love you," he chokes out and hangs up the phone.

Tears stream down my face. I love Jagger. I hate this happened. There is no one to blame, it just happened. It is a price the rich and famous have to pay for being on top of the world. When you sign up for the R&F club, they take a piece of your soul away. It's almost as if signing on the dotted line makes you a demigod. We are no longer looked at as mortal humans. We are toys, and so people play with our lives.

***

Jagger's jet finally lands, and my heart kicks into high gear again. My car is parked at the hangar on the private runway. I open the passenger door and walk to the hood to sit. Once the small jet comes to a complete stop, the steps are lowered. I see Jagger take the steps with his shoulders slouching as if he carried the entire world on them at this moment. He looks in my direction, but doesn't see me. He looks so defeated. I start walking towards him, but he doesn't see me for a few minutes. I finally call out his name, and he looks up, startled. He has tears in his eyes, so I run to him, jump, and wrap my arms around his neck and legs around his waist. He holds me so tight, and I squeeze back. I begin to cry, and I can hear him sniffle. Today, we both almost lost each other. That isn't taken lightly, and the fear doesn't subside with the truth. Today, we are reminded that we are indeed mortal, but we are also toys and people can fuck with our lives whenever they wish, with no regard for our wellbeing.

"I thought I would never see you again," he says with a raspy voice.

"I thought I would never see you again," I say back.

"Please don't ever leave me Henley," he says.

"Please don't ever hurt me."

"I wouldn't dream of it. You have always been the woman I wanted to fall in love with and marry. I want to live my entire life with you. I would never hurt you," he says.

***

When we arrive at my house, we hold each other tight. We don't speak, we just hold each other. We don't even make love. I'm so afraid to let him go.

When I wake this morning, he is leaning up on one arm, watching me.

"What?" I groan.

"You are not a morning person."

"You just now getting that?" I ask.

"I think it's cute."

"Cute?"

"Yup. I have missed you so much Hen. I miss waking up with you in the mornings. I miss hearing Kip hit on you. I miss your brother rolling his eyes at us. Life on tour has been shit without you there. Please come back with me today," he pleads.

"Okay."

I immediately agree because I miss all of those things too. I miss the smell of Jagger and his morning coffee and cigarette, but I miss our connection. The world seems to be a bit off its axis when I can't breathe the same air as he does.

I pack quickly as Jag makes plans to take a private jet back to Portland. I call my parents and text my friends to let them know where I'm headed. We are at the airport by twelve, and we will land in plenty of time for him to make the gig. We cuddle on the plane and watch a movie. As soon as we land, I turn my phone on, and a text from Jessica waits for me.

"Look at Sam's statement over the stripper scandal," she says. I have to be honest, it still stings a bit.

I show Jagger the text, and he raises his eyebrows. We both know what Samantha is capable of when you piss her off. We are ushered to a waiting limo, and once inside, Jagger opens his iPad. He types in his own name on Google. Yes, it is just as weird for us as it is for you to stalk us. He finds the article in reference to Sam's statement and opens it.

Yesterday, a story was released by TMZ citing bad boy rocker Jagger Carlyle was photographed the night before in a strip club with stripper Heidi Rosenberg. He was then cited to be photographed leaving the club with Rosenberg. Carlyle's publicist, Samantha Davenport, issued a statement this morning:

"It saddens me that my work deals with keeping good people out of harm's way. Fourteen months ago, I was contacted by Heidi Rosenberg regarding the night in question. Mr. Carlyle did indeed visit the Toy Box, and he did leave with Rosenberg. However, this occurred fourteen months ago. Rosenberg was asking for a substantial financial settlement in exchange for the photographs. My client declined to associate any further with Ms. Rosenberg. I advised the dancer that Mr. Carlyle is a public citizen who has every right to visit a gentleman's club, and he would not pay to keep the public from knowing he is a human being. Mr. Carlyle felt as though his rejection of Ms. Rosenberg outside of his hotel on said night led her to harbor ill will towards him. When I brought the accusation to the table, Ms. Rosenberg behaved irrationally and disconnected our call. My firm, nor Mr. Carlyle, has received any further communication from Heidi Rosenberg. My client is involved in a relationship and is asking that his privacy and his right to carry on a relationship be respected. If you have any further questions regarding the allegations against Mr. Carlyle, please forward them to my firm."

The beloved bad boy of rock-n-roll is currently linked to the gorgeous Guitar Goddess, Henley Hendrix. The two have been spotted all over the country as she tours with Broken Access. Four weeks ago, Hendrix was assaulted by a Broken Access fan in St. Louis and sustained a severe head trauma that lead to a brief hospitalization. A friend close to the family stated Jagger never left her side and was beside himself until she gained consciousness again. Other than the statement from the publicist, there is no indication of the effect of the scandal on their relationship.

"Don't you love how they always say 'a friend close to the family,' and people have no idea it is our publicists?" he laughs.

Samantha is really good at what she does.

"So I'm linked to the gorgeous Guitar Goddess, huh?" he teases.

"You haven't been lately, no," I tease.

"Are you saying you miss being linked to me?" he asks.

"Jagger, my vagina hasn't been touched in four weeks, so I'm definitely saying I miss being linked to you. A girl has needs is all I'm saying."

He rolls the privacy window up to block the driver's view and presses the intercom button to tell the driver to take the long way back. Please take the long way down while we are at it.

Jagger kisses me softly. "I didn't want to hurt you. You were so weak. Don't think I didn't want you. Jerking off like a teenager is getting old."

I smile and kiss him back. I climb over the seat and straddle him as we continue to kiss slowly. He takes my top off, and my bra slowly follows. He kisses my chest and then my breasts, sucking and licking my nipples softly. I remove his shirt and unbutton his pants. He pulls out a foil and then unbuttons my pants. He kisses my mouth again, and I moan as his hands play with my breasts.

"Henley, I have been tested, and I'm clean. You were tested in the hospital, so I know you are clean. Can we stop using the condoms? I want to feel you." I trust Jag with everything, so all he really had to do was ask.

I slide down on him as my way of an answer, and he moans loudly. It feels so damn good. I relax my hips and start grinding on him. He places his hands on my hips and digs his fingers in. I love it when he does that. I ride towards my release when his head falls back and his dick jumps.

"Fuck you feel so good. You are so warm and wet."

Then he explodes inside me. I ride until that tingly feeling begins, and I know I'm on the brink of my own release. I close my eyes, and my head falls back. The tingly sensation is accompanied by a light-headed feeling, and my body feels light as a feather as the muscles tighten in preparation for my climax. Then I dive over the edge. My breathing is irregular, and I shake a little. I whisper his name and keep grinding until the tingles go away. Then I collapse on him.

"Jesus Christ, that was beautiful. I love watching you come. I need to record it so next time we have to be apart, I can use it as jerk off material," he says.

I let out a little laugh while trying to catch my breath.

Chapter 18

Jag and the guys are so happy I'm back on tour. After our little scare with the stripper, who is of course named Heidi, I feel a little needy. I just need to be with him. As I watch them play that night, I know I need to get into the studio. I never made it to Memphis, so I never had the "Let's make another album" conversation with Griffin and Rhys, and they didn't press me about my intentions.

I stand on the side of the stage and listen to the song Jagger wrote about giving his heart to me. I wonder if the world knows he is talking about me.

Dale, the bassist from Resin, approaches me as I listen to Broken Access. "Hey, Henley. Glad you are feeling better after St. Louis."

"Thanks, Dale." I give him a little hug.

"Look, I know you get asked all the time for favors, but I figured it is worth a shot." His South African accent is really hot.

"Shoot." I say.

"Shaun's birthday is coming up, and I think he would be really surprised and stoked if you sang with him at one of the gigs," he says.

"I would love to. What song?" I ask.

"*Broken* would be a great song since it's already been sung as a duet."

"Isn't that song a little tainted for him?" I ask.

"Nah. It wasn't written for her."

"Why don't we just surprise him at the next gig? I don't know if I will be on tour for sure on his birthday," I say.

"Yeah, great. Sounds good. Thanks Henley," he says. I really could listen to the guy talk all night. Maybe Jagger would work on a South African accent for me? Dale and I plan out how to best surprise Shaun at the show two Saturdays from now in Los Angeles. I think we work out all the details, and I'm really excited for the chance to play with the band. They are an amazing group of artists.

When Jagger emerges off stage, he is shirtless and sweaty. Did I mention hot as hell? We party with the other bands after the show. I'm so happy to see them and the road crews. I get attached to people. We play Bullshit with Shaun, Dale, John, Koi, and Jagger. These guys are a lot of fun. Their mouths are as dirty as ours, which is pretty common in the music industry.

Jagger and I go out of the game about the same time and find an empty room to be naughty in. We step behind a bookcase that holds sheet music, and I drop to my knees. I unzip his pants and set his manhood free. I'm still impressed at the sight of it. I lick the underside of his shaft all the way down to his balls. Then I place all of him in my mouth and suck slowly.

"Shit, Hen that feels so good." I keep sucking and pick up my pace in increments. Then, I embrace my inner porn star, and I take him all the way to the back of my throat.

"Holy fuck!" he says.

Yeah, so he likes it a little. So I suck from the tip of his dick all the way down. I keep deep throating him and sliding back up the length.

"I'm going to come baby." I keep sucking. He knows I'm going to swallow his load like a good girl.

"Fuck yes!" he yells. Then he blows his load in my mouth, and I swallow every last drop of it. I put him back to right and zip him back up.

He kisses me on the cheek and pulls me to him. "I'm feeling romantic tonight. Has anyone ever told you, you can suck a man dry?" he asks, and I burst into laughter.

"Quite the silver-tongued one."

"Hey, not all guys can pull off romance like I do."

***

The next morning I wake in typical Kip style.

"Oh yeah dad-dy. Put you fist in me. Fist me like whore. Tell you friend to put cock in my mouth," a Russian-accented woman says.

"Oh yeah? You like that fist don't you Nadia?" Kip asks.

"You put cock in my pussy. I like big cock."

"Yeah, daddy's gonna give you big cock. Where do you want it first?" Kip asks Nadia.

Nadia groans and squeals a little. "You stick it in my ass like dog."

"Yeah I'm going to stick it in your ass, you bitch." Kip told Nadia.

"If you don't shut that bitch up, I'm going to stick my foot in *your* ass." Koi says, and we all roar with laughter.

"He hasn't done that shit the entire time you have been gone," Koi announces from his bunk.

"I haven't needed to. You see, when Henley is here, her proximity keeps me in a constant state of hard. I just use the porn as a cover so she doesn't know I'm really jacking off to these lacy boy shorts taped on the top of my bunk. When she isn't here, I don't need cover. I pretend I'm really spraying her in the face with my load when I shoot it on the top of my bunk on her pictures," he says.

"I just vomited in my mouth a little," I say.

I exit the bunk and head for the restroom to get as far away from Nadia as possible. When I emerge, Jagger is holding my cup of coffee and as I slide down, he places the ashtray between us. He hands me a cigarette and lights it for me. I smile the biggest smile I'm capable of in the morning.

"What's that smile for?" he asks, giving me an equally big smile.

"I missed my morning coffee and cigarette."

"Me too."

"Well, I miss you letting me toss your salad. You haven't told me how much you miss it back, buttercup," Kip says.

I hold my hand up at Kip and he ceases talking for the time being. Jagger chuckles.

We are currently on the road headed to Los Angeles. It takes close to 18 hours to travel from Portland to L.A. by bus. We are scheduled to arrive around seven tonight. I cook the guys some breakfast and settle in to finish writing a song.

***

L.A. hasn't changed since the last time I was here. I still have a house in the area, but I only stay when I need to come here for a photo shoot. I own a house in Pacific Palisades. If I was going to live in California for any amount of time, I was buying a house on the beach. My house has a bungalow feel to it. I love the modern setup and my artistic additions to the décor over the years. Jagger has roomed with Koi for the last two years, so he decides to stay at my house since he isn't attached to anything at Koi's.

Jagger and I hang out on the beach for most of the evening and decide at the last minute to go out in search of food. I put on a messenger cap and find him a Yankees cap. Jagger drives my Range Rover towards Santa Monica Boulevard. We blare Red Hot Chili Peppers the entire way to Dan Tana's. This joint has the best Italian food known to man.

"Stay put," Jag orders when we arrive. He crosses in front of the car and opens my door for me. I smile.

He holds my hand as we walk to the front door. This place has been open since 1964 and has red booths you would imagine in a Rat Pack movie. The tables are donned with red checkered table clothes, and it had an old, familiar vibe to it. The best thing about this place is that it's open until 1:30 in the morning. I have even begged the managers to stay open a bit longer after a long stint in the studio. We are instantly recognized and subsequently seated immediately. I order my usual, spaghetti with meatballs. I finally tell Jagger about my plans to speak with Griffin and Rhys about recording another album, and he doesn't look the least bit surprised.

"How will you go about finding another guitar player?" he asks.

"I honestly don't know. It is something we need to do as a band. It won't be easy to choose another guitarist. I know a lot of bands decide to go the probationary route, but I need to feel secure in our choice. I need to be secure enough to bring someone into the fold fully," I answer.

"I get that. It can't be easy to do this. We have always been lucky. None of us have ever done any shit crazy enough to make the rest of the band want him out. I really can't imagine losing one of them. I don't know how you fill shoes like Caleb King's. Those are mighty big shoes to fill," he says with a sad little smile.

"They most definitely are. I don't even have anyone in mind right now. I need to talk to Maria and Donnie first. I don't want it to seem disrespectful. I know that Caleb would have wanted me to record and keep playing a long time ago."

"Can I ask you a question?" he asks.

"You know you can."

"Henley, I don't know how to ask this without coming right out and saying it. Did anything ever happen between you and Caleb?"

The question doesn't shock me. I have been asked this a million times before. I'm not even exaggerating the amount of times.

I sigh. "I never saw Caleb like that. I loved him, sure. I just never saw him as anything but my best friend, a brother even."

"And Caleb?"

"If he felt that way about me, he never shared. He never gave me any indication that he saw me as more than a friend. Why?"

I'm suddenly curious where his train of thought stemmed from.

"When you two played on stage together, there was a cohesiveness that usually only lovers share. When you two got lost in the guitars, it was intimate. There are times it felt like I shouldn't watch, almost like I was watching you two make love. The chemistry you two had musically is rare. I have played music with your brother for almost as long as you played with Caleb, and we know each other. I know by his facial expressions if he is going to deviate. I know by his body language, which way he is going on that guitar. You two closed your eyes, and you just somehow knew what the other was doing. I don't mean practiced songs, recorded songs, or something the two of you played countless times. I'm talking about the unplanned guitar solos. When you decided it was time to step away from the mike, the two of you would go on forever."

"That's why I had no desire to play music again," I confess.

"I think I get that now."

We finish our meal, and I pay the bill since Jagger pays for most things. Paparazzi surround my Range Rover when we emerge. Shit on a stick. Jag grabs my hand, and we keep our heads down as we walk the distance to the car. They know it's us within seconds. The berating began.

Henley, how do you feel about the stripper?

Is it true she is having Jagger's love child?

Will you leave him now?

Jagger, how does she taste?

Jagger stills at this comment, and I know he is ready for a fight. I squeeze his hand, look up briefly, and shake my head. "Please don't," I'm pleading him silently.

We wade through the idiots, and when I say wade, I mean it. They don't move out of your way. They stay in your face every second they can get access to you. All for a fucking shot on TMZ tonight. It is really big news that Jagger, and I went out to eat. By the time the story develops, they will know exactly what we ate and drank.

Jagger, are you still in contact with Heidi Rosenberg?

Henley, since Jagger loves fake breasts so much, are you considering having yours done?

Jagger is it true that you and Koi Hendrix aren't speaking as a result of Heidi?

Jagger finally gets me to the Range Rover and opens the door. I quickly jump in, and he closes the door. It takes him a minute to get around to the driver's door, but he manages. Once inside, he turns the radio all the way up, and we pull our caps down even lower. We pull onto Santa Monica Boulevard, and he cuts the radio when we are paparazzi free. I burst into laughter. Jagger smiles, but looks a bit confused.

"Jagger Carlyle and Henley Hendrix are spotted eating at Dan Tana's tonight. She ate the Spaghetti with meatballs, and he devoured the manicotti. They even had tiramisu for dessert. She is getting close to thirty, she better start watching those hips. Oh look, here they are now. Jagger, can you tell us how you feel about Henley's vagina?" I thrust my imaginary microphone into his face.

"Well, I'm glad you ask. I'm in love with her vagina," he says with a grin.

"Does the carpet match the curtains?" I ask and thrust my imaginary mic back in his face.

"I wouldn't know. She waxes very regularly. It is as smooth as a baby's ass," he winks.

"Is it true you two were married in Vegas last night?"

"No. Her mother would kill me if I eloped and married her daughter in front of Elvis." Isn't that the truth!

"What do you say regarding the allegations that you are expecting a child later next year?" I hammer him with another question.

His smile drops, and he stares ahead for a minute and doesn't say a word. What's up with him?

"Jag?"

"That's enough Henley. It's not funny anymore," he chastises me like a child. What the fuck?

"I'm sorry. I didn't mean to offend you," I apologize. What did I do?

"You don't offend me. You just took it too far," he snaps at me.

"What are you talking about?" I ask.

"You don't think I noticed? The questions about marriage and children. Something you would like to tell me?" He is beyond pissed.

"What in the hell are you accusing me of exactly, Jag?" My voice does nothing to hide my hurt.

"You want to get married and have children? If you want to know if I want the same things, why don't you have the decency to ask me instead of beating around the bush like a fucking idiot?" he speaks through his tense jaw.

I decide it is probably best to just stop speaking to him all together. I take my hurt feelings and shove them down as far as I can. Maybe he's just upset about the paparazzi. I lean into the window and watch the world go by.

"So, now you aren't fucking talking?!! You wouldn't shut up two minutes ago!" He raises his voice, but I keep quiet because talking will only make it worse.

"Do you hear me talking to you?" I can see him look at me out of my peripheral vision.

"Great, now you are just going to shut down. Classic Henley! Any little thing happens in your life and you check out. How long is it going to be this time Henley? How long will you not speak for now? How far away will you run from your problems?" He is screaming at me, and he can scream all he wants, but what he says cut deep… all the way to the fucking bone.

I try to keep the tears at bay, but there are too many to keep from spilling over. I continue to look out the window. I try to sniffle as quietly as possible so he doesn't know I'm crying.

"Jesus fucking Christ. Poor Henley. She has had such a hard life being a guitar prodigy and then making it big before she was even old enough to fucking vote. She is just so damn pretty, and it is hard on a girl to be that damn pretty. It's not easy having EVERY straight man on earth wanting to stick his cock in you. Poor Henley." His voice is so cold, and it makes me feel like I don't know the person in the car next to me.

I know from my surroundings that we still have at least ten minutes before we arrive at my home. He finally quiets down for a few minutes, but the silence doesn't last long enough.

"You don't want to ask me any questions Miss Paparazzi? How many children would you like Henley?" He pauses. I won't answer him, so he begins hitting the steering wheel and screaming. "I asked you how many fucking children you want Henley! Answer me, God dammit!"

I refuse to speak to him. This has to be a bad dream. Five minutes. For some reason he doesn't speak those last five minutes. My face is covered with tears that I'm too afraid to wipe off. I'm afraid that if he sees me crying, he will only berate me more. Is this how women end up in abusive relationships? Do the men treat them like a fucking queen and then flip the script one day and act like a fucking jackass? I won't be a victim, that's for damn sure. I didn't do anything wrong. He pulls into my drive, and as soon as he puts the car in park, I jump out of the car and run for the door. He is out of the vehicle and in front of my face before I know it.

"Aww. Henley is crying. What, you can't handle the truth? You think you can make an album after all these years without Caleb and it be worth a shit? Everyone is already starting to forget who you are! The only reason anybody is talking about you now is because I'm fucking you! Your fame now depends on whether I'm on your arm. Not the other way around. What are you crying for?"

I keep walking towards the door. I have to stop and start another path in an attempt to get away from him. Once I make it to the door, I realize Jag has my keys.

I look up at his beautiful crystal blue eyes so full of rage. "Can I have my keys, please?"

"That's all you have to say to me right now? Keys please? You aren't going to respond to anything else I've said to you? Avoidance is now your thing, yeah? I think that is just as unhealthy as you entering a catatonic stage."

And just like that, I snap. I've had enough of this shit. Poor Henley, my ass. I lean back and swing on him. I throw an uppercut straight to his right eye, and it dazes him. You didn't see that shit coming, did ya' sparky? He drops the keys, and I quickly pick them up. And just for good measure to ensure he won't follow me into the house, I kick him in the knee knocking him off balance. He falls down the four concrete steps that lead to my front door. I take that as my cue to get the fuck out of dodge.

Chapter 19

I lock the door and make sure every window and door in my bungalow is locked. If he gets in here, I'll fucking kill his ass. I go to the pantry and turn on the light, praying to everything holy that something in there is strong enough to take the bite out of his words. They play on a constant repeat in my head. Four bottles of Roscato stare back at me on the wine rack. Thank you, baby Jesus.

I open the first and stuff the other three in the freezer. I hate room temperature wine, especially red wine. I don't give a shit what the rules say either. That's the way I like it. I would have to make do with the first bottle and some ice. I found the biggest wine glass in the house and fill that motherfucker up to the rim.

I hold my glass out to no one. "To proving him wrong."

It takes me an hour to go through all four bottles. I'm as fucked up as a football bat. His words jumble around in my head, but I can't remember how the whole ordeal began anymore. His words still hurt like hell. So, I'm not the life of the party for the first time in my life. I have become the depressed woman who sits at home, drinks wine, and eats chocolate to soothe her broken heart. I don't have any chocolate. I should get some. I need some cats too. Yup, I will go to animal shelter tomorrow and get a bunch of fucking cats. I will just call them all Thing. Thing 1, Thing 2, Thing 3… you get the gist. No. I will not be a cat lady! I'm still young and hot and talented. Fuck Jagger Carlyle. Yeah! Fuck Jagger Carlyle! I scream to no one. I bet he isn't at his house acting all pathetic. I bet he isn't drinking alone. He is probably in a strip club paying some herpes infested whore to blow him. Oh yeah? Well, I can go drink with other people too! Fuck him. I begin to walk to my front door, but I realize I am in no shape to drive. Come to think of it, I'm not really in any type of shape to walk either. Staggering is probably not sexy these days. I should just go to bed.

***

I wake with a heavy heart, and an angry stomach. I jump out of bed and run to the master bathroom in time to heave up four bottles of wine. They were so much tastier going down. I brush my teeth and find a bottle of water. I need to hit the market for food. My cell phone is going crazy on the bed side table. I take a peek at the clock. Shit, it's 5:00 in the afternoon.

I ignore the calls and texts. If it is Jagger, I can't talk to him right now. I click to the home screen and find Jessica's number.

She picks up on the second ring. "Hey, sexy."

"Well hello to you too gorgeous," I say.

"Oh, you sound like shit."

"Yeah, four bottles of wine will do that. I just woke up," I croak.

"Ah, the life of the rich and famous. Hey, I saw you and Jag were in L.A. last night. Well, I saw you on the tele. I really love the hat you were wearing."

When she saw Jag and I on TV, all was right in my little world. I was in love with a kind, beautiful man. Now, I don't know if I ever want to see him again.

"Look, I need you in L.A. You busy?" I ask.

"You pay me not to be busy. I will book a flight now. What's going on, Hen?"

"The Guitar Goddess is back. I will call the guys," I say, and she shrieks with excitement.

She books a flight while we talk. She will be here tomorrow at 6 p.m., L.A. time.

I'm already slowly trying to get back to me again, but Jagger single handedly pushed me over that cliff. I won't ever be "Poor Henley" again. It is time I stop hiding and show the world what I'm made of. His words still eat away at my heart, and he might not like the result. I put in a call to Griffin, and he is booking a flight. He will be here in three days. My next call is to Rhys.

"Yo, gorgeous, talk to daddy," Rhys answers.

"Yo, yourself. You busy?" I ask.

"Not for you. What's the plan my friend?"

"It's time to make music Rhys."

He grew quiet on me for a beat. "You still in L.A.?"

"Yeah, can you get here?"

"Let me look at flights. Hold on sec." I hear him typing. "I can be there in a couple of days. I need to take care of some stuff in Mactown first. This is going to be amazing Henley," he says.

I order some food from a local delivery joint and jump in the shower. As soon as I stand under the steaming hot water, the memories of Jagger and I showering together wash over me. He loves, well, loved to wash my long blonde hair. His fingers always massaged my scalp, and it was surprisingly sensual. We were never able to take a shower without making love. I love seeing his big, tan, muscular body under the water. He is a sight to behold. The tattoo of an abstract guitar begins at his right hip bone and winds its way up his rib. It touches slightly on those rock hard abs. The head of the guitar tucks under his arm on the rib cage, and then it morphs into small black crows that run under the underside of his arm. They morph into music notes that sweep across his arm and then down his forearm. They are beautifully tucked into the mass of other tattoos. I would often kiss the music notes while we laid in bed wrapped in each other. I have often thanked Stephanie for the beautiful tattoo she inked onto his skin.

I shake the happy memories of Jagger and the shower. By the time I finish and dress, the doorbell rings. I creep through the dining room and look through the blinds. A small Asian kid stands impatiently while he rocks his head back and forth to whatever is coming out of the Beats on his neck. I grab some cash and open the door as his mouth falls open.

"Holy shit! It's you," he says.

Then I hear a song off of Abandoned Shadow's second album blaring from his headphones. That makes me smile, and I think, maybe they haven't forgotten me after all. Maybe, just maybe, I don't need to be on Jagger's arm to be somebody. I pay for my meal, and he hands over the goods. Mmmm, it smells like heaven.

"Ms. Hendrix?" he begins.

"Call me Henley. I'm not old enough to be Ms. Hendrix yet."

"Henley, I just want you to know I've waited a long time for you to put out something new. I really love your music. I know you hear this all the time, but I really am your biggest fan."

I step onto my porch and kiss the boy on the cheek. He blushes, and I smile.

"You may not have to wait much longer. Thank you for your kind words." I step inside, close the door, and devour my food.

***

If I'm going to show the world who I really am, I'm going to do it right. The sad thing about being a celebrity is that you have to always look your best. I've had over four years to slum it, and it is time to embrace the inner goddess. Going to the supermarket doesn't give you an excuse to slum it, so I don't. I dress in dark wash skinny jeans, black boots with a ridiculous heel, a sparkly baby blue racer back tank, and a lightweight black leather jacket that only comes to the middle of my ribs. I put on baby blue dangly earrings, a black necklace, and style my hair and makeup to the nines. It is high time to let the paparazzi take pictures of me in my best.

I take my time in the supermarket. I slowly load up my cart. Several of the other shoppers smile, and I know they recognize me. I always smile back. When people stare, I look straight ahead. Then I spot them...the men with the big cameras are outside the market taking pictures through the window. I knew they would show. They are such predictable little creatures. I load up the cart with bottles of my favorite wine and check out at the register. On my way to the car, I see an older lady is having problems getting through the paparazzi. I push my cart to my car and turn back to help her. These assholes are relentless.

I approach her, and she looks upset. The idiots are screaming my name and asking questions I pay no mind to. This poor woman had to be eighty.

"Can I help you ma'am?" I ask.

"They are just making it difficult to get through," she says short of breath.

"Let me help you. Just hang onto the cart, and I will push us through. Where is your car?" I ask.

"I take the bus darling."

Well, that just won't do. I push through the paparazzi as they continue their assault on me. I finally manage to push her cart behind my own cart and the Range Rover.

"May I take you home, ma'am?" I ask.

"Oh no, that is quite alright. I usually just push my cart to the stop, and the driver helps me load them on and off. The young man inside retrieves the cart for me from the bus stop over there." She points to an area about 500 feet away.

"I would really like to take you home so these men don't pester you any further."

"Well, I guess that would be alright. I get quite winded these days anyhow."

I help her into the passenger seat and load our bags into the car. This is all my fault. If I hadn't pranced my ass around the store waiting for the scum of the earth, this woman wouldn't have gotten so upset. I push the carts back to the metal racks that hold them in the lot. The paparazzi follow me the entire time with their cameras shoved in my face.

Henley, where is Jagger?

Do you know what happened to his face? Yeah, I decked his ass.

Did you do that to him? Yup, I did.

Did he cheat on you with another stripper? I continue to look straight ahead, but I don't speak a word.

Where were you last night while he was drinking half the bar at The Airliner surrounded by women? Oh, that hurt. So that's how they saw his face.

He told the bartender he was nursing a broken heart. Did you break his heart?

Is this the end of Henley and Jagger?

I reach my car and quickly jump in. I slowly back up so I don't hit one the fuckers behind me. I'm not going to be their payday because they jump behind my car. As soon as I'm clear of them, I speed up and get the hell out of there. The older woman name is Lilly, such a beautiful name. I take Lilly to her home. She lives in a condo about twenty minutes from my home. I help bring her groceries in and unload her bags. I even help her put them away.

Before I leave, I find an old business card I previously kept handy. It has Jessica's information on it so people won't bother me. I write my name and number on the back of it and ask her to call either one of us if she needs to go to the store, or if she needs anything at all. She thanks me for my kindness, and I go home. Alone. It hurts to know that Jag is so malicious towards me, and yet he is so unaffected by what he did. He spent his evening drinking with beautiful women hanging from his limbs. My tears didn't affect him last night. They only made his behavior escalate. The revelation that I may not really know Jagger at all, after all these years, is crushing.

I unload my grocery bags and put them away. It's getting late, and I'm still hung over. So I lie in my hammock on the deck and listen to the waves of the ocean. It really is beautiful here. The ocean is incredibly peaceful, yet I feel anything but. My heart beats a steady ache, and I can't seem to find a place in my mind where it gives me any reprieve. I decide to take a peek at my missed calls, voice mails, and texts. I might as well see where Jagger's head is after last night. Koi, Kip, and Cam are the only missed calls. There are none from Jagger. That hurts like hell. I have a few voice mails from Kip who claims to serenade me on the guitar. It hurts my ears. He'd need a lifetime worth of lessons. Koi left several messages checking on me. He wants to know if I'm okay. I don't know what he knows, and I'm not going to drive a wedge between him and Jag. Jagger once told me if we ended badly, it ended badly for a lot of people. He was right, and I'm not going to bring others into whatever is going on with us.

I check my text messages.

Kip:

I need lessons woman!

Listen to your voicemail. I'm getting good at this shit. I will be your man before you know it!

Want dinner?

You okay, gorgeous?

Don't know what's going on… call me okay?

Koi:

Did you give him that shiner?

Samantha:

Why is he at a bar drinking all night without you?

I need to issue a statement. Please call me. I don't know what is going on between you two, but I know a swollen eye handed to a man courtesy of you when I see it. I would like to keep in mind your current situation when I issue a statement. Call me. Love you.

Mom:

I love you baby girl. I'm here if you need me.

There are no texts from Jagger. Everything we had is bullshit. It is all a fucking lie. He is living out some teenage dream. How do you say the things he said and not apologize? This hurts so much. I feel the anger rising up. I stand and find my MacBook to Google Jagger's name. Lo and behold, the pictures from last night are staring me in the face. He is surrounded by women, most of them incredibly beautiful. Fuck you, Jagger. He appears to be having the time of his life. He is all smiles in every photograph posted. Broken heart my ass! He is using that line to get laid. I slammed the computer shut and stood to pace the floor. Anger doesn't cover this. Rage is more like it. I swipe the candles, pictures, and figurines off of a nearby hall table. They crash down to the floor, and the glass breaks. It doesn't make me feel any better, so I punch the wall. OW! How do men make that look so fucking easy in the movies? Fuck you, Hollywood! Fuck all of you! I hold my hand. It throbs like a bitch. Shit, I have to play with that hand. I quickly wrap it in a towel and ice.

I make my way to the walk-in pantry and turn the light on with a little more force than is really necessary. There sits a big, beautiful bottle of Crown Royal XR Heritage Blend. I open it and take the biggest gulp I can manage. I wipe my mouth on my sleeve. Lady like, I know. I pick up my phone and reply to Koi.

"Yeah, I hit his ass. Then I kicked him off my fucking porch. And if you tell him to come over, I'll gladly hit him again. I will run circles around his pretty boy ass. Fuck Jagger Carlyle! If you see him, you tell him I said just that." I hit send.

I drink my whiskey straight from the bottle with my left hand and keep my right covered in ice. I need to smoke. I don't normally smoke in my homes, but I find an ashtray in the kitchen, sit in the middle of my living room floor, and light up. I find the remote between swigs of alcohol and turn on a Five Finger Death Punch album. I turn the volume up as loud as it will go. My phone rings, and Koi's face lights up my screen. I send it to voicemail and send him a text.

"I can't talk right now. It's too loud in here," I text. I'm not turning down the radio to have a conversation with my brother about "Poor Henley."

Koi: Where are you?

Me: Leave me alone Koi. I don't want to be bothered.

Koi: I will hunt you down if I have to. You are pissed off which means that motherfucker did something pretty damn bad to get you there. WHERE ARE YOU?!!!

Me: I'm at home. I'm fine. Perfectly fine. Better than fine. Don't come over here Koi!

Koi: That is not an option.

Me: Oh, it is. I won't let you in if you show up. I want to be left alone. Don't bother showing up.

Koi: I will break down the goddamn door!

Me: And I will beat your ass too!

Koi: I will see you in a few minutes.

Me: Don't come over here Koi!!!

He doesn't respond. Fuck. I need to respond to Sam's text.

Me: I couldn't care less what you say in your statement about Jagger's behavior. Please issue a statement telling the world, which cares so fucking much about when I wipe my ass, that Jagger and I are announcing our split. You know, splitting as friends and all those stupid lies publicists tell to paint a pretty picture for our fans.

Samantha: I'm coming to L.A.

Me: Don't bother. I'm perfectly fine with my bottle of whiskey

She doesn't respond anymore either. Great.

Me: Issue the statement before you get on the plane please. I want this over with as soon as possible.

I drink some more and smoke two more cigarettes before Koi starts banging on my door like a lunatic. If he would think for a second, he would remember he has a key. He can't see me from the front door. Then I hear a tap on the deck French doors. Kip stands there with a sad smile on his face. He holds up his key asking for permission, and I nod. At least he is smart enough to remember he has the damn thing. He lets himself in and locks the door behind him. Koi continues to beat on my door. Stupid ass.

Chapter 20

Kip doesn't say a word. I hand him the bottle of whiskey, and he turns it up. He grabs a cigarette tucked behind his ear and lights up. We sit in silence while FFDP screams, and we listen to Koi attempt to beat the door off the hinges. Kip and I pass the bottle back and forth. Koi stops beating on the door, and I hope he will just go home. A few beats later, Koi taps on the French doors. We both look at him, and it is clear he is pissed that Kip is inside. Kip digs his keys out of his pocket and holds them up while smiling at Koi. Realization spreads across his face. He pulls his own keys out and lets himself in.

He doesn't scream and yell at me. He extends his hand in a silent request for the bottle. I hand it to him, and he sits on the ottoman. He lights up his own cigarette. We sit in silence and listen to music, smoke, and drink. My heart isn't numb enough yet. Kip and Koi finally notice the mess from the hall table. Kip nods and smiles with approval. Koi sees the hole in the sheetrock and looks at my hand wrapped in ice. He bends down and takes the towel and ice off. I wish he hadn't. It is a bloody swollen mess. I hope I didn't break it.

Koi steps out onto the deck with his phone in hand. I don't care who he is calling. I turn the TV on E! News, muting the sound. Kip and I drink more whiskey and read the subtitles. FFDP is still screaming. Angry music. I really like it. Koi enters the house again and re-wraps my hand with ice. Then the story breaks

I turn the music off and the TV on.

A statement has been issued by Henley Hendrix's publicist citing the relationship between her and Jagger Carlyle has come to an amicable end. The two remain longtime friends, and will continue to support each other musically and personally. I can't say this split does not disappoint me. Although they were still very early in their relationship, the pictures of the nearly four month courtship shows the two were clearly in love. What happened? Late last night, Jagger was spotted at The Airliner heavily intoxicated. He was all smiles and surrounded by fellow partygoers. He must not be taking this split too badly after all. He was sporting a black eye, but it didn't slow him down. Is the bad boy rocker returning to reclaim his title? Henley was spotted earlier today in Pacific Palisades at a local market. The photographers waited outside and bombarded her with questions regarding Jagger's whereabouts last night. She doesn't offer any commentary. Earlier tonight....

I mute the TV. There it is. It is over. I can finish off this bottle, climb in bed, and wake up a single woman tomorrow. I can begin to reinvent myself. Koi opens my front door, and an older gentleman walks through. He carries a physician's bag, and Koi directs him to me.

He instantly notices the mess all over my floor and the hole in the wall.

"Mr. Hendrix has some concerns about your hand. May I have a look?" he smiles at me.

He must know a broken heart when he sees one. I put my hand in his. He moves it around and asks about my pain level. He asks me to move my fingers in several fashions. He can't be sure it isn't broken without an x-ray, but his exam doesn't lead him to believe it is anything more than bruised and beaten a bit. He advises me to take Advil for the pain and swelling and to call him if my condition worsens. I wonder if he has a miracle shot that can take away the swelling and pain in my heart.

When the doctor leaves, Koi and Kip sat in silence for a beat.

"So it's over?" Koi asks.

"It appears so," I answer.

"What happened?" he asks.

All the words from the night before punch me in the gut. The look on Jagger's face as he berated me, and talked to me like I meant nothing to him, slaps me in the face. I wish I could forget how he looked when he beat his fists on the steering wheel. The tears stream down my face, and Kip moves over to me. I throw my hand up to stop him, and he backs off. I can't tell them what Jagger said to me last night. I won't come in between them.

"I know you guys are worried, but it's over with now. I'm going to wake up tomorrow and live my life without him. I mean, it isn't like we were together for years. It was only four months. I know it is hard to see me upset, but this is between Jagger and me. You cannot let this interfere with the band or the music. This will pass just like each of your breakups has over the years. Just give it some time, yeah?" I hope that is enough to convince them to stay out of it.

"Yeah. I guess I can do that Henley. He may be my best friend and our guitarist, but you are my sister. I'm here. Breakups are rough. Jag being your friend for most of your life doesn't help matters. If you want to talk, or if you need me, I'm here."

I hug Koi and Kip and usher them out the door with promises that I would go straight to bed and meet them for breakfast in the morning. I leave the mess in my living room for the morning and pad down the hall to my room, where I will sleep alone again.

***

Sunlight wakes me. I look out my windows to see a beautiful California day waiting for me. My heart still aches, but I'm bound and determined to get up and live today without Jag. I know better than anyone that time heals a broken heart, and this time will be no different. I sit up on my bed and stretch. Ouch, my hand hurts. It doesn't look as bad I thought it would though. My phone chirps with a text message from Kip.

Kip: You up?

Me: Yeah.

Kip: We still on for breakfast?

Me: Definitely, I'm famished.

Kip: Dogtown Coffee?

Me: Can we take it down to the beach and eat?

Kip: You know it.

Me: Thank you.

Kip: I will pick you up in an hour. Koi had something come up with a guitar he is having custom made. He is running into downtown to follow up. He says he will text you later.

Me: K. No problem. See you soon.

I open my closet, and a dress I bought years ago is begging to be worn. It still had the tags on it. I pull the grey and blue striped Coachella dress from the hanger. The dress is a short halter dress with an open back. It is a short little number and perfect for a warm November California day. I love the year round warm weather here. I find some silver sandals to go with it. I jump in the shower and decide to pull my hair over one shoulder in a loose braid so sand won't wreak havoc on my tresses. I apply some lip gloss and keep my eye shadow a natural color. I also apply some liquid eyeliner. I pull my long eyelashes out with the mascara and throw a little bronzer on my cheeks. Aviators on, I grab my phone and purse, and I send Kip a message advising him I will be on the deck in the back.

I head outside and sit at the patio table. I light up my morning cigarette and lean my head back to bake in the warm sun until Kip arrives. The sound of the waves and seagulls are so relaxing. I might just take a nap in the hammock after breakfast.

"Hen?" I hear him say.

I shoot up from my chair. Jagger stands in front of me with a black eye and scratches on his face and arms. He looks tired and disheveled. I scoff at him and turn on my heel to the French doors. If he thinks he can just show up at my home unannounced, he has another thing coming. I manage to make it a few inches from the door when he grabs me from behind. He pulls my back into his chest. God, I already miss his touch. My body attempts to betray me.

"Let me go!" I scream.

"Henley, just talk to me for a minute," he pleads.

"I don't want to talk to you."

He turns me around and squeezes my body tight against his, places his hand on the back of my head, and the other around my back. "Please. I know I fucked up."

"Let me go Jagger," I demand with venom dripping off each word.

"No. Not until you talk to me."

I push against him as hard as I can, but the solid wall of muscle that is Jagger doesn't budge. "Let me go!" I scream again.

"No," he says softly.

I pick my foot up and slam it down on the top of his foot. He doesn't let me go though.

"You can kick and scream as much as you want to. You can beat my ass for everything I'm worth. I deserve every damn lick, but I'm not leaving here until you talk to me."

"Fine. You want to talk? Let me go so I can see your face when you spew your bullshit at me," I say, and he releases his hold on me, unsure if I would bolt on him.

He finally takes a few steps back and gives me some space. I walk around him and sit back on the seat I vacated at the patio table. I don't say a fucking word. Instead, I cross my arms and refuse to look at him, like a petulant child. He apparently has something to say, but I'm not going to give him the satisfaction of beginning this conversation. He sits in the chair across from me.

"You look so beautiful. I always love your beach look," he says.

"Yeah, well, you didn't come here to reminisce, so start talking Carlyle," I snap at him.

"Why did you issue the statement, baby?"

"I'm not your fucking baby," I growl, and the hurt registers on his face.

"Why?" he asks again.

"I just saved us both a great deal of heartache and time. You think you can speak to me the way you did two nights ago, go on a bender with a smile plastered on your face, and take pictures with every pussy in the place, and not call? You think you get to do all of that and not bring your ass to me to show me the respect of saying you're fucking sorry? You think all of that doesn't end us? What world do you live in?" I ask.

"Bab… I don't know what came over me. I have so much shit going through my head right now. The paparazzi pissed me off with their rude ass questions, and I lost it. I unfortunately lost it on you. I went out on a bender because I needed to get my head straight. I didn't call or text because I didn't think you would talk to me. I was trying to give you time to cool off. I almost called you a million times yesterday. I haven't seen you in over 24 hours, and I miss you."

"But you didn't call. That told me everything I needed to know. You let me think what I wanted about the pictures from The Airliner, and you stayed silent. You let me sit over here to stew in my own misery, and you did nothing to fucking stop it!" I yell.

"You are miserable?" he asks hopeful.

"Yeah, I was. I got it all out of my system though. The shelf life is short. No more 'Poor Henley.' You missed out on your window of opportunity buddy." He flinches at his own words from two nights ago, but those words can't possibly cause the same level of hurt that it caused me.

"What happened to your hand?"

"Now that isn't really any of your business anymore, is it?"

"Yes it is. I don't want anything to happen to you. I want to protect you," he says.

"You did a really fine job of it two nights ago," I say, and his shoulders slump. "I'm over it."

"No. You don't stop loving someone overnight. Tell me you don't love me anymore, and I will walk off your deck. You will never have to see my face again."

The thought of never seeing Jagger hurts like hell. I almost falter, but his words come back to me.

Do you hear me talking to you? Great, now you are just going to shut down. Classic Henley! Any little thing happens in your life and you check out. How long is it going to be this time Henley? How long will you not speak for now? How far away will you run from you problems? Aww. Henley is crying. What, you can't handle the truth? You think you can make an album after all these years without Caleb and it be worth a shit? Everyone is already starting to forget who you are! The only reason anybody is talking about you now is because I'm fucking you! Your fame now depends on whether I'm on your arm. Not the other way around. What are you crying for?

It still hurts like hell, and they make me angry all over again.

"I still love you Jagger, but I don't want to be with you." I don't even know if I believe the words coming out of my mouth. He looks at me with his poker face.

"If you still love me, then this isn't over," he growls.

"Yes it is. Most of what you said the other night has some truth to it, but it doesn't mean I deserved it. Especially not the way you said it. But your words sparked something inside of me I'm so very thankful for. I will never put myself in a position to be recognized because you are fucking me or are on my arm. And, I can handle the truth. I will never be able to replace Caleb, and I won't be able to make the same music with him, but I can make music that someone will love. You want to know how far I'm going to run this time? I'm running away from you and all that filthy shit you hit me with. I may love you, but I will never put myself in a situation where you can hurt me again. So, I'm going to run back to music, my career, and my life. I don't need you to get there. I never did. I'm *the* Guitar Goddess. I earned that fucking title. It wasn't handed to me on a silver fucking platter. I learned every note, chord, and song right on my very own. I will make it back to the top on my own, and I will look down at *you* from my pedestal. Get off my porch," I bite out with rage in my voice.

"Henley, I didn't mean those things. You have to believe me. I love you." Tears run down his cheek.

"She asked you to leave, Jag." Kip says from behind me, and it startles me since I never heard him come through the doors.

"Stay the fuck out of it, Kip. This is between her and me." Jagger says.

"I know it is buddy. She made that very clear to me and Koi last night after she put a hole in the wall and busted up her hand. That is also after she broke half the shit in the house. I promised her I wouldn't get in the middle, and I won't. She is hurting, you are hurting, and it is difficult to watch. I love you both. Let me take her to breakfast, and you go home and get yourself cleaned up. Give it some time, yeah?" Kip pleads.

Jagger stands there for a beat and mulls over what Kip said. He turns to walk away, and as he hits the second step down, he turns back to me.

"I meant every word I ever said to you, except what I said two nights ago. I have loved you since the first time I laid eyes on you in sixth grade. I won't ever stop loving you. I won't ever stop trying to win you back."

Jagger disappears down the steps, Kip wraps his arms around me, and it becomes tempting to break down and cry, but I wouldn't. I won't ever be "Poor Henley" again.

"It's going to all work itself out," Kip assures me.

Kip and I have breakfast on the beach. We people watch and make up stories about each of them. We often did this as teenagers, but our stories got dirtier with age. We stay on the beach for a few hours, and thankfully Kip doesn't bring Jagger up. We decide to hit the market for steaks. I keep a fire pit on the beach, and Kip wants to grill steaks and drink around the fire tonight with Jessica and Samantha. They are arriving on the same flight at six tonight. I sent a limo to retrieve them, and Kip and I work on repairing my sheetrock to kill some time. I never would have thought a drummer would know how to make repairs of any sort around a house. He is so cute covered in sheetrock dust. Koi joins us around four and helps Kip finish the repair. After that, we lounge on the deck and nurse our beers. At around five, the doorbell rings. I hurry from the back of the house to answer it and open the door to a floral delivery.

"Ms. Hendrix?" the man asks.

"Yes, that's me," I answer.

I sign for the arrangement and set them on my hall table. I pull the card from the center and instantly know the handwriting is Jagger's.

Two days ago, I made the biggest mistake of my life. I will spend the rest of my days trying to make up for that mistake.

Love,

Jagger

Tears prick my eyes, but I quickly shake them away. Koi and Kip check on me, but I push all the emotions whirling around inside of me as far down as they will go. I won't let him ruin a great day. Samantha and Jessica arrive around seven, and we get the obvious questions right out of the way. I enjoy the evening. Kip masters the grill. Koi takes care of the salad and potatoes and orders us girls to relax. I'm going to live in L.A. for a while now, and the camaraderie, food, love, and music is what I want to be surrounded by.

Chapter 21

I wake, and when I attempt to turn over, I quickly realize there is an arm draped across my hip and wood in my back. Shit. I went to bed alone, so I panic. I quickly attempt to locate the closest object that can be used as a weapon. My poor heart is about to explode in my chest. I assess the distance from my place in the bed and how long it will take me to grab the gigantic, solid wooden lamp on my bedside table, turn around, and knock the shit out of this asshole.

Do you remember when you were a kid and sounds scared you in the middle of the night? For some reason, those are the nights you have to pee something fierce. You have to hype yourself up enough to throw the covers back and lunge from the bed so the monsters under it can't grab your feet. This all has to be done in one quick sweep, of course. But how long did you lie there gaining the courage to throw the covers off? That is where I am right now.

My game plan is to roll quickly from under the arm, throw my feet to the floor, reach to my right to grab the massive lamp, and chunk that motherfucker at this asshole before he can get his hands on me. I bet this is some crazy ass fan who thinks I love him. I just have to get to know him and all that psychobabble. Here goes nothing. I take a deep breath and count to three, but I haven't gained the courage yet. I start over with the breath and the counting and decide to end at five instead of three. Still nothing.

The first time I ever bungee jumped, I walked hundreds of steps to the top platform. Three men jumped in front of me. When it was my turn, the man ensured my harness was hooked properly, instructed me to turn backwards, grab hold of the bars, count backwards from three, and then let go. I looked back to see the big red air bubble below that would catch me, and I wondered why I ever thought this was a good idea. Oh yeah, Kip teased a sixteen year old girl and said I wouldn't do it. The man counted back from three, and as he said "one," he followed with a "go." I then wondered, am I supposed to let go on "one" or "go." Shit, I'm so confused, and scared to death. When the man said "go", I was still holding on for dear life.

"So do I let go on 'three' or 'go'?"

"Which would you prefer?"

"Um, not sure."

"How about 'go'?"

"Can you just push me? I don't really want to know it is coming. I'm having an issue with committing to letting go and plunging to my death and all."

The man laughed. "I can't push you."

"Please."

He laughs again. "I can't. Let's try it again."

"Three, two, one, go!"

I let go this time. I don't know how I found the courage to do it, but once I did, it was exhilarating. My stomach felt as though it were in my throat, and each time the bungee cord reached its end, it would throw me back in the air. I now lie in my bed attempting to conjure up the same damn courage. I wish this asshole would haphazardly push me out of my bed. I can crawl under it until he leaves. Okay, three, two, one, go! I tell myself.

My plan does not go as planned. Grace is obviously not my middle name. I roll out from under the arm, but as I do, the arm moves and heavily lays weight on my throat and chokes me. The stalker is still sleeping, so I slowly roll back towards Mr. Snuggles and start again. I roll quickly again, and as I try to find the floor with my feet, I realize my roll doesn't have me rolling off the bed on the right side. The next thing I know, my face is flat on the damn floor, and it fucking hurts.

"What the fuck?" Mr. Snuggles says with a sleepy voice.

Now or never princess. I search deep within myself… okay, not that deep, I just woke up, I'm about to piss on myself, and Mr. Snuggles is stalking me. Let me start over. I search as quickly as I can for my inner Bruce Lee. I push up quickly from the floor, grab the wooden lamp, and come down on Mr. Snuggles face like a ninja! I even made the whole "Hey Ya!" sound. Take that, Daniel son! I got this shit covered.

As the lamp comes down on Mr. Snuggles, he lets out a yell. The lamp bounces off him and then off the bed, landing with a thud against the wall. My cat-like reflexes kick in, and I get my little ass the fuck out of there. As I walk through the threshold, I hear Mr. Snuggles.

"Jesus Christ, Hen. You just hit me with a fucking Mac Truck!"

Shit. I know that voice. I stop dead in my tracks, turn around, and see Rhys holding his face and blood pouring from his hands.

"You snuck into my bed! I thought you were an intruder!" I yell back.

"Fuck! You knew I was coming in early this morning!" he yells.

"I didn't know you would be in my bed. I have a lot going on and I temporarily forgot. I'm sorry," I pout. I didn't mean to hurt my friend.

"Why didn't you just turn over and see who the hell it was before you hit me with… what in the hell did you hit me with?"

"That big ass lamp Kip got me for Christmas that one year," I answer with a cringe.

"The one made of solid fucking wood?" he growls. He was starting to look a little angry.

I look up at the ceiling and begin whistling.

"You hit me with a fucking tree!!!" he screams.

"Your dick was in my back!!!" I yell back. It was the only thing I could come up with to be mad about on such short notice.

"What in the hell is going on?" Griffin walks in scratching his balls.

Gross.

He looks back and forth between Rhys and I and seems unable to form words for a few minutes.

"What happened to your forehead, Hen?"

I instantly reach up and touch my forehead, which causes the damn thing to start hurting. I run to the mirror in my bathroom and see a big ass red whelp mark in the middle of my forehead. Damn floor! I walk back in, and Rhys is explaining why his nose is bleeding. Griffin is laughing entirely too hard and is gasping for air.

I shrug my shoulders at him and offer the only excuse I have. "His cock was in my back."

Griffin really loses it. He rolls onto the bed, and tears spill from his eyes. "Oh God, I can't wait to tell this story."

I clean Rhys up and assess the damage. It doesn't appear that his nose is broken, but most of the left side of his face is already bruising. I apologize repeatedly for the violence, and I really try not to laugh or even crack a smile. Griffin doesn't have so much gumption. He breaks into fits of laughter each time he looks at Rhys.

Since I beat Rhys with a tree, I figure the least I could do was make him and Griffin some breakfast. Rhys seems to start towards forgiveness with the coffee. Luckily, I make extra food since Koi and Kip show up unannounced.

"Bruh', what the fuck happened to your face?" Kip asks so eloquently.

"Henley hit me with a fucking tree!"

"In my defense, I went to bed alone, woke up with an arm over me, and a cock in my back. I was scared," I say.

Koi and Kip look between us for several seconds and finally at Griffin who is busting at the seams to laugh. He doesn't hold it in long.

"How did you hit him with a tree?" Koi asks.

"I hit him with the lamp Kip gave me several Christmases ago," I answer.

"The one made out of solid fucking wood? That damn thing weighs a ton," Koi adds.

"Yeah, no shit," Rhys declares.

Kip and Koi howl with laughter for a few minutes, and suddenly a very serious look takes over Kip's face.

"Wait a minute. Why were you in Henley's bed?" Kip asks.

"I landed at two a.m. When I got here, I came in here to let her know Griff and I arrived. She looked so damn comfy, and I wanted to snuggle with my friend. So, I climbed in and snuggled. Then I got my face smashed in by Jackie Chan over here. She even screamed 'hey ya!' at me," Rhys explains.

Griffin, Kip, and Koi let loose with their howls once again. Now it is Koi's turn to get serious.

"Bruh', why the fuck was your dick in my sister's back?"

"Man, I was having this dream about a certain tattoo artist, and she was going at it with this tattoo model, and they were letting me watch. They had just asked me to join when Kung Fu Hen over here smashed my face in."

"I can't wait to tell Stephanie," I shriek.

"Nu uh, you ain't telling her shit! That woman will smash the other side of my face in," Rhys says.

After a late breakfast, Koi and Kip depart and the three of us lounge on the back deck. Rhys turns on Bob Marley, and we chill out while listening to the waves and the seagulls. This is the life. There have been several moments when I wish Jagger was in this hammock with me, and I fight the urge to cry. I miss the way he envelops me in his arms. I miss the way he smells and the sweet kisses he places on the top of my head or cheek throughout the day. When thoughts of Jagger seem to be too much, I decide to take my mind off it by taking care of business.

"So, are we going to record an album or not?" I ask, breaking the relaxation.

"Fuck yeah, we are!" Rhys exclaims.

Quiet settles in around us, and we all have the same thought.

"How do we replace him?" I ask.

"I don't know, Hen," Griffin offers with a sad smile.

"We should talk to Caleb's parents so they don't hear it from someone else first," I say.

We are all in agreement. We begin talking about the sound we would like to go with and the possible ways in which we can begin a search for a guitar player. Part of me is incredibly sad that my music career will go forward without Caleb. I had a connection with him that I could never in a million years find again. I will still enjoy making music, but it will never be the same. I have come to accept it, but it doesn't make it any better.

Tonight, we all agree to party like rock stars. Jessica and Samantha show up in time to doll up. This is the first time in four years that the three surviving members of Abandoned Shadow will be photographed together. The three of us being together will fuel rumors of another album, and I have no idea how or when it is best to broach the subject with Caleb's parents.

I wear a little black dress that barely covers my ass. I throw on some Jimmy Choo black stilettos with skulls on the straps. My makeup is smoky, and my hair cascades down my back in loose waves. I spray a little perfume in the right places, and it is time to meet the limo out front. We drink champagne on the ride over to Cashmere's night club and toast to Caleb who will be missed tonight.

Once the limo pulls up to the front of the club, the attention of the line and the paparazzi turns to us. Rhys and Griffin exit first and then help me and the other two ladies out of the limo. The crowd goes wild, and those flashes from the cameras blind me. We huddle into a group and quickly make our way inside.

Alcohol immediately flows freely in our little group. Some of Hollywood's elite are already going strong in the club. We enter the VIP area and are seated by the hostess at an empty table. The stares from the rich and famous don't go unnoticed. I ignore most of the pompous assholes. I do not consider myself in the same league as most of them since I actually know how to treat other human beings. They aren't all bad, don't get me wrong, but I have no tolerance for the ones who have god complexes. The good ones are usually really eccentric, which most artistic kinds are.

An hour after our arrival, a very attractive man who looks to be my age approaches the table.

"Hi. I want to send over a round of whatever you are having." His smile is concentrated solely on me.

"Oh, thanks man. Who are you by the way?" Rhys asks.

The gorgeous man extends his hand to Rhys. "Kai Scott."

"As in, THE Kai Scott?" Rhys clarifies.

The man lets out a humble chuckle. "I don't know about that, but I'm a producer."

"Then you are THE Kai Scott," Rhys states.

"Then I guess I am," he says genuinely flattered.

Griffin extends his hand in greeting, and Kai then takes Jessica and Samantha's hands and lightly shakes. I think they are both swooning a little, which says a lot since Sam is gay. His eyes land on me, and there were visions of me leaned over a sound board in this little black dress. Hey, I may have a broken heart, but this bitch ain't blind... or dead.

He extends his hand to me, and I accept it. He gently shakes it, never letting his eyes fall from mine.

"Henley Hendrix, it is such a pleasure to meet you," he finally says.

"Likewise."

"I never thought I would see this group out together again. It is really an honor to meet all of you," he says to the entire table.

Rhys and Griffin engage this man, who they obviously know of, in conversation about apparent albums he has produced in the past. If you are wondering why these two have a man crush, it has nothing to do with his looks. Great music producers in our world are famous amongst their peers. This is actually a higher status than being famous to the public. If Rhys and Griff have infatuation in their eyes, then this guy must be one of the best producers in the industry. I will have to ask more later.

Jessica leans over and whispers in my ear, "I would do shit to him you wouldn't do to a farm animal. That motherfucker is so damn fine. Did you look at the bulge in the front of his jeans? I bet he is packing at least ten inches under there."

I laugh at my audacious friend who so refreshingly tells it exactly like it is. Jessica excuses us to the ladies room.

"I do not bat for that team, but damn I can appreciate beauty when I see it. He was all humble and shit. I actually considered asking him to take his clothes off for a moment. Then I realized as soon as I saw his dick, I might vomit." Samantha laughs.

"He is pretty damn hot," I say.

"Oh, honey, what is hot is the look that man was giving you. I think I just saw you engaging in foreplay, and it felt really naughty to watch him undress you with his eyes." Jessica fans herself.

We decide to join the main dance floor once we refresh our drinks at the bar. My heart hurts when I long for Jagger to be here with his arms around me. I try to be strong and shake the yearning. Once a slow song blares out, Samantha and I dance together since a Laker just asked Jessica's gorgeous ass to dance. I went to my first and only prom with Samantha since the conservatives in our school had an issue with her bringing a female to the prom. Being the rebel I am, I begged to be her date. I danced as nasty as I could all night with her, just to prove a point. I'm not gay, but I have no problem with my friend being gay. And subsequently, you shouldn't either.

After a few more songs, we return to our table, and whiskey shots flow freely. We are approached by several actors and fellow musicians, and I enjoy the short conversations with them. I hear repeatedly how each of them hopes we plan to put out another album, and I just smile, keeping it secretive for now.

Towards the end of the evening, Rhys leans over. "Kai Scott said he wasn't getting in our business, but if we are ever recording another album, he would be honored to produce it. Hen, this guy is like the Rick Rubin of modern rock. He is the shit, and he wants to work with us. Our first album back couldn't be produced by a better man."

"Rhys, do you have a man crush?"

"I certainly do, ma'am," he plainly answers.

"We have to find a guitarist first, Rhys."

"I brought up to Kai a hypothetical situation of us recording another album, and his recommendation was to record when you are ready and not delay. You can record all the guitar parts, and hopefully we can find someone who is the right fit while we are still in the studio. I know you want the newest member involved in the creative process, but I agree with Kai. We shouldn't postpone recording based on that."

"I think it sounds like a good idea, but I don't want the search for a guitarist postponed by recording either."

"I agree, Hen."

A man interrupts our conversation and introduces himself as Jeff Davis, the new Vice President of our record label. Here we go. He looks to be mid to late forties, attractive, but in that stuffy, arrogant way. I'm immediately put off by him.

"Ms. Hendrix, how lovely to see you out and about."

I simply stare at him and offer no pleasantries. Bitch, I know.

"I just want to remind you, Ramses Records is owed another album by Abandoned Shadow per your contract. The record label felt it only right to provide you with enough time to grieve over the death of Caleb King, and I think four and half years is quite enough time. I will have my secretary call and schedule an appointment with you since you are in town."

He extends his hand once again, and Rhys and I look at one another and begin another conversation like the douche bag isn't standing there.

"Hey, Hen did you hear about that dick Jeff Davis over at Ramses Records? Apparently he has a little dick, so he dresses in $20,000 suits, and talks down to people to make himself feel more like a man. Apparently penile implants aren't even an option. Sad really."

"No Rhys, I haven't heard about him yet. I wonder if he has been advised not to fuck with me because my grandfather owns a controlling share in the company. It would be nice if someone would tell him so I don't have to deal with little man syndrome."

"Ms. Hendrix, Mr. Donovan, I by no means meant any harm here, I simply…"

"Jeff, you were probably about to say something like, it is only business, nothing personal, and all that jive. When you bring up Caleb King, you better fucking have known the man, or someone at this table will beat the shit out of you. It's personal to us. I'm sure you saw the videos of his death at some point. Hell, most of the globe has seen them. And if from that video you could not deduce how personal of a loss we felt, then you might want to consider some serious classes in interpersonal skills. You don't get to tell us how long we can grieve. Hence, the record company has not pushed for another record just yet. For your information, we have discussed very recently recording another album. We will record when we are ready, we will use whatever producer we want, and we will release when we are ready. So, if you don't mind, have a nice night and go fuck yourself," Rhys said in a very businesslike manner. The smile on his face almost had me rolling in laughter.

Jeff Davis turned on his heels and left. It is clear the man is not accustomed to being spoken to so frankly.

Chapter 22

"What do you mean you are replacing me?"

"Caleb, I thought you would want us to move on. I never thought I would, but this little boy Noah made me realize that life is short, and I have to live it to the fullest. Music is all I know."

"Henley, I'm right here. I'm still the guitar player."

"What are you talking about?'

"Hen, what's wrong with you?"

"Caleb, you are... you're gone. You can't play anymore."

"I most certainly can. Watch this."

Caleb picks up a strat and plays Jimi Hendrix's Red House. I close my eyes as the bluesy notes wash over my soul, and the warmth from the music takes over. I feel every last riff and am afraid to open my eyes. He might be gone if I open them. I haven't heard him play in four years. I miss the sound of him playing. When the song is over, I still haven't opened my eyes.

"Henley, open your eyes."

"I can't. You will leave me again."

"What are you talking about?"

"You always leave me."

"I'm right here, baby girl."

I feel him touch my face, and my eyes fly open. His face is just as I remember it. When he frowns, the area between his brows scrunches up, and it always makes him look so young, younger than he really is. I lift my hand to touch his face, but I can't seem to make contact.

"I can't feel you Caleb."

"I'm always right here."

"You always leave."

"You haven't been looking."

"We have to hire another guitar player."

"I know."

"But you said..."

"You aren't listening."

"I don't understand."

"I'm always your guitar player. I will always play music with you. You won't replace me. You won't ever be able to. You have to supplement the music, not replace. It's always been right in front of you."

"What has?"

"You will know it when you see it."

"Caleb, stop with the cryptic shit. What in the hell are you talking about?"

"See that right there? That's the fire that has always burned inside of you. You will never replace me or the bond we have. You will find someone who has a different bond with you. It will fit, and it will feel more right than anything you have ever felt. You will know when Henley."

"I'm scared."

He kneels down in front of me, and touches my face again. I want to touch his face too. I lift my hand once again, and when I reach his face, it goes straight through him. I jump back, startled, and he fades away. I scream for him not to go. He always leaves me. I just need a little more time with him. I scream again and again. I need him to come back.

"Henley, wake up!"

I shake my head. I need to go back and find Caleb. I need to know if I can hire another guitar player.

"Henley, wake up baby."

Someone is shaking me. I want to scream for the person to stop, but my eyes pop open and Rhys instantly brings me into his arms. I claw my way to get even closer and I sob. I sob loudly. I sob until my body can't physically cry any longer, and I fall back into sleep.

I wake with the California sun in my eyes. I stretch and pad my way to the kitchen for some coffee. Rhys is standing in my kitchen with a cup already in his hand. He pours me a cup and adds sugar and creamer, but he sets in on the counter and envelops me in a hug.

"I didn't know you were still having the nightmares."

"It's not like it used to be. I have them infrequently."

"Do you want to talk about it?"

"Not really."

"I get it."

After our morning coffee and cigarette, I find my phone to call my grandfather to inquire about Jeff Davis. A text from Jagger is waiting on me when I touch the home screen.

"I saw the photos from last night. You looked so gorgeous as usual. It made me smile to see you out with Griff and Rhys. I hope you enjoyed your evening. I miss you so much. I'm so sorry I hurt you."

I sigh and throw the phone on the bed. I miss him too. It hurts to breathe when he isn't around. The steady ache in my chest hasn't subsided yet, and my daily life seems forced without him here. I feel a song here somewhere. I lounge around in bed for a few hours and try to pull the song from my thoughts.

You held my hand through it all

With your gentle touch and kind eyes

I knew all I had to do was call

And you would hold me while I cried.

The days without him are so damn long

I can't remember the last song.

Will you cut me with your words,

And show me who I really am?

Will you tell me how I failed,

And remind me of why I ran?

Will you scream my faults,

So I can know you never really gave a damn.

Seeing me through your eyes,

Shows me what the world must think.

I was once the one, who shined,

So brightly against the background.

I let it all slip away in time,

Just to find some measure of peace.

Will you cut me with your words,

And show me who I really am?

Will you tell me how I failed,

And remind me of why I ran?

Will you scream my faults,

So I can know you never really gave a damn.

I won't stand by any longer and wait,

For the world to make sense of it all.

I can't leave it all to fate,

And let you destroy me.

The decisions are now mine to make,

I have to leave you behind.

Will you cut me with your words,

And show me who I really am?

Will you tell me how I failed,

And remind me of why I ran?

Will you scream my faults,

So I can know you never really gave a damn.

Rhys and I spend the afternoon on the beach with his drum sticks and my guitar. We manage to write some chords and a beat to go with it. I usually write on an acoustic guitar to gain some semblance of what the song will sound like. Lyrics are words on paper until you pick up an instrument. Instruments somehow guide us into what the song will evolve into. The song begins as a ballad, and then I scream through the chorus with all my emotions pouring into the words on the piece of paper. This is the first song I have completely written and began the music process with in four years.

Chapter 23

I keep good on my promise to Dale, and that Saturday night, I join Shaun on stage for *Broken*. He is so surprised when I walk on stage with an acoustic guitar. It takes him a few moments to speak. The crowd grows crazy loud as I sit on the stool Dale places in front of a second mic.

"So, I hear your birthday is in a few weeks? I figured I would join you on stage tonight before you leave L.A. for the last few gigs of the tour if that's okay with you?" I ask, and the crowd grows even louder.

Shaun smiles and nods.

"You originally sang this song with a very talented artist, but let's see if we can make it better." I begin picking the guitar. Shaun and I sing our hearts out, and the crowd is lit up by their lighters and cell phones as they sing along with us. When the song ends, I take the strap off and hold the guitar by the neck. I wish Shaun a happy birthday again through the mic and hug him. As I kiss his cheek, he requests my favorite Resin song.

"Definitely Gasoline. I like the grittiness of it." I smile.

"Let's do it then, yeah?" he asks.

"Yeah."

We rock the fuck out. Shaun, Dale, and I extend the song and shred like metal gods on our guitars. Dale eventually stops playing, and Shaun and I keep going. It lasts for over ten minutes, and the fans are wild. I'm pouring sweat from the lights and the energy I poured out on stage. God, it feels so good to be back up there. I'm back! Shaun walks me off stage and hugs my neck again.

"That is the most amazing birthday gift ever! I have a penchant for female musicians," he says with a wink.

"I'm happy to do it. Maybe I can hit you up for some collaboration on my new album?" I ask.

He is excited at the possibility, and I exchange numbers with the guys. As I exit stage right, I follow the black curtain behind the stage and see Jagger standing stage left with Koi, Kip, and Cam. Most of the other musicians on the tour are there too. I guess they showed up to watch me play. I don't see anybody else though…I only see Jagger. He is so gorgeous, but he looks empty. His blue eyes are void of their usual fire. I smile at him, and he returns a sad smile of his own. He steps forward as though he is going to cross the area between us and speak, but Koi and Kip jump in before he goes any further. They are full of hugs and smiles for me. I never get tired of hearing how awesome I am from these guys. The rest of the musicians are full of hugs and smiles too. As the guys trickle out, I search for Jagger, but he is gone. I really try not to be disappointed, but it is consuming me. Seeing him makes my resolve waver. I miss him so much. I miss his smell, his smile, his touch, his eyes, his body, his heart, and the sweet little things he does for me. That familiar ache in my heart is now front and center. Maybe I overreacted two weeks ago. Maybe I should've let him apologize and rebuild what we had. I hug my brother and Kip goodbye since they are leaving in a few days to play the last two gigs of the tour.

I wind my way around the backstage area until I find the exit. I carry my guitar on my side and am still riding high from performing. You have no idea what a screaming crowd and music will do for your soul.

"I miss that smile," I hear him say.

He sits on the side of his Black BMW M6 hood with his legs crossed. He looks so fucking gorgeous. I want to tear his clothes off right then and there and ride him to kingdom come on that hood. I don't care if the world watches me fuck his brains out. I need him like I needed air in my lungs. "Poor Henley." My subconscious says. I wish she would shut the fuck up. I'm horny, but those words pester me. He holds up a bouquet.

"You looked amazing out there. The Guitar Goddess is back," He smiles a small sad smile at me again.

The empty eyes are what tug at my heart strings most.

"Yeah. It felt good," I finally say.

He moves the side of his car, and walks towards me. He reaches down and grabs my guitar case. As he does, his touch on my hands sends tingles down to my toes. And, might I add, all the parts down south are screaming at me that my principals don't mean a damn thing in this very moment.

"These are for you." He hands me the bouquet.

"Thank you," I say quietly.

"Come on, I will load this up for you."

We walk slowly to my car. I can see him glancing down at me every few steps, but I can't meet his eyes. Whatever resolve I'm holding onto will snap and leave me stranded holding my heart in my hand.

He holds his hands out for my keys, and I hand them over. He opens the back hatch on my Range Rover and sets my guitar in the back.

"Will you sit and talk to me for a minute?" he almost whispers, but he won't meet my eyes.

Jagger may have hurt me, but he is hurting too. I have known this beautiful man since the sixth grade, and the sentimental part of my heart takes over.

"Yeah." I sit beside him.

"Whatever I say tonight, I mean from the bottom of my heart. The only ulterior motive I have is to get you back in my life. If that means I can only ever have you as a friend, I will take it. Okay?"

"Okay."

"I have some heavy shit weighing on me. It's not something I can share with anyone right now, but it's there. I snapped that night. It isn't anything you did. You definitely didn't deserve it. When I say that I didn't mean those words, I mean it, Hen. I don't even know where they came from. I just saw red and was left lying at the bottom of your porch wondering how in the hell I let it get that far. I picked myself up and went straight to the bar. You know what it's like when we walk into a place. I was alone and vulnerable, and I hurt the only woman I ever loved. I know the bartender, and he took one look at me and knew I was nursing a broken heart. The people just started hanging off me, and I tried my best not to explode. I wanted to tell them to leave me the fuck alone, but I couldn't. The only picture that ran through my head again and again were the tears rolling down your face, and I was holding back my own tears the rest of the night. I poured as much alcohol down my throat as I could to stop seeing you cry. Everyone wanted to take pictures, and so I just smiled through it. I smiled to keep from breaking every one of their necks. The bartender finally called me a cab, and I rode by your house several times trying to get up the courage to grovel. It isn't that I was afraid to grovel. I was afraid of what you would say. I couldn't handle you leaving me at that moment. I checked into a nearby hotel and passed out. By the time I woke up late the next night, the pictures from that night were all over the news, and your statement ending our relationship was playing on repeat. I went crazy. I trashed the entire fucking room. I screamed and cried until I didn't have anything left. And do you know what I saw next?"

"What?"

"I saw you on TMZ being hounded by the paparazzi. I saw the sadness all over your face, and yet you were more concerned about getting an old lady away from them than you were your own broken heart. So, all those things I said that night are bullshit. I never meant them. I hurt you, and I was a weak coward who can't deal with his own shit so I took it out on you. While I was drinking and fucking up our relationship, you were selflessly giving yourself to others. That isn't 'Poor Henley.' The girl on that TV is the girl who told me in sixth grade that I needed to toughen up against Brian Carrington right before you punched the bully in the nose."

We laugh at the memory. "I had forgotten about that. The look on his face was priceless. He was such a mean kid, and he got his ass handed to him by a girl."

"You made sure he never forgot that either." Jagger smiles. It is a real smile this time.

"Hell no, I didn't. I even wrote it in our eighth grade annual."

"You didn't?"

Dear Brian, middle school has been a blast. I hope you remember you should always play nice with others. I will kick your ass again if you don't.

"I drew a little heart and signed my name under it. His mom called my mom a week later and read it to her. She took my guitar away for a month. It almost killed me."

"I remember that. You were all of a sudden very interested in taking up the drums. She said you couldn't have your guitar so you beat the shit out of Kip's drum kit for a month."

"I will never be a drummer."

"No. You are the Guitar Goddess." His face is full of pride for me.

We grow quiet for close to ten minutes. Both of our gazes are focused straight ahead, lost in our own thoughts. I swing my legs as I often do when my feet don't touch the ground. He reaches down and gently grabs my hand, and we remain quiet for another little while. This man still holds my heart whether he knows it or not. His gentle touches and simply holding my hand makes my heart swell.

"I'm sorry Hen. For everything."

"I know."

I hear someone shouting next. "Where the fuck are you?"

It sounds like Koi. "Jagger!" His voice grew even louder. Jagger stood from the back of my SUV and rounded the car.

"Oh. Alright." Koi sees him at my car.

"Hen?" He called out.

"Yeah."

"You okay?"

"Yeah, I'm okay."

"Alright." He paused. "Jag we go on in 25. You ready?"

"Ready to go."

"Alright. See you inside."

Jagger walks back around the car to me. He holds his hands out to me, and the old familiar feeling takes me over. I put my hands in his, and he stands me up.

"I know this shit doesn't go away overnight. It doesn't go away with one apology. Time mends all wounds though. I don't have the right to ask you for anything, but I would like us to at least try to get back to a place where we speak, and maybe eventually we can be friends who don't feel awkward or angry around each other. If we have the chance to build something else one day, then we will just let it happen. Can we do that?"

"Yeah."

He pushes my hair behind my ear and runs the pads of his fingers down my face. I close my eyes and my face leans into his hand. I miss this so much. He touches me like I'm the only woman on earth.

"Hey," he whispers, and I open my eyes.

He stares into them and then looks at my lips.

"I love you, friend," he says, and my eyes burn with tears.

"I love you too," my voice cracks.

"Hey. You don't cry any tears for me. I don't deserve them."

He runs the pads of his fingers down my face again, and then he leans down to put his forehead on mine. His lips are only a few inches away from mine. I can feel his breath on my mouth.

"I'm so sorry, Henley. I will regret that night for the rest of my life. You have no idea."

I think I do.

I lick my lips because that's what I do when Jagger is so close to me. I didn't mean to. My body betrays me every time I'm around him. He leans in the last few inches, and his lips touch mine. They aren't pursed in a kiss. No, his lips just simply touch mine. His lips are parted, and my own parted lips are between his. He doesn't move for the longest time. His hands are on either side of my head. I part my lips a little more, because again, that is what happens around Jagger Carlyle. The tips of our tongues touch and he pulls back far enough to change his angle. His lips lightly touched mine again, and then our tongues briefly touch. This went on for God knows how long. Just our lips touching and parting and the tips of our tongues touching. I have never felt so overwhelmed by love like I do right now.

"Five minutes Jag!" Cam yells.

Jagger continues the kiss for several more moments, and then he pulls away slightly, his eyes still closed, our breaths ragged. He opens his eyes, licks his bottom lip, and lets his lips softly touch mine one more time. He pulls away slightly once more and rests his forehead on mine.

"Thank you for hearing me out," he says.

I just nod because I can't form words at the moment. He pulls his forehead back and brushes my hair from my face again. He looks my entire face over and kisses my forehead. He steps back a couple of steps. He closes my hatch, grabs my hand, hands me my keys, and opens the driver side door.

"Hey." I look up into his big crystal blue eyes, and he touches my face again. "Be careful going home, okay? Will you text me and let me know you arrive safely?"

I stare into his baby blues for a minute.

"Look," he shrugs his shoulders, "If you don't want to text me, will you let Koi and Kip know you are safe?"

"I will text you, Jagger," I say softly.

"Okay. I gotta go." He leans down and kisses my forehead again.

He hesitates as he takes a few steps back, but he finally turns around and walks towards the venue. I watch him walk away. Even his back side is beautiful. When he reaches the entrance, he touches the door frame with his hand, turns and looks back at me. I don't drop my eyes from him. He smiles, and I smile back, and then he is gone.

I slump into my seat a quivering mess. I hope I can remember the way home.

Luckily, I remember the way home, but the drive is one big blur. I'm still lost in that kiss. I pull into the garage and close the door behind me.

Once, inside, I stare at my phone. Should I wait to text or just text him now? I don't want to give him the wrong impression. Hell, I don't even know what impression I have of us anymore. I know he is sorry for what happened, and I doubt my reaction again. Did I overreact?

Fuck it. I pick up my phone and text him.

Me: I'm home safely.

I set my phone on the ottoman and pad to my bedroom to change into a pair of yoga pants and a tank. I return to the living room and settle in to catch up on The Vampire Diaries. I can't help it. The Salvatore brothers are smoking hot. Not that I would know anything personal about one of them. My phone chirps.

Jagger: Good. Doors locked?

Me: Are you on stage?

Jagger: Yeah, between songs.

Me: Ok. Doors are locked.

Jagger: Sweet dreams.

Me: Play beautifully.

I send Kip and Koi a message to inform them that I made it home safely. I fall asleep during the second episode of TVD. My phone chirps and wakes me at some point. When I look at my phone I discover it is 3:30 a.m.

Jagger: You up?

Me: Yeah.

Jagger: Did I wake you?

Me: Yeah, but it's okay. I fell asleep on the couch watching TV. I need to get up and go to bed anyways.

Jagger: Are you going out to smoke now?

Me: Are you spying on me?

Jagger: I just know you.

Me: I just lit up.

Jagger: No, I'm not stalking you. I promise. Can't sleep.

Me: Wired from the show?

Jagger: Yeah. We've had two weeks off, so I'm not exhausted like I normally am.

Me: It always takes me hours to find sleep after a show, no matter how tired I am.

Jagger: I remember. Caleb wouldn't go to sleep until the sun came up. I remember him staying up all night playing Xbox or….. with a pretty lady.

Me: He was such a playboy.

Jagger: Every woman wanted to fuck him, and every man wanted to be him.

Me: He was really humble about it though. I have seen musicians treat women like shit. He was always such a charmer.

Jagger: He had major game. He could talk a nun out of her panties.

Me: Yeah, he could.

Jagger: Go back to sleep. I'm sorry I woke you.

Me: It's okay. Sweet dreams.

Jagger: Always.

I toss and turn for an eternity thinking of Jagger. I wish he were here holding me because I would find sleep instantly.

Chapter 24

Three days later, I'm awoken in typical Kip style.

"Stick it in me. Oh yeah. Oh God, right there," a woman demands, followed by a man grunting.

"Oh God, I want to piss on you," the woman says and the man grunts again.

Then I can hear a steady stream of piss.

"Oh, that is beautiful," the man says.

I finally crawl out of the bed and look at my cell. It's 8:00 in the morning. I'm going to kill him! I was up all night writing. I make my way to the master bath, but I can't piss because the porn is streaming through my home's surround sound system. Jesus Christ.

"Lick it out, big boy," she says.

I can hear a human tongue lapping and hope it isn't really urine he is lapping up.

"That's a good boy. Now lie back. I'm going to sit on your face you fat fuck," she says.

I'm sorry you have to hear this, baby Jesus. I can hear the muffled groans of the man.

"You like when I ride your fucking face, don't you? Fuck me with your tongue!" Then I hear the sound of a slap on skin. It sounds like it hurts.

"You like it when I beat you? You are such a worthless fuck. Do I have to do this all myself? Turn over!" she screams.

When I walk into my living room, I discover it is filled with Koi, Kip, Cam, Jagger, Samantha, Jessica, Kathrine, Griffin, and Rhys. They erupt in laughter. They haven't been up all night. I narrow my eyes on Kip. He smiles and wiggles his brows at me. Sometimes I just want to throttle him. I start towards him, and the dumb ass just stands there grinning. I walk up to him and grab his hand. It is time to teach Kip a lesson about waking me up in the morning. I lead him down the hall to my bedroom and push him onto the bed. His eyes are as big as half dollars. I pull out a few scarves from my closet, and straddle Kip on the bed. His dick is hard. Men can be so predictable. I tie one hand up to the headboard, and then the other. I do this with slow precision, so he thinks I'm trying to be sexy. I'm making damn sure the little shit can't get out of it. I stand from the bed and head to the door.

"Are you closing it so you and daddy can have more privacy?" He has the smuggest little smile on his face, so I turn and wink at him. Then I yell for Samantha and Jessica. "What are you doing?" he asks.

Samantha and Jessica enter my room anxious to see what I have done. "Uh oh," Sam says.

"I need you to retrieve your bag of toys," I say to Samantha.

"What bag?" she plays coy.

"The bag you keep in the back of your car for bad little girls, you fucking freak," Jessica says. Samantha rolls her eyes and leaves to retrieve the bag.

"Sit with him and make sure he doesn't move." Jessica sits down with him, and rubs her hands all over his stomach to mess with his head. Both of them.

I return to the living room and turn the annoying porn off. Who pisses on people? I find some Bury Your Dead and turn it up in only my bedroom. I walk back to my room and see Jessica has discovered a feather in my bedside table. She is using that on his stomach now, and Kip looks like he is temporarily in love.

I'm finally able to pee. I return through the living room to the kitchen. I need coffee, badly! I smell coffee before I round the corner to the kitchen. Jagger holds out a cup of coffee to me, and I kiss him on the cheek. I take a swig and head to the deck to smoke a cigarette. The guys follow, and I discover Shaun, John, and Dale lounging around. They are so hot!

I light a cigarette when Samantha walks through the French doors and sits a huge duffel bag on the table in front of me. I open it and almost have a heart attack. Jesus, I knew she was a freak, but really? Who needs this much stuff? I discover she has a small sex store in a bag. It would definitely do the trick. I put my cigarette out and turn towards the house.

"Can we watch?" Koi asks.

"Absolutely, I might need help holding him down."
"I can't wait!" Rhys exclaims.

We return to the bedroom, where the only sounds audible are death metal. I chose this music for a reason. When I return, Kip smiles until he sees the men following me. A look of panic crosses his face again.

I sit the bag on the bed, and the guy's crowd around staying close to the walls. I open the bag and pull out a ball gag. I straddle Kip and force it over his head and into his mouth. Next, I pull out a collar and leash and put it around Kip's neck. He really looks scared now. I lift off of him and look at Jessica. She knows that look. She reaches down and unbuttons his jeans, sliding them down his legs while running her tongue across her teeth. Kip just closes his eyes. He doesn't know whether to be afraid or excited. Then, I pull out an ankle restraint bar and bind each ankle in them. Over the death metal, I can hear the roar of laughter behind me. Next, I pick up a strap-on and throw it at Jessica. She puts it on. Bless her. Kip's eyes are about to pop out of his head, and he struggles against the ties at his wrists. He is about to be my bitch. I look back at Koi and Jagger, and I motion them over. Once they are close enough, I yell over the music.

"I need to flip him over on his stomach and restrain his hands behind his back. Let's take his shirt off while we have his hands untied."

The guys take a hand each, untie one at a time, and I take his shirt off. They force him on his stomach and then put his hands behind his back. I put another bar restraint on his wrists behind his back. I'm so thankful Sam is a freak. I find a riding crop and smack him on the ass. About the same time the music ends on the current play list, we hear Kip scream through the ball gag. The room erupts in laughter.

"Up!" I say to Kip, and he bends his knees and puts his ass in the air. Jessica starts thrusting the strap-on in and out of his face, which solicits a whimper from Kip.

"How many times have you done this to a girl?" Jessica yells at him.

She is really good at this. He makes an "I don't know" sound, and Jessica orders me to hit him on the ass. I do, and he screams again through the ball gag.

"No," Jessica says, and pulls his boxers down exposing his bare ass. "Now hit him."

Kip's eyes grow large again, and he shakes his head "no". Slap! He screams again. Jessica reaches in the bag and pulls out a long black paddle and begins thrusting the strap-on in and out of his face again.

"How many times have you shoved your dick in a girl's face?" she asks again.

He whimpers again. She hits him with the paddle in the left ass cheek, and I follow behind with the riding crop to the right cheek. He screams again. His white ass is bright red. Jessica climbs on the bed behind him with the strap-on pointed at his bare ass, and I pull my camera out. I take picture after picture of her thrusting it in and out, pretending to insert it in his nether region. I also take several of her hitting his red ass with the paddle and riding crop. The best pictures show Kip's face, and the fear is plainly there, ball gag firmly in place. The guys each take disturbing pictures with him. When I have had enough fun, I have Koi and Cam place Kip on his back, and I take the ankle restraints and the ball gag off.

"Now what did we learn today Kip?" I ask.

He looks up at me with puppy dog eyes. "Wake you with porn every morning so you and that hot little Dom over there can tie me up and beat my ass?"

Jessica is obviously not satisfied with his response, because she calls his name, and when he turns his head to the opposite side of the bed, she rams the strap-on in his mouth. I lost it. That is the funniest thing I have ever seen, and it causes me to double over with laughter. The entire room is having a tough time of it as well.

"Tastes like cotton candy," Kip says, and we all lose it again.

***

We spend the morning and afternoon at the beach munching on food, drinking beer, and listening to music. Kip proposes marriage to me and Jessica several times and is now a self-proclaimed Mormon. We play volleyball and corn hole, and we each got our own nap in at some point. Jagger and I don't speak a great deal, but when we do, it isn't awkward. I catch him looking at me several times, and he simply smiles. The smile reminds me of our last kiss. It is super panty-dripping, I mean dropping, hot!

When night falls, we build a fire in the pit. The guitars come out, and we play into the night. I sing and play mostly cover songs with everyone there. Some of the guys sing and pick songs they are writing.

As the intoxication grows, we play less and less and collectively decide to take a stroll down the beach. Cam and Kathrine disappear in the opposite direction of the group. Ten-four! Koi grabs Jessica's hand, and Samantha slaps Kip in the arm when he attempts to grab hers. Jagger and I walk closely to each other, and I find myself wanting him to grab my hand. We don't walk far before Shaun, Dale, and John stop by a party a few houses down. It appears to be a bunch of college kids are going on a rip. Samantha's eyes hone in on all the women at the party. She likes college girls, so experimental. She nods at me, and I smile back in understanding, so she hauls Kip off to the party.

Koi, Jessica, Jagger and I continue down the beach. Jagger and Koi are arguing about a Pink Floyd song, and I take the moment to give Jessica a smile. She winks back. I know these two would end up hooking up. Jessica jumps into their dispute and agrees with Jagger. Smart move girl.

"You are really agreeing with this ass hat?" he points to Jag.

"Yeah. I am! Right is right. This isn't a grey area. That is the correct interpretation of the song!"

"Yeah?" Koi asks smiling down at her.

She backs up as he moves towards her like a predator, and then turns and takes off running, but Koi chases her down. He picks her up and turns her around, which is when my best friend wraps her legs around my brother. I try not to think too much about it. Otherwise, I will begin planning their wedding tonight. Koi drops them into the ocean and takes her under water. She comes up shouting expletives at him, but she is interrupted when he kisses her. I give them their privacy since Koi doesn't get it often enough.

Jagger and I continue walking, and he finally reaches down and grabs my hand. I smile but don't look at him. I can't. We walk in silence for a bit before he finally breaks the ice.

"So Koi and Jess?" he asks.

"Yeah. I kinda knew something was going on in New Orleans."

"They would be good together. She wouldn't put up with his shit. She also knew him long before he hit it big. Her intentions wouldn't be questioned."

"They would be great together. I would be lucky if I ever managed to get her as a sister-n-law. Sister-n-law and best friend in one package is every sisters' dream," I say.

"You think Koi will ever get married?"

"When he meets the right one and is ready to settle down, I think he will."

"He hasn't ever talked about it."

"He's been too busy playing rock star. He's had the world at his fingertips for ten years. He wouldn't pursue Jessica if he didn't want something serious from it. Too many people get hurt if it ends badly." I repeat his words from months back. "That tells me he is ready to settle down."

Jag agrees, and we continue our walk towards a little rock cove that separates this private beach from the public beach. From the time I bought the house, a cave had been shaped and maintained in the rock wall. The last time I was here, Caleb made me swim into it. The tide was up, and he dragged me along. He wrote our names and a bunch of vulgar things on the rocks. That was a month before he died, and I wonder if it is still there.

"There is a cave in the rock wall. When the tide is up you have to swim into it," I say.

"Let's check it out."

"Uh-uh. I'm not going in that thing at night."

"You scared?"

"Of what critters could be in there? Definitely!"

"Come on, I will protect you. Stop being such a girl."

"I am a girl."

"You have never acted like one before. Too damn tough."

"Fine, but if I'm eaten by a sea monster, my death is on your hands." I march ahead of him and reach the entrance of the cave before he does. I stop at the entrance, my resolve giving way.

"You have to go in."

"You can't see anything in there."

"I have my cell; I will use the light on it," he pulls his cell out of his pocket and illuminates the cave. "Come on sissy."

"Sissy my ass." I push myself forward but he grabs my hand.

I walk over to the wall Caleb had vandalized, and wouldn't you know, it is still visible. Jagger laughs. "No he didn't!"

"He did."

Call for a good time is still on the cave wall along with a previous cell number of mine.

"Henley, look at me." I turned my head to him, and he hit something on my shoulder.

"I don't want to know do I?"

"Nope."

"I told you I was going to get eaten by a sea monster!" I ran for my life, and out of the cave.

Jagger runs after me. "Come back, you sissy."

"I'm not a sissy; I just don't want to die." I yell over my shoulder. He catches up with me and scoops me up from the sand, throwing me over his shoulder. I'm only wearing a bikini, so my ass is literally in his face.

"You just want to look at my ass!" I say.

He leans over to my ass and bites me on the cheek.

"I'm so kicking your ass. Where are you taking me?"

"Back to the cave we shall go! You have to face your fears and all that good shit," he says.

I kick and squeal trying to get loose and then give up. Jagger is a big man, there is no use.

"I'm being a good friend here and making you face your fears. You cannot let the sea monsters win!"

"If you put me back in that damn cave, this is war!"

"What are you going to do?"

"Did you see what I did to Kip this morning? I will plaster pictures of you in very compromising photographs all over the internet!"

He sits me down in the cave. "Good point, but you are already here."

I close my eyes. I have no idea what was crawling on me, but I don't want to see it again. Then it hits me.

"Was there really something on my shoulder?"

Jagger smiles a mischievous little grin, and I know I've been had. I push him, and he laughs. So I step forward and push him again, but he grabs my wrists.

"You really are a sissy!" He pulls my wrists to him. "You are really cute when you throw a temper tantrum."

"I'm not throwing a temper tantrum. I'm not a toddler. When you are a grown woman, it's called a bitch fit."

"Thank you for the clarification."

He is smiling down at me with that bad boy rocker smile. Those smiles that can make your panties drop on the spot. He could be across a room, and your panties would drop. You could stand with a friend having a perfectly normal conversation. If you were to look up and see his smile for two seconds, BOOM! You are now standing in a room full of people with your drawers around your damn ankles!

"You are very welcome," I say all breathy.

It's not fair! All he has to do is smile, and I get overheated. He hears it too. His smile slowly fades, and he brings my body closer.

He is inches from my lips. "Henley…"

"Shut up, Jagger."

He leans down and touches his lips to mine. His tongue eventually finds mine, and he slowly laps his tongue against it. His hands are on my lower back, and it doesn't help the whole panty dropping situation. I'm so screwed. I want him so bad, so I pick up the pace, and he follows my lead. He inches us to the cave wall and leans his tall body down to mine and kisses my neck. When he continues across my shoulder, I arch my back because that is what I do when Jagger is kissing my body. I can't help it. It's an involuntary response. He pulls my face to him again and kisses my lips. I gently bite his bottom lip, and he growls in response. Have I ever told you his growl makes me lose my sanity temporarily? I moan into his mouth, and he growls again as he picks my petite body up by my ass. Saying the cave wall isn't comfortable is an understatement. Who really cares when the hottest man alive is pressing you against it with his dick pushing into your thigh? Not me, that's for damn sure.

"Henley…"

"I need it. Please," I beg. Don't say no. Rape is so not cool.

"I can't."

You what?

"You can't what?" I ask between kisses.

"I can't just fuck you like it doesn't mean anything," he says.

"Do you see me sleeping with anyone else?" I ask through gritted teeth and sexual frustration.

"What are you saying?"

"I'm saying I can't sleep with anyone else when my heart still belongs to you."

He thinks on that for a beat, then charges back in quickly, bruising my lips and pushing my bottoms to the side. I feel him reach below and dip a little to pull himself out. He doesn't enter me immediately, but continues kissing me, slowing down the pace.

"I love you, Henley. I always have."

"I love you too."

He looks me in the eyes as he enters my body and slowly pushes his pelvis into me. It has been way too long. He takes his time and balances me off the wall. I wish I could see this from the outside looking in. He is standing straight up, balancing the entire weight of my body, and thrusting slowly in and out of me while also kissing me. Now that takes skill. I feel his muscles begin to shake after several minutes.

"Kneel down," I say.

He brings himself to the sand and leans back on his calves while holding me in place. Once I get my footing, I begin to grind on him. He watches every move I make. I look straight into the eyes of the man I love, and I know I've made a big mistake. He finally starts kissing me again, and I have that overwhelming feeling of love and adoration.

"Koi! Stop!" I hear Jessica say.

I look to my left and see her standing there, a little shocked she found us. "We don't need to go in there. Just take me back to the house."

And just like that, they are gone. Thank you Jessica!

I look down and smile at Jagger, and I start moving again. Not long after, I feel my orgasm building. When the full body tingles start, I let my head fall back and hold on to his neck. I have no idea what I cry out, but good God, Buddha, Allah, and everything that is holy thank you for this man… and his penis. I hear Jagger growl, he grabs my hips and thrusts into me as hard as he can. He thrusts again and again until he finds it. He reaches around to my back and pulls me flush to his chest, where I put his head on my shoulder. He thrusts some more, and I feel him empty his load inside me.

We stay like that for quite a while, all tangled up in each other in the sand. People who bitch about sex being difficult in sand have never had sex with Jagger Carlyle. Sand is the last thing you think about being in your bathing suit. He runs his hand up and down my back as we both catch our breath. His head remains on my shoulder. When he catches his breath, he showers kissed along my collarbone.

"Let me come home Henley."

"Home?"

"You are my home."

"Okay, baby."

Chapter 25

After the night in the cave, Jagger and I reconcile. He apologizes repeatedly for the things he said that horrible night. Our friends and family are more than elated we make peace. Jagger has to leave a couple of days later for two gigs. Broken Access only has two more gigs before they will be home for a while. There is already some talk about recording a new album.

Light streams through my window. I love sunshine. I attempt to move, but a solid muscular arm draped across my body pulls me back.

"I have something for you."

"You do? I really like presents. What is it?"

"I will give you a few hints. You suck on it, but it can't stay hard forever. Sometimes it evens stains your lips."

"Oh I love popsicles!" I attempt to jump out of his hold and out of the bed, but he grabs me by the hips and pulls me under the covers as I squeal. I find myself under him, and he pulls the covers over our heads.

He presses himself into me. "Does that feel cold to you baby?"

"No. Why don't you just say 'dick'? I always like that surprise."

"Yeah?"

"Yeah."

While he removes my panties, he kisses a trail down to them. He removes his own boxers, and thrusts into me, pulling in and out of me at a moderate pace. He runs his hands down my inner thighs and pushes my knees towards my chest. He can't be any deeper in me.

"I have to go without this for five days baby. You sure you can't go on tour with us?"

"Shut up, Jagger."

"I love it when you get so bossy. I like it when you order me around in the bedroom."

"What about in caves?"

"Just one cave in particular."

"Okay, shut up, Jagger. I'm almost there."

He leans down to my ear and whispers, "I want to feel you quiver on me. Your pussy is so wet. Is my head hitting that spot baby?"

"Yes!" I yell gripping onto the sheets for dear life....or an orgasm.

"That's it. Come for me. Come on my cock. God, I love it when you scream."

He picks up speed and the friction increases, and tingles start at my toes and slowly rise to my center.

"Come baby. Stop holding out on me. I need to feel you come. I need you to give it to me."

I arch my back and scream out his name along with motherfucker, shit, ass, bitch, fuck yes, and Jesus Christ! Sorry baby Jesus. I'm a limp mess when it is all over with, and that piece of visible knowledge strokes his ego if the smile on his face is any indication. Smug ass. He finds his release and says fuck about twenty times.

A few hours later, I drop him at the lot where the bus is parked. I hug all of their necks.

Cam approaches me for a hug. "I need your help."

"Of course."

"I need you to find me a ring."

My mouth drops, "Like the ring?"

"Yes. The ring."

"You're proposing to Kathrine?"

"Yes. Please tell me she will say yes."

"I'm sure she will. You guys are so great together. Want me to put out a feeler?"

"Yeah. That would calm my nerves a bit."

"Did you ask her dad?"

"He is excited. He gave me shit at first, and it scared the crap out of me. He is talking about a freaking dowry for his first child."

"That sounds like Big Daddy."

"So, I will text you a price range. See if you can find several pieces for me to look at. I would like to do it on Thanksgiving. I'm trying to think of a really memorable way to propose."

"I will think on that too."

***

I'm over the moon for Cam and Kathrine. They are both amazing people who deserve each other. I pick up Jessica on the way from dropping Jag off so I can hit up a jeweler I've used in the past. I don't tell Jessica where we are going because I want to see the look on her face when she figures it out. I have Cam's price range, and he isn't holding back which makes my job really easy. I want to do a little dance and sing "Kathrine and Cam sitting in a tree."

"What you buying?" Jessica asks.

"I'm not buying anything."

I ask the jeweler for engagement rings in the price range Cam specified, and he disappears into the back. Jessica is trying to figure out why I'm here. I instantly see *the one* when the jeweler returns with a case. It's a vintage-inspired five carat emerald cut platinum ring. The diamond is surrounded by crusted diamonds, and the band is also crusted.

"What do you think? It looks really vintage, and vintage would be really cool since they fell in love in New Orleans. It also looks really artsy, like her." I give her all the hints I possibly can.

"Shut the fuck up, bitch! Is he really asking her?"

"Yup. He just told me. We have to think of the best way for him to drop on one knee. He wants to do it in a couple of weeks on Thanksgiving."

"Aww that is so freaking romantic. He is giving thanks for their love!" She can be a hopeless romantic too, but don't tell her I told you so.

I ask the jeweler to hold the ring after I text Cam several pictures. He agrees it is definitely *the one*. I put a hefty deposit on it since Cam can't be here. I don't want him to lose out on the ring. Jessica and I instantly put our heads together to plan the perfect proposal.

My mom calls later that evening.

"Hey, sweetheart. How are things?"

"Great mom, really great."

"Good. Well look, I have an idea for Thanksgiving. All the parents had dinner last night for our monthly get together. We thought it would be a great idea for us to fly out since so many of you kids are out there. It's really cold here in Georgia, so we would rather have a warm California Thanksgiving."

"That sounds great, mom. Who all is coming out?"

"Everyone!" She is so excited.

"Donny and Maria?"

"No, baby. I don't think they can deal with that just yet. They don't come to many of our dinners either. It reminds them too much of Caleb."

"Yeah, I get it."

"So why don't I call you with some ideas for dinner and let's put it together?"

"Sounds good."

We prepare for the holidays while the guys are out on tour and decide dinner will be at my house. I organize where everyone will stay during Thanksgiving. We all have enough houses and rooms to accommodate our families.

Cam and I speak back and forth all week about the proposal. Kathrine loves the beach. He really wants to do something to incorporate Thanksgiving into it so that it is a really memorably moment. Kathrine is really close with her dad, so I figure it would be a really neat to tie him into the proposal.

The bell rings from my front door late Friday night. I'm not expecting anyone. When I open it, the love of my life stands with his guitar in hand and a bouquet in the other. I jump on him and throw my legs around his waist. I really missed him.

"What are you doing here?" I ask.

"Water main busted in the venue this morning. As soon as they found it, the show was cancelled. I caught the first flight home."

"I missed you."

"I missed you too, baby."

We go to bed and tangle into each other and then just lie in bed and talk for several hours after. I tell him all about Cam and Kathrine. He thinks my idea is genius and is sure Cam will be on board. I show him the pictures of the ring, and he agrees it suits Kathrine.

"You really are excited about this," he says with sleepy eyes.

"Yeah. Go to sleep baby."

"K."

He is out soon after. I watch him sleep for a while. His buzzed hair is a little longer than it normally is. He hasn't shaved in days and has bags under his eyes. He is clearly exhausted. As I watch him sleep, I realize how connected I am to him. I can't imagine my life without him. We spent a few weeks broken up, and my heart never stopped aching. I love this man so much.

Chapter 26

Our parents arrive on Monday morning, and they help me set my house up for Thanksgiving. Decorations are everywhere. It turns out beautifully. The men lounge on the beach and drink beer each day. Several try their hand at surfing, and it is truly comic relief. Jagger, Koi, and Kip grill for us each night, and Griffin and Rhys cook the sides. Dinner time is the reserved for the women to relax. Each night, we gather around the fire pit, snuggle into our blankets and partners. I set up horseshoes and corn hole for whoever wants to play, but mostly we just play our guitars and sing. My grandparents even stay late on Wednesday evening, and Red, my grandfather, plays the guitar and sings for us. His musical abilities still mesmerize me, and I know I will never be the guitar player he is. I leave Jag to snuggle up to my Grandfather that night. He is the most amazing man I have ever met. The nights around the fire feel so much like Caleb's last Thanksgiving. So much has changed in each of our lives since his death, and I wonder what he would think of Jagger and me. He would be jealous of Jessica and Koi. He always had a thing for her. I don't think he would be surprised by Cam and Kathrine at all. They fit so well together.

Thanksgiving morning rolls around, and Kathrine's mom talks her into shopping before the Black Friday crowds hit. Kathrine is not excited when her mom says she wants to find a bathing suit. She knows her mom will take all day, which is exactly why the plan was enacted. Koi, Kip, and Jagger make us breakfast that morning, and the moms show up with Kathrine around two to start cooking the feast. We drink wine all day and are riding high on the impending proposal. Cam is a nervous mess, and Kathrine is starting to notice. I send Jagger and Koi down to the beach with him to calm him down. Each time Kathrine mentions it, I just chalk it up to him being nervous being around her parents.

When dinner is ready, we gather in the dining room. Jagger holds my hand the entire time, and rubs his thumb in my palm. The joy is so contagious and very present in the room. At the end of dinner my mother asks each of us to describe what we are thankful for.

Mom: I'm thankful for my wonderful parents, and the influence they had on my children. I'm also thankful for my loving husband who I have loved since the day I saw him play the guitar in my dad's studio. I'm most thankful for my two beautiful children who have grown into amazing, happy, healthy adults.

Here! Here

Dad: What she says. And rock-n-roll!

Here! Here! We all toast again.

My Grandfather: I thought raising my daughter was the most amazing experience of my life, and she is the best daughter a man can ask for. She did well in school, never got in trouble, and married a good man. She gave me the two things I'm most thankful for, my grandchildren. They took to the guitar at such a young age, and when they wanted in the industry, they didn't ask for it. They worked for it. They climbed to the top of that rock-n-roll mountain on their own. Even though they far surpassed my celebrity in this world, you both remembered the values you were raised with. You are kind to others, you give to those in need, and you love with everything you have. I'm also thankful that the woman I married fifty years ago loved me at my worst. She loved the music as much as I did, and through our love, all of you sit here together as a family.

Here! Here

The toasts went on and on.

Koi: I'm thankful for my loving family, my career, our very talented band, this beautiful woman who sits beside me. I think I have had a crush on you since I was 16.

Awwww! We all say and then lift our glasses.

Jagger: I'm thankful for my family and the music. I'm most thankful for Henley. She is the most amazing woman I have ever met. I treasure every day I'm allowed to spend with you. I know I can be an idiot, so I'm extra thankful that you put up with me. I love you so much! And I have loved her since the sixth grade, so I win Koi.

Here! Here! And our families toast while he kisses my lips.

Me: If you told me our Thanksgiving five years ago would be Caleb's last, I would have called you crazy. It was an amazing Thanksgiving, and this one reminds me so much of that week. I'm thankful for the amazing memories of Caleb. I'm also thankful to each one of you for loving and supporting me through my journey to find peace in his death. I will never forget that. I'm thankful for a grandfather and a father who gave me music. I'm also thankful for my mother and grandmother who held it all together so the crazy musicians in the family could chase their dreams. You kept us grounded and never let us forget where we came from. I'm thankful for my brother who always has my back and loves me like a big brother should. I'm thankful for the love in this room tonight. If you take a look around, someone is holding someone else's hand. There isn't a soul at this table that isn't holding the hand of someone they love. Life is crazy, and our lives are even crazier, but it is these moments that we hold closest to our hearts; the moments when we are surrounded by unconditional love. I'm very thankful for Jagger. You are the love of my life. I'm also thankful for a little boy named Noah, who gave me the biggest gift I have ever received.

"I'm holding my mom's hand," Kip says. "I should've hired an escort."

"You what?" my grandfather asks.

"You know Red, like a woman you pay to be your lady friend for the night?" he winks at my grandfather.

"You mean like a street walker?"

"No sir, we don't call them that anymore. They are called prostitutes or hookers now. An escort is someone you can hire to give you companionship for a set amount of time. You aren't buying hanky panky, just her time."

"So, what do you do with her? Talk?"

"Well, it depends on what language you speak, sir."

"What in the hell are you talking about, boy?"

"Well, if you speak the language of love, you can definitely talk… ALL NIGHT LONG!" Kip lets out a yelp when his mother hits him in the back of the head.

"Was that boy dropped on his head as a child Paxton?" My grandfather asks Kip's dad.

"I think they gave us the wrong child at the hospital. I have tried to talk her into taking his ass back for 28 long years."

While everyone else cracks up, I narrow my eyes at Kip's father. I know his words cut my friend to the bone. He's a piece of shit father.

"I said nice things about you people in my toast. Shame on you! I'm so not feeling the love tonight," Kip deflects with humor.

"Maybe you should hire one of those escorts, so you can feel loved," my grandfather says, and Kip has finally been rendered speechless.

We busy Kathrine with washing dishes and wrapping the food. Jessica, Sam, Cam, Koi, Jagger, Kip, and Big Daddy state we are going on a big ass liquor run. Everybody makes up their own convincing excuse as to why they need to go to the liquor store. We set up the lights on the beach. We then wait on the beach out of sight while I send Big Daddy in to retrieve Kathrine. Once he goes in, the remaining guests know to join us on the beach.

I see Kathrine exit the French doors with her dad, fussing about the dishes still left in the kitchen. Her dad points to the lights on the beach. They read, "He asked me. I said yes. What will you say?" She looks at her dad in confusion, and I hold my breath. He points down to the beach where Cam is waiting amongst the lights. Her dad kisses her on cheek and escorts her down to Cam. He steps over to our crowd, and Cam drops to one knee. I throw my hands over my mouth to suppress my squeal of joy. I want to jump up and down, but she can't see us in the shadows, and I don't want to take away from their moment.

"I have felt so lost these last few years. The music was great, but it just didn't make me feel whole anymore. I couldn't put my finger on what was missing. I have known you a long time, but when you came to New Orleans, I found what I was missing. When you left, I felt lost again, but each time I heard your voice or saw your face, I was whole again. Please do me the honor of being my wife and making my life whole, always. Will you marry me?"

I hold my breath. If she says no, I'm kicking her ass. She starts saying yes as she nods her head vehemently, and he places that gorgeous ring on her finger. Our massive group finally lets out the hoots and squeals. Kathrine turns towards us in shock, and the fellas light the Tiki torches so she can see us. She hugs her parents and makes her way through the family and friends. When she gets to me, I hold her tight. We jump up and down holding each other squealing like teenage girls. Jessica and Sam join in our hug and squeal fest too.

Chapter 27

Two weeks after Christmas, I'm still shopping. Luckily, the guys have chartered a private jet back to Georgia. So, I can just wrap presents here and take them with me. I still haven't figured out what to get Jagger. Jessica and I are out shopping today for Jag and Koi. They aren't easy to shop for, so we need the moral support and lots of coffee. My phone chirps as I leave Starbucks after lunch.

Jagger: What ya doing?

Me: Still trying to find the love of my life the perfect gift.

Jagger: The love of your life already has the perfect gift. You.

Me: Awww… I can't think of a damn thing to get you that you don't already have.

Jagger: I've given you some ideas, baby.

Me: I know, and I have bought everything you asked for. I just need to find the big gift. The special one.

Jagger: You will find it. You always figure it out.

Me: What you doing?

Jagger: Running some errands. Want to meet me for dinner after you shop?

Me: I would love to. I will text when I'm finishing up.

Jagger: K. I love you so much.

Me: Love you too babe.

Jessica and I hit Saks to finish shopping for our moms. Our moms love clothes and perfume as much as we do. We spend hours in Saks, and I buy everything I see that I think mom would like, and I even pick up some jeans for Koi. After I check out, the manager approaches me. She is a beautiful woman with shoulder length grey hair. Her smile is so warm that it makes her feel familiar.

"Ms. Hendrix, Can I ask you to step into my office for a moment?" she asks.

I frown. "Is something wrong?"

She hesitates. "Uh, no ma'am. I have a call for you in my office."

A call? What is she talking about? Jessica's phone chirps as I look at her for help with the manager. The look on her face is one of horror.

"What is it, Jessica?"

"Nothing. Let's go take that call."

"Let me see the message."

"Come on, Hen. Let's just go to the office."

"I swear to everything holy if you don't show me the message I will make a scene." She flips her phone over for me to see.

Samantha: Get her the fuck out of Saks. Shit just hit the fan!

"What is she talking about?"

"I honestly don't know, Hen."

The paparazzi begin banging on the windows and call out my name. What the fuck is up with them? The manager is waiting impatiently.

"Ms. Hendrix, for your own safety, I'm begging you to follow me to my office."

Jessica and I look at each other, and shrug. The manager escorts us to her office, but she stops Jessica outside the door. She whispers something in her ear, and Jessica struggles with her poker face. I can see the second the shock and anger pass over her face, and I know no matter what I do, she won't tell me what she heard. So, I sit in the middle of Saks wondering what the hell is going on in my life that the paparazzi act like I'm a cat in heat, and two of my best friends feel the need to be cryptic.

An alert sounds on my phone letting me know there is an update with my name on it. I sit my bags down and take a seat in the chair in front of the manager's desk. I open the alert and Google takes its time connecting me to the story with my name in it. I'm in the middle of the building inside another room, so the signal isn't stellar. I wait some more. What now? Did someone hear me fart? Did I pick my nose in public? Did I forget to pay something?

Google finally connects me the article.

"OH MY GOD! OH MY GOD! NO! NO! NO! NO! NO!"

Jessica rushed to me. "Breathe, Henley. Breathe. Seriously take some deep breaths."

"Please call Samantha."

Jessica calls Samantha's L.A. office, but she doesn't pick up her direct line. She tries her personal cell, but she doesn't pick it up either. She then phones her secretary who also doesn't pick up. They are avoiding me. This is what Samantha does when she is dealing with the mack daddy of cluster fucks. This can't be happening. I need to talk to Samantha. Jessica spends the next ten minutes blowing up every phone Samantha can be reached on.

When she finally answers her cell, she sounds defeated. "Hen?"

"Yeah."

"Where are you?" Her voice is so soft it scares me. Samantha is soft when the world is about to implode.

"Saks."

"We gotta get you out of there. I'm going to work on an escape…"

"Shut up Samantha." She rambles when she is nervous. She stops talking. I finally ask the one thing I need to know before I can figure out how in the hell I'm going to deal.

"Is it true?" I ask.

She doesn't say anything for a long minute. "Yeah, Hen."

The tears run down my face, the phone drops, and I begin to shake my head. "No. No. No. No. No. I can't do this. I can't do this. I just can't."

"I know, Hen," she says.

Guitar Face Series
Guitar Face

There's No Crying in Rock-n-Roll

Walking Back to Georgia

River of Deceit

Roosevelt Series

Speak Softly

If you enjoyed this book, please consider leaving a review on Amazon and Goodreads. Indie authors rely on reviews from readers to tell others the book is worth reading. Thank you for reading my book.
-Sasha

Follow Sasha Marshall

Join the Mailing List

Website

Facebook

Twitter

Goodreads

Acknowledgements

To my husband: You've stood by my side through this ridiculous process of writing, and have read every write, rewrite, and ridiculous notion I've written. You were so involved in this book, you would question everything that would happen next. Sorry for toying with your

emotions. Thank you for understanding me, loving me, and supporting me while following my

dreams. You are the best partner-in-crime a girl could ever wish for. Kip was for you.

To my mother: Thank you for believing in me and supporting this crazy journey. You have read, edited, and gushed about this book. You have always been my biggest fan, no matter how crazy the journey might have been. I love you and am so thankful for you. The pirate was for you.

To my father: I'm sorry I made you blush. Thank you for supporting me and always being so incredibly proud of me, no matter how insane my dreams are. I love you so much. Thank you for rock-n-roll! From the time I remember, I played with your CD's, and through that I discovered Jimi Hendrix, Led Zeppelin, Pink Floyd, Aero smith, The Allman Brothers, Metallic a, and so many more. Throughout the years, I enjoyed playing the "Can you guess who this is?" game by the first chords of a song. It really shaped my ear for amazing music, and my need to be surrounded by it at all times.

To Jessica: You were the third person to read this book all the way through. Your early morning text messages about what would happen next were hilarious, at times profane (which I always appreciate), and downright livid. I will always remember them. You have read, edited, and lived this journey with Henley. We have had many front porch conversations about the book,

and what could happen in the rest of the series. I also need to thank you for being an

amazing friend. You are such an amazing human being, I had to write you in as a character. Koi

is for you, my sister.

To Samantha: You are the first person I ever spoke with about this book. You are the only person who saw the story evolve into what it is now. You are my best friend in the entire world and have always been my rock. Thank you for all of your support throughout the years, and for understanding the creative, artistic mess that is me. Since you are one of the most amazing people I know, I had to write you in as the one who holds it together for everyone. You have always been the glue. Samantha was for you.

To Meghan: You are one of the kindest people I know, and even with the distance, you remain such an amazing friend. I will always cherish your daily texts requesting more chapters so you could get your Henley fix. Thank you for reading this book and loving it. You were also written into the book because of how incredible you are. You have always lent an ear or a shoulder when needed, and that was something I knew Henley would need throughout her journey.

To Grush: We have been friends a long time and have seen each other's live change so much. Thank you for supporting my dream, and for loving Henley. I always appreciate you being

stuck in another city because I know you will read and text each thought you have. Thank you

for reading. Kip is also for you.

To Hillary: Ian was for you. Not many people may have gotten the two references, but I know you were panting through them. Henley, had to have him as a past conquest. We must live vicariously through her.

To Heather (Spanx): You jumped on the chance to read my book and even edited for me. Thank you for loving the book, and the late night texts about the characters, and where the story could possibly go. I can't wait for front porch and beer time with you, my friend. And, screw soccer coaches!

To Kathrine: You are amazing at everything you do, and an incredibly kind person. Thank you for always supporting and believing in me. You have edited way more than this book. I couldn't have gotten my graduate research paper done without you, at least with any sanity still intact. Thank you for everything! Cam is for you.

To Stephanie: My girl! I've known you for a long time, and absolutely adore you and your family. I'm so proud of y'all and the journey you have been brave enough to take. I wrote you in as a character, because Henley needed someone who is tough as hell, and could handle

anything and still come out on the other side of it. You are a fighter, and your character was needed. You are also as horny as I'm, and well that was also needed in the book. Thank you for

reading my book.

To my favorite bands: If you are mentioned in the book, it is a compliment. I hope that none of the bands or individuals were offended by the references. I asked several of my guy friends, "If you were a rock star, would you care if a woman you didn't know gave you a shot out for your amazing talent, and for being sexy as hell? Or if she had fictional naughty thoughts and/or sex with you?" The unanimous answer was, "Hell no!" My imagination runs wild, especially when it pertains to sex, and tatted rock stars. I hope that my readers, who are not already fans of yours, will read this book, know Sasha Marshall has high standards when it comes to music, and subsequently leads more fans to your music. Keep on rocking the fucking out!

Redemption Tattoo Parlour: While, I often request some of the most difficult tattoos, like the Library of fucking Congress on my leg, you have always blessed me with gorgeous art work. I have enjoyed every second I've spent at the studio, and just wanted to give a shot out to some of the best artists in the industry. True artistry is not appreciated enough. Thank you. Macon, Georgia: I've lived almost my entire life in this city, and I adore her spirit. I'm thankful for her history, art, music, festivals, people, food, and her willingness to overcome obstacles. Remember to move forward in a positive spirit.

The Rookery: For years, I've sat outside your front doors in the cold and in the sweltering heat, drinking beer and eating your amazing food. Since the character is from Macon, Georgia, I had to mention my favorite restaurant. Keep on keeping on and thank you for keeping the music alive.

To anyone else who read this book before it was published: Thank you for reading it and loving it. I do need to mention a few more names. Alesha, Tiffany, Katie, Tracie, Leta, Kelly, Melissa, and Ashley each read the book in their free time. You are my girls for a reason!

About the Author:

Sasha is an indie author who loves to write romance novels with an edge. She appreciates bad boys with tattoos and lickable bodies. I mean, what woman doesn't? She has a degree in history and thought about joining the U.S. Marshal Service when she graduated, but she chose to work with troubled youth instead. Shooting people wasn't really appealing, there's a lot of paperwork to fill out. She loves animals and secretly prefers them to most humans... or not so secretly because it's on the website now so it's out there. She traveled with well-known rock acts as a photographer during her undergraduate work and wants to clarify that she was not a groupie. Groupies wait in the wings hoping to get a night with one of the guys, she was a rock princess. She traveled right along with the guys hopping from tour bus, to plane, to hotel, to venue.

Sasha settled down and married Dane, who's her favorite idiot in the world. He is a true partner-in-crime, and sometimes their dialogue appears in her books. They both have a lot of Kip in them. Dane is a musician and Sasha loves to fan girl on him, so I guess she's now his groupie. And, yes ladies he's covered in tattoos. She often gauges a man's attractiveness by the amount of tattoos he's sporting. She's currently attempting to talk Dane into recording some of the songs she wrote in the books, but her persuasion techniques are seriously lacking. You should drop Dane a line to encourage him. Cleavage shots work well with him, and she's giving you permission to fan girl him if it gets the job done.

She reads a lot and has lots of favorite authors, but tends to stick to indie books. She's a nocturnal ninja, and frequently throat chops Dane when he snores. What? She's a light sleeper and his snoring messes with her beauty sleep. This is entirely his fault, her martial art skills in a king sized bed are obviously a reaction to his action.

Sasha has three dogs who think she is their own personal human. She spoils them a little. Her American Bulldog is deaf and marches to the beat of his own drum. He's part goat and part monster, eating inedible items such as bricks and destroying things when

Sasha ignores him. He is particularly fascinated with her socks and shoes. She frequently addresses him as "asshole" when he does these things. She also has a Miniature Schnauzer who has amazing old man eyebrows and a magnificent beard. He recently began fantasizing about being a troll as he likes to hide under the house from the American Bulldog who aggravates the ever living shit out of him. Last but not least is the Black Lab who lounges on the front porch snoring as she writes, brings her his tennis ball when it is time to fulfill her humanly duties, and flirts with the cows that live on the farm. He's a real ladies man and has a tendency to be attracted to heifers.

She's currently finishing book three in the Guitar Face series, Walking Back to Georgia. The book took an unexpected turn for many characters, but she is merely a vessel for the sex, literature, and romance gods. They tend to take over her mind, and even body at times, and crazy shit ends up in Microsoft Word.

Sasha & Dane live in Georgia on a cattle farm and love the peace and quiet. There's usually music playing in the background in their home. Their musical tastes are quite eclectic but Sasha prefers rock, blues, and New Orleans jazz. Bands that you'll hear in the Marshall household are Theory of a Deadman, Five Finger Death Punch, Seether, Tool, Muddy Waters, Etta James, BB King, Buddy Guy, The Allman Brothers Band, Butch Walker, and Johnny Cash. You'll often find them hanging out with friends (beer in hand), many of who are in the books, yes these people really exist in their lives. They enjoy watching television from time-to-time with their tastes ranging from Shameless to The Walking Dead to Scandal to Sons of Anarchy (tattoos, bad boys, and Harley's make Sasha hot). They also enjoy shooting their many weapons, which they have collected in preparation for the Zombie Apocalypse. Sasha is a better shot than Dane, this fact must be stated.

Sasha's dreams are to be a full-time author because working for the metaphorical man blows. Her dreams also involved getting Kurt Sutter to read her books and making a kick ass television show about them. Who else is there? Once the television shows pay her major loot, she'll retire from her day job and write from home. Well, she'll probably stalk the hot actors that play her characters, too, but that's to be expected. Fo' sho.

She loves to hear from her readers, it makes her all giddy and shit. Making Sasha giddy makes her feel like a literary goddess and helps her write better, so by all means shoot her a mother fucking email by either using the contact page or emailing her directly at sashamarshallauthor@yahoo.com

Printed in Great Britain
by Amazon.co.uk, Ltd.,
Marston Gate.